Jill Marie Landis
Jo Leigh & Jackie Braun

Destination: Marriage

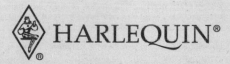

ISBN-13: 978-0-373-83725-0
ISBN-10:   0-373-83725-9

DESTINATION: MARRIAGE

CONTENTS

TROUBLE IN PARADISE

Jill Marie Landis

This story is dedicated to my hula sisters one and all, who seem to have no problem getting into trouble in paradise. Dance on, girls, dance on.

Dear Reader,

"Trouble in Paradise" takes place on Kauai, an island near and dear to my heart. Destination weddings are held all over Hawaii—on sandy beaches, cliffs overlooking the expansive blue waters of the Pacific, in grottoes lush with ferns, fancy hotels, family-style in the backyard, parks and quaint historical churches.

Just the other day I watched a wedding photographer take photos on the beach. The lovely bride had to grab the billowing organza skirt of her formal white gown and dash barefoot out of the reach of the foaming tide line. Her barefoot groom, wearing a black tux, ended up with wet trouser cuffs. He didn't seem to care in the least as they shared a laugh together, gazing into each other's eyes.

Except for the photographer, they were alone. I was reminded that a wedding isn't really about the guest list, the formal reception, registering for gifts or even the bridal gown and flowers. A wedding is, first and foremost, about the couple exchanging their vows and their commitment to each other.

In "Trouble in Paradise" Carrie Evans becomes convinced the island is giving her signs and warnings not to go through with their wedding. Suddenly groom Kurt Rowland finds himself with just hours left to convince his reluctant bride to say yes all over again.

I truly hope you enjoy this glimpse of island magic and romance.

Aloha,

Jill Marie Landis

"PLEASE FASTEN YOUR SEAT BELTS in preparation for landing. Please remain seated until the captain has unlocked the forward cabin doors and turned off the Fasten Seat Belts sign."

Carrie Evans locked her tray table into position, shifted in her seat and reached up to twist a wayward lock of hair back into the casual upswept knot she'd anchored atop her head with a chopstick. Not just any chopstick—a hand-carved rosewood piece with an enamel design—a new item she was featuring at Time After Time, her upscale, all-things-beautiful eccentricities shop on La Cienega in L.A.

Then she returned to reading a *Spirit of Aloha* complimentary in-flight magazine article that had caught her eye.

Ho'ailona, she read, was the Hawaiian word for signs and symbols, omens sent from the world of spirits to those discerning enough to recognize that they were far from natural occurrences.

"In Hawaii, it's believed that nature provides signs and omens that sound a warning for danger, misfortune, or trouble ahead on one's intended path."

Signs and omens.

Good thing she didn't believe in such nonsense. If she did, she might see the fact that her fiancé, Kurt Rowland, hadn't been able to make the flight for their wedding trip as a very bad sign.

Tossing the colorful airline magazine into her carry-on bag, she left the comfort of her first-class seat behind and smiled at an exotically lovely Hawaiian flight attendant in the doorway. The young woman's makeup was flawless. She wore a vanda orchid tucked behind her ear and both the flight attendant and the orchid looked as fresh as when they took off from L.A. five hours ago.

Carrie wished she could say the same about herself.

The young woman smiled. "Aloha and welcome to Kauai," she said, handing Carrie a map of the island.

"Thanks." Almost in disbelief, Carrie added, "I'm getting married on Saturday. On the beach. At sunset."

"Congratulations." The flight attendant wished her much happiness.

Southern California seemed light-years away as Carrie stepped out of the jetway and into the air-conditioned comfort of the waiting area at the Lihue, Kauai, airport. Exiting the building, she bumped along with the crowd toward the baggage claim, enveloped by the heady scent of plumeria blossoms floating on a blanket of sultry humidity.

Reality hit her as hard as the tropic heat.

I have a wedding to pull off in four days.

A wedding that was taking place two thousand miles from home.

And her groom, who should have been at her side, was still on the other side of the Pacific.

"It's not every day a guy gets the opportunity to be featured on the cover of the *Los Angeles Times* Sunday magazine," she'd reminded him that afternoon as he drove her to Los Angeles International Airport. She was proud and happy that Kurt been chosen for the honor, far more than she was disappointed that they couldn't be on the same flight.

After years of struggling as an unknown artist, Kurt's bold, primitive work was in high demand, but they were both realistic enough to know that fame was fleeting. However, right now he was hot and the *Times* article would really put him on the map. His massive creations graced upscale hotel lobbies and corporate offices all over L.A. Even A-list celebrities were commissioning him to work his magic on their mansion walls.

Carrie made her way to the baggage carousel and edged closer, braced to grab her bag as soon as it trundled past.

Ten minutes later, all but four people had exited the baggage claim area and those left behind were beginning to look forlorn. Carrie's suitcase hadn't come tumbling down the chute onto the carousel as expected. It wasn't oversize. It wasn't overweight. She had the claim tag.

But she had no bag.

Just then, her cell phone rang as if on cue. She glanced at the caller ID and smiled when she saw that it was him.

"You made it." He sounded as if he were right beside her and not an ocean away.

She glanced around at the nearly deserted baggage claim area. Across the carousel, some very pale tourists were helping themselves to complimentary Kona coffee from an air pot on a shelf against the far wall.

"The flight was easy. I took a nap, watched *Spiderman 3* again and went through my folder of wedding plans. Now, here I am."

"Great. The photographer's assistant promised that he'd take care of getting me on the very next plane to Kauai. I'll catch the red-eye and meet you in the morning. Have some champagne on ice and we'll have mimosas and breakfast in bed."

"That sounds fabulous. There's only one little hitch. My bag is missing." She glanced at the ramp that was no longer spewing luggage.

"It'll show up." Kurt's optimism was one of the things she loved most about him.

"I know." She glanced around the baggage claim area. It was only March, but Kauai was extremely hot and muggy. Her parents didn't do hot and muggy well. "I'm beginning to wonder if this was such a good idea after all," she mused aloud.

There was a sudden, ominous silence on the other end of the line. Then Kurt said, "You're not having second thoughts, are you? Look, honey—"

She realized what he was thinking and cut him off. "Oh, no! No. I'm not talking about getting married. I was just wondering if having the wedding all the way over here was such a good idea. I mean, destination weddings are in, but I feel so far away."

Everything was set. Their immediate family and her best friend, the maid of honor, had purchased their airline tickets and reserved rooms. Still, she couldn't help but worry.

"What if my bag doesn't show up? My wedding gown is in it." Simple, elegant ivory silk, her gown was a Vera Wang. It fit her like a glove. "So are the place cards and the photos of arrangements I wanted to show the florist."

"No turning back now. Your bag will get there. Don't worry. You're just exhausted from the long flight. Get some sleep. Things will look better tomorrow."

She sighed. He was always so positive. He made things sound so easy. "You're absolutely right. I love you, Kurt."

"Love you, too, hon. Keep your eye on the goal."

They said their goodbyes. She hung up. She *was* tired. But everything would work out.

She'd never failed at anything in her life and she wasn't about to start now. The sunset wedding on a secluded stretch of beach—the prelude to their marriage—would come off without a hitch. With the help of the Hawaiian event coordinator she'd found on the Internet, she'd planned everything in minute detail.

A destination wedding had been her idea. Having Kurt's bohemian father and brother meet her conservative parents on neutral ground was a far better plan than what would surely become a horrific scene from an unscripted *When Worlds Collide* if she'd opted to hold the reception at her parents' country club outside Chicago.

She didn't have to remind herself that Kurt Rowland was a dream come true. He was not only her fiancé, but her lover, the man of her dreams, her best friend. Just the sound of his voice over the phone had worked its magic.

She was calm. She was refocused now. Everything would be fine.

She'd never believed in love at first sight until the moment her eyes had met Kurt's across a crowded gala in the upscale lobby of L.A.'s latest boutique hotel. The hotelier had ordered gift baskets for VIP guests from Time After Time, and Carrie had received an invitation.

The hotel's automatic door had whisked closed behind her that evening and she'd barely stepped inside the lobby when she'd recognized Kurt, the celebrated artist who had created the floor-to-ceiling mural in the lobby across from the reception desk. His stare was so intent, so sizzling hot, that her high-heeled pumps seemed to have suddenly been Gorilla-glued to the terrazzo marble floor. She couldn't take another step.

It was a second or two more before she even realized he had a woman on each arm, bracketing him like well-placed bookends. One was a striking brunette, the other an icy, glamorous blonde. Both, Kurt explained later, were models. Their attendance was set up by his publicist so that he made a statement walking into the reception.

Barely breathing, she watched as he smoothly left the two women, snagged two glasses of champagne off a passing waiter's tray and carried them across the room to her.

He wore his dark wavy hair long enough to tease the collar of his black Armani T-shirt. He was the only man at the gala in jeans, yet he looked perfectly at ease. He was male-model handsome, but exuded a bad-boy roughness around the edges. Once she got to know him, she found that he laughed easy, loved hard and was a hopeless romantic.

The mural behind him depicted the settlement of L.A., from its early history to the present, the diverse mix of the city's ethnic groups, the grandeur of the miles of sparkling coastline and the lavender, snow-covered mountain peaks that rimmed the L.A. basin.

One glance at his work and she knew they were from two different worlds. She was traditional: classic white on white, vanillas and crèmes, calm on the exterior but a cauldron inside.

He was eclectic: bold colors that bordered on neon, bright blues, reds, sunset oranges and purples, primitive and earthy. He wore black, took chances with his art and his business dealings. Inside, he was as tranquil as a tropical shoreline at sunset.

From that night on, when they weren't hard at work establishing their careers, they were inseparable, forging a relationship that both hoped would last a lifetime.

She learned his parents were back-to-nature hippies from Vermont who'd pledged their undying love to one another while standing naked under the summer solstice moon. Though they'd never bothered with a legal ceremony, Trini and Bogie had devoted their lives to each other and their twin sons until Kurt's mother passed away three years ago.

But unlike his parents, Kurt held traditional beliefs when it came to marriage.

Carrie was the woman he wanted to share his life with—he told her he'd known it from the moment he'd seen her walk into the hotel lobby—and he wanted a legal and binding union.

Two weeks after the gala, they moved in together. A month later, he proposed.

It had taken her nearly two years to say yes. She was fearless on all fronts—except when it came to the idea of marriage. Her parents' marriage had lasted nearly forty years, but only because their mantra was "divorce is not an option."

It wasn't love that frightened Carrie. She knew how much Kurt loved her. It was the notion that marriage would somehow change everything that frightened her. It had taken him over a year and a half to talk her into accepting his proposal and setting a date.

To the casual observer, her parents, Dorothy and Edward Evans, had a marriage as picture-perfect as their privileged lives. But only Carrie knew the truth. Behind closed doors, her parents coexisted in a cocoon of polite, icy exchanges. Any passion, laughter or love had died long ago. As far back as Carrie could recall, they hadn't even shared the same room.

Kurt had finally convinced her that just because her parents hadn't had a loving relationship, that didn't mean their marriage wouldn't be as successful as everything else she'd ever attempted in her life.

Now, as she tried to ignore the humidity in the Lihue airport, she tucked her cell phone back into the outside pocket of her carry-on, looked around and thought, *By week's end, we'll take our vows on a beach on this romantic, magical island.*

But first, she had to track down her bag.

The man behind a Dutch door beneath the Lost Luggage sign wore the placid expression of someone who had heard one too many complaints and was no longer listening.

"Fill this out," he mumbled as he plunked down a form in front of her. "Sign here, and here."

The sheet was covered with drawings of numerous styles and sizes of bags. Many looked exactly alike. Finally she chose what she hoped was her bag type, checked the box, signed and handed back the form. Behind the man in the door, a heavyset woman in a purple- and yellow-flowered muumuu had her back to Carrie as she worked at a computer. Images of bag identification pictures filled the monitor.

"My wedding dress is in that bag." Carrie sighed.

The woman in the muumuu shot her swivel chair around. "Wedding dress, eh? Congratulations, den."

"Thank you. Realistically, how long do you think it will be before my bag arrives?"

The two airline employees exchanged a telling look. Both shrugged.

"Pretty soon. Tomorrow, maybe, at the latest," the woman offered. "Worst case it went to Samoa. Get next week."

"Next *week?*" Carrie gasped. Her fluttering hope began to die. "The wedding is on Saturday night."

Tuesday was nearly gone.

Suddenly what the woman had said dawned on Carrie.

"Samoa?"

The woman burst out laughing and slapped her knees. "Just having some fun wit you. It'll be here… mebbe on da next flight. Somebody will call."

"But it *will* arrive, right?" Carrie glanced between them, seeking reassurance.

"Go get one mai tai. When we find it, we'll call you and have someone deliver it to—" the man paused and glanced down at her form "—to the Hanalei Plantation Hotel."

"Thanks," Carrie mumbled. No way was she having a fruity rum drink with an umbrella stuck in it. It was bad enough Kurt wasn't here. Now her bag was floating somewhere in luggage limbo.

Or, heaven forbid, making its way to Samoa.

Recorded Muzak, typical tourist fare, filled the Alamo Rental Car building.

The young Hawaiian female clerk behind the counter couldn't have been nicer, or more apologetic, as she smiled at Carrie.

"Sorry, ma'am, but the Town Car you reserved isn't available. We'll put you in a nice Jeep, though. If you'll just sign here and here. Will you need extra insurance?"

Jeep? There are nice Jeeps?

Carrie shook her head. Hearing herself called ma'am was bad enough.

"I don't need extra insurance. I need the Town Car. We'll be picking up our folks. And my fiancé has an elderly aunt who—"

"Tourists love our Jeep. It has four-wheel drive and the option of a convertible top."

"I really don't think…"

The clerk continued to smile but she tapped her long, bejeweled nails on the counter. Her hair was glossy black and hung loose down her back to her waist. "This is the only car we have available right now. We're completely booked. Take the Jeep and maybe check back in the middle of the week."

"Do you think one of the other rental agencies—"

The young woman shook her head. "Everybody's choke."

Carrie stared, not sure she understood. "Choke?"

"Booked. There are a couple of big conventions on island. Better you take the Jeep and be sure you have a car."

Carrie sighed.

No fiancé beside her. No bag. No dress. No Town Car.

She remembered the in-flight magazine article.

So far, the signs were definitely *not* good.

BY THE TIME she'd pulled out of the Alamo parking lot driving a bright, bumblebee-yellow Jeep that screamed "I'm a tourist, rip me off," the sky began to sprinkle. She ended up circling the small airport twice before she hit the correct exit lane, made it onto the two-lane "highway" and headed north toward her destination at Hanalei.

When the sprinkles escalated to a downpour, she was forced to pull over and deal with the Jeep's zip-on top. It was like wrestling with a vinyl alligator. After fifteen exhausting minutes, she gave up. The rain came in squalls, so between downpours she drove along in a string of traffic at what appeared to be the island's top speed of forty miles an hour. Occasionally she would pull over beneath the biggest tree she could find and wait it out.

She figured she was over halfway there when it began to rain so hard she was forced to stop in the small town of Kilauea. She took refuge in an old stone church built during the town's plantation days. She'd no sooner stepped through the double wooden doors and into the hushed, quiet coolness of the lava-rock walls when her cell phone went off.

She recognized her mother's number.

"Hi, Mom." Carrie didn't dare let her mother hear the exhaustion or frustration in her voice or Dorothy Evans, whose hobby was making mountains out of molehills, would pounce.

Her mother was a self-described charity fund-raiser who still couldn't hide the fact that she was disappointed Carrie had opted for something other than a traditional church wedding and a five-course dinner at the Willow Creek Country Club. The Evans family had been members for nearly seventy-five years.

Her father, Edward, a conservative stockbroker, had been presented a membership by his father as a wedding gift. Edward had held the office of board president for four years running.

"How is it going, darling?" Her mother wanted to know.

"Great." Soaked to the skin, her crème-colored linen dress looking like something a bag lady would wear, Carrie stood in the open church doorway staring out at the pouring rain. At least she didn't have a suitcase getting soaked in the Jeep. "I'm on the way to Hanalei Plantation."

"Kurt is there, isn't he?" Her mother almost sounded hopeful that Kurt *wasn't* there. She'd been waiting for a crack in Carrie's relationship almost since the beginning.

"The *L.A. Times* called wanting a last-minute interview and photo shoot. He's coming on the next flight."

"Oh, *really?*"

"Yes, really. It's a great opportunity for him. For us," she amended.

"I suppose marrying an *artist,* you'll have to learn to adapt to a more…*fluid*…lifestyle."

Her parents were convinced that marrying an artist was one of the single most foolhardy things Carrie could ever do. What she'd tried to explain to them was that Kurt wasn't a scattered, flaky artist. He was a man with a vision who set goals and didn't lose sight of them until he'd accomplished success. But her parents only believed what they wanted.

She reminded herself that Kurt was *her* choice and this was *her* wedding. Her and Kurt's. She wasn't going to let her mother dampen her spirits. Besides, the rain was doing a great job of that already.

"You know," her mother was saying, "when I went to the Arnold wedding at the club last week, it was just lovely. They served the most wonderful salmon with a creamy artichoke sauce. The bride chose carrot cake. I thought it very untraditional, but then Mary Ellen Franks told me that carrot cake is quite popular at weddings now. Are you having carrot cake? Can they even *get* carrots over there?"

Carrie decided now was not the time to tell her mother that she'd ordered what the event planner had declared an island favorite—a *liliko'i* or passion fruit cake, with white icing smothered in toasted coconut.

"Carrie?"

"I'm here, Mom."

There was a long sigh on the other end of the line and then, "I wish you were getting married here. It would have been so wonderful. Your father always dreamed of walking you down the aisle at St. Augustine's where we were married."

Carrie doubted her parents knew what each others' dreams were anymore.

"Well," Carrie said, trying to stay positive, "the wedding is in four days and I'm here to get the ball rolling, so I'd better get back on the road."

"Call me, dear."

Carrie promised to call again before her parents left Chicago. When the rain let up, she ran back to the car. She tried to ignore the squish of the wet seat beneath her linen skirt as she sat down.

Twenty minutes later she was checking into the

Hanalei Plantation Resort high on a bluff above the Hanalei River. The view was spectacular. Feeling like a drowned rat, she was escorted to the private Honeymoon *Hale* Bungalow by a young, dark-eyed bellman attractively wrapped in the male version of a sarong.

He appeared to relish explaining how to correctly pronounce *hale*.

"Hah-lay," he said with a sloe-eyed wink of his bedroom eyes.

"Ha-ha." She rolled her eyes, too exhausted to appreciate his joke.

Once she'd made herself comfortable and helped herself to the complimentary toothpaste and potions in a welcome basket, she ordered breakfast and a bottle of champagne for tomorrow morning, then called and left Kurt a voice mail.

"Aloha, honey. I've got the champagne ordered and I'll see you in the morning. Sweet dreams on the plane."

She walked to the poolside café where she ordered a light salad for dinner. Afterward, a simple pink tank top and khaki shorts, some flip-flops and slip-on rubber reef walkers caught her eye in the hotel gift shop. She bought them, along with a fun, extra-large, men's tank top with a colorful Kauai rooster printed on the back.

As she was about to walk out the door of the shop,

she noticed a rack of cards and books on Hawaiian customs and myths. Remembering the interesting in-flight article, she grabbed a few books, too. Since much of Kurt's art incorporated blending the past with the present, she hoped he might find something inspiring in them.

Returning to the cottage, she slipped into the oversize tank top and turned in early. Sometime during the night, her cell rang. The LED numbers on the bedside clock radio glowed 11:00 p.m.

It was Kurt. He should have been in midflight.

"Where are you? Are you all right?" She was drowsy and hot but more concerned about him. Clutching her phone, she wandered across the room in the dark, patting the sliding door to the *lanai* as she searched for the latch in the semidarkness.

"I'm fine. I made the flight…"

"Can you speak up a bit? I can hardly hear you."

"I don't dare." His voice was hushed. "We've been sitting on the runway for two hours…"

"Kurt!" Carrie switched on a light, forgetting about opening the doors. "You haven't been hijacked—"

"Of *course* not."

"Then why are you whispering?"

"There's a lady with a toddler beside me and the little guy *just* stopped screaming. The airport's fogged in. They predict it's going to lift soon, but I wanted you to know I'll be getting in late. How is everything going?"

"Okay." She had a vision of herself navigating the miserable topless Jeep down the highway in the pouring rain.

No Kurt. No bag. No Town Car. No top. No sun. Fog shuts down LAX.

Signs and omens.

"Hon? Carrie? You don't sound okay."

"I'm fine." It was impossible to sound upbeat when it was 2:00 a.m. in her previous time zone. "I'll set the alarm and come pick you up in Lihue."

"There's no guarantee when we'll be taking off. I'll get a cab and meet you at the hotel." He made kissing noises over the phone. "All better?"

She couldn't help but laugh. He was the best.

"Yeah. Thanks, honey. See you tomorrow."

Wide-awake now, she opened the slider and the tropical breeze billowed the sheer white drapes against her bare legs. Somewhere in the distant darkness, drums pounded with a primitive, carnal beat.

Carrie walked back to the bed, picked up the in-flight magazine she'd carried off the plane and slid beneath the crisp sheet. She hoped staring at glossy photos of beaches and endless expanses of ocean would help her drift off again.

Of their own accord, the pages shifted open to the

article about the mystical side of island life. Carrie read the first few lines again and then shoved more pillows into place to prop herself up. She glanced toward the wide double doors open to the *lanai,* watching the white sheers dance on the night breeze as she read the article teaser again.

"In Hawaii, it's believed that nature provides signs and omens that sound a warning for danger, misfortune, or trouble ahead on one's intended path."

Exactly what kind of signs and omens? she wondered.

Hurricanes and volcano eruptions? Or simple everyday things like last-minute delays? Lost luggage? The wrong car? Rain? Fog? Tardy fiancés?

Carrie closed the magazine and tossed it on the table. She clicked off the bedside lamp and shut her eyes. The sound of water rushing down the lava-rock waterfall into the pool outside the *hale* was meant to be soothing, but all she could think about was driving around with rain blowing into the Jeep for the next four days. She reached out to Kurt's empty side of the bed and sighed.

He should be here. This was their wedding trip.

So what? She told herself not to sweat it.

After all, she was a doer. An organizer. When *L.A. Magazine* covered the opening of her store they'd called her "one of the sharpest, most inventive and perceptive entrepreneurs to come on the scene in decades."

She'd have no problem pulling off the wedding of their dreams and they'd live happily ever after.

But deep inside that sharp, inventive, perceptive woman, there existed a niggle of doubt when it came to truly believing love could stand the test of time. She knew firsthand about the failure of marriages in today's world, knew the odds weren't good. A niggle of doubt plagued her the way a grain of sand in the wrong part of a sandal could worry itself into a blister.

What if the island is trying to tell me something?

As she lay in the dark, lulled by the sound of gently falling water, caressed by the scent of plumeria on the night wind, her worry mounted.

What if Kurt's last-minute delay, not to mention all the other little setbacks that have occurred since I arrived, are signs and omens foreshadowing disaster ahead?

Ridiculous, she thought as she tossed the magazine back onto the bedside table. *Absolutely crazy.*

She punched her pillow, lay down, closed her eyes.

Ten minutes later she gave up, padded across the room toward the table where she'd left the books on Hawaiian lore and carried them back to the bed.

"Aloha! You've reached Happily Ever After Events. I'm Rainbow Roberts and I'm not here right now, but wait for the beep, leave a message, and I'll get back to you as soon as possible. Have a sunshine day!"

Carrie waited for the beep. And waited. Finally the recording came on again and this time a generic automated voice announced, "Machine full."

She'd slept fitfully until dawn when she gave up trying and went for a walk along the beach. Afterward, she returned to the gift shop and bought a few more books on Hawaiian myths and legends. Leafing through them over breakfast, she found there was much that was forbidden and mysterious about the islands—and nothing very reassuring.

Back in her room, she checked on Kurt's arrival time only to learn he was going to be far later than he'd estimated. At least he was on the way.

She hadn't gotten where she was in life by assuming everything was under control, so she tried calling the caterer that Rainbow Roberts had booked. When no one answered at Island Grinds Kau Kau Katering, she looked up the address in the phone book and decided to drive to nearby Anahola and take one last look at the menu for herself.

Nearly twenty-five minutes later she was making a third U-turn on a small residential street near the beach. With a map in one hand and the steering wheel in the other, she tried to locate the caterer's headquarters, but the neighborhood of modest dwellings nestled around a bay was clearly residential. She'd passed the same row of houses four times. Kids playing in the yards openly stared as she drove by.

Clearly there was no warehouse, no restaurant, no substantial building that might house Island Grinds Kau Kau Katering. She checked the address again, looked up and finally noticed a small square of worn plywood propped against a rock in the yard in front of a faded green house. The address had been spray painted on the wood with neon orange paint.

Carrie pulled over. According to the map, she was in Anahola and this was the address of Island Grinds. She grabbed her straw bag and stepped out of the Jeep.

The front porch was minuscule and covered with rubber thongs, work boots and tennis shoes of all sizes. She stepped onto the threadbare mat in front of the sagging screen door and knocked.

And waited.

Eventually she heard the sound of heavy footsteps inside. A plus-size elderly woman in yards of ruffled floral fabric opened the door. Silent, she scowled up at Carrie as an episode of *Family Feud* blared out of a television in the background.

"I'm sorry to bother you." Carrie lifted the map and gave it a wave. "But I was looking for..." She suddenly remembered that when Rainbow pronounced *Kau Kau* it had sounded like cow-cow. She wasn't brave enough to give it a try. "I was looking for Island Grinds…" She let the rest of the phrase drift away.

Immediately the woman smiled. "Dis da *kine.*"

"*Kine?*"

"Place. Da *kine.*" She opened the screen and stepped outside. "You wanna talk my daughter, Leinani, but she gone *holoholo.*"

Carrie had no idea what going *holoholo* meant. Either the woman had left for a place called Holoholo or, for all Carrie knew, she'd gone crazy.

"Has she been *holoholo* long?" she dared.

The woman shook her head and laughed. "Jus' since yesttaday."

"Is she going to be all right?"

"She'll be back couple'a days. Mebbe more. Mebbe not."

"She's not here?"

The woman laughed again and patted Carrie on the shoulder. "No. She gone *holoholo* to Big Island to see her cousin. Took all da *keiki.* Da kids."

Carrie mentally ticked off the days. Today was Wednesday. Three left until the wedding. "My wedding is on Saturday. Rainbow Roberts assured me things were all set—"

The woman cut her off. "Dat one *lolo.* For sure."

"Rainbow is *holoholo,* too?"

"No. Rainbow is *lolo.* Crazy. I don't know if she gone *holoholo,* too, or not."

Carrie knew one thing for certain. If she wasn't off this porch in two seconds she might be going *holo holo lolo* or whatever herself. She pulled out a small notebook and pen, wrote down her name, the name of the hotel and her cell number.

"Have your daughter call me the minute she gets back, okay? Thank you *so* much." She forced a smile and pressed the paper into the woman's hand and bid her goodbye. She was off the porch when the woman called out, "Eh, no worry, yeah?"

Carrie waited until she'd climbed back into the Jeep before she dug her cell out of her purse and dialed Rainbow's number again.

The answering machine was still too full to leave a message.

Carrie started the engine and headed up the hill toward the highway.

The first thing she planned to do when she got back to the hotel was buy a Hawaiian dictionary.

"ELVIS PRESLEY made three films on Kauai, *Blue Hawaii* being the most remembered. Our next stop will be the famous Hanalei Pier where not only *South Pacific* and the *Wackiest Ship in the Army* were filmed, but also *King Kong*. Let's all sing along to the theme song of *Blue Hawaii* as we head to Kauai's lush North Shore…."

There wasn't a cab to be found and all the rental cars were booked when Kurt's flight had finally touched down four hours behind schedule. He walked out to the highway and flagged down a white minivan with a brightly painted sign that read Movie Tours.

The driver was a Hawaiian named Kimo. His dark scowl became all smiles when Kurt offered to pay him and the tour guide, Danny, aka Mr. Perky, the $110 attraction fee just to hitch a ride out to Hanalei.

Kurt figured no amount of money was too much with Carrie waiting for him in bed in the Honeymoon *Hale* she'd described over the phone last night. He would have paid double—until he bumped his way down the narrow aisle to the only empty seat at the back of the luxury van.

There was no place for luggage, so he was forced to sit with his suitcase on his lap. Beside him, a woman with a violent sunburn scooted close to the window. She pulled her straw purse up off the floor, scowled and crossed both arms over her bag.

He nodded in her direction. A tight smile came and went across her lips.

So much for aloha.

As advertised on the side of the van, there was air-conditioning, but comfort was short-lived since Mr. Perky, in baggy shorts and a bright pink and orange aloha shirt, felt obliged to fill every single second with corny banter. When he wasn't talking, he was showing clips from movies filmed on Kauai on a small television mounted at the front of the bus. Between the clips, Danny led the passengers in repetitious choruses of old movie tunes. Just now, they were working their way through the theme from *Gilligan's Island.*

Had he signed on for the entire five-hour tour, Kurt was sure *his* last stop would be the nearest psychiatric ward.

He shifted the suitcase on his lap and stared out the window, ignoring six Texans who had already mutinied and segued from singing "Gilligan's Island" and "Blue Hawaii" to "Hound Dog." They were happily bellowing off-key, ignoring Danny's pleas for them to stop.

Outside, the sky showed intermittent patches of blue between dusty-gray rain clouds that occasionally dropped a gentle mist. Kurt's seat was *maka'i,* the ocean side of the bus. On the other side, the land swept toward towering green mountain peaks.

Kauai, he realized, was a place of majestic views and tropical lushness. It was easy to imagine King Kong stomping his way through the misty fog encircling the tops of the mountains. As the Texans ignored a video clip of *South Pacific* and continued to sing Elvis tunes, Kurt found his attention drawn to a bright yellow Jeep parked on the side of the road beneath the canopy of a huge tree.

It took a second before he realized Carrie was seated behind the wheel of the car holding a map over her head in the drizzling rain.

He reached across the woman beside him and tried to slide the window open. When that didn't work, he gave a shrill whistle, hoping to get Danny's attention, but he couldn't be heard over the Texans.

Trapped in an airtight refrigerated nightmare, Kurt tossed his bag into the aisle and stood up. The woman beside him clutched her purse to her bosom and pressed herself into the corner of the seat.

"You have to sit down, sir," the tour guide bellowed over the microphone.

The Texans stopped singing and swiveled in their seats to stare at Kurt.

"Stop the bus. I want off," he told Kimo.

The van continued to sway down the narrow two-lane highway. Kurt gripped the backs of the seats on either side of him to keep his balance.

"My fiancé is in that yellow Jeep back there. Let me out and I'll walk back." He stooped to glance out the back window as the van rolled on.

"We're not supposed to stop." Mr. Perky had become Mr. Snarly.

Kimo exchanged a telling look with the guide and then backed up Danny.

"No unscheduled stops. Sorry." Kimo shrugged.

"Okay, how much?" Kurt reminded himself it was only money.

Kimo and Danny exchanged another glance.

"Fifty." Kimo had the shoulders of an NFL lineman and was twice as wide around the waist.

"You got it." Kurt reached for his wallet.

Kimo pulled into a turn-out at the top of a hill. The automatic door whooshed open and steamy air was sucked inside. Kurt grabbed his bag, headed up the aisle, and shoved a fifty into Kimo's meaty hand.

"T'anks, bra," Kimo mumbled.

"Buh-bye. Make *every* day a *movie* day!" Danny flung his left arm toward the bus door in a dramatic gesture worthy of Judy Garland.

Kurt hopped out of the van and headed back down the road on foot. The rain was now just a slight mist. The air was warm. He didn't mind getting soaked. Within a few seconds, the rain stopped entirely. He watched the yellow Jeep pull back onto the highway and sat his bag down. Then he started waving his arms over his head.

ONCE THE RAIN ENDED, Carrie swiped her wet hair out of her eyes, started the Jeep and pulled out from beneath the shelter of a huge tree blanketed in red blossoms. She hadn't heard from Kurt, but she hoped he'd be at the hotel when she got back. Her cell hadn't picked up a signal since she entered the Anahola area where Leinani, the caterer, had gone *holoholo.*

Carrie was soaked, her tank top plastered to her skin like a contestant in a wet T-shirt contest. The map she'd picked up at Alamo had almost disintegrated. While fiddling with the air-conditioning control knob, she caught sight of a man in a black shirt standing very close to the edge of the road. He was waving his arms, whistling an ear-piercing whistle. As she drove by, he started running after the Jeep calling, "Carrie! Stop!"

Her heart executed the same flip-flop that it always did whenever she saw Kurt.

She glanced in the rearview mirror. There were no cars immediately behind her, so she braked and pulled over. He came around to the driver's side and reached over the door, laughing and kissing her at the same time.

"I was afraid you weren't going to see me." He wiped a raindrop off the end of her nose.

"What are you doing out here? How did you get here?" She looked in the rearview mirror and spotted his suitcase standing next to the highway.

"Let's just say I nearly witnessed an Elvis sighting, but I was spared." He glanced around the wet interior of the Jeep. "Why didn't you put up the top?"

"I tried. It has a life of its own." When she noticed his gaze locked on her nipples, she reached down and pulled her sopping wet tank top away from her breasts.

"Wet looks good on you." He winked. "Maybe we should just pull off onto a dirt road and not waste time going back to the hotel."

"Are you kidding? You'd have to be a contortionist to make love in this thing."

"I'm willing to try." After one look at her face he added, "Let's go back to the hotel and get you out of these wet clothes. What do you think?"

"I think I'm really, *really* glad to see you. It doesn't matter how you got here."

"Let me run back and grab my bag. I'll drive to Hanalei."

She watched him jog back down the road a few yards, grab his suitcase and head back to the Jeep. He tossed the bag in back and as if he wrestled vinyl alligators every day of the week, he quickly zipped the top and windows into place. She was happy to relinquish the wheel and climb into the passenger's seat.

"Did you get any sleep on the flight? Are you awake enough to drive?" She reached over and ran her fingertips through his hair where it curled over the collar of his casual polo shirt.

"I'm wide-awake now. I finally got some sleep after the toddler in his terrible twos passed out." He spread his palm possessively over her thigh and began to slide his hand up her leg toward the hem of her shorts. She shivered.

"So why are you driving around in the rain, anyway? I thought you'd be waiting at the hotel."

"It wasn't raining when I left." She sighed and glanced out the window at the endless expanse of ocean. "I don't even know where to start."

"How about with this Jeep?"

"Two big conventions on island. The car companies are choke."

"Choke?" He started laughing and reached up to readjust the rearview mirror.

"Never mind." She waved away the explanation. "They didn't have the Town Car we ordered. The event planner, Rainbow, has an answering machine that's so full it's not taking any more messages. Rather than sit around, I decided to drive to Anahola to talk to the caterer myself."

"What did he say?"

"*She* wasn't there. She went to the Big Island. Actually—" Carrie smiled "—her name is Leinani and her mother told me she had gone *holoholo*. I thought that meant she'd gone crazy, until I found out *lolo* means crazy." She took a deep breath and then said, "Do you believe in signs?"

"What? You mean like stop signs?"

"No, *signs,* as in omens. Warnings."

Kurt stared back at her as if he had serious doubts about her sanity.

He reached over and pressed his palm against her forehead.

"What are you doing?" she asked.

"Checking to see if you have a fever. You sound delirious."

She wished her mounting fear would dissipate like the rain now that he was here, but she still felt edgy. Losing sleep while reading about ancient Hawaiian beliefs and myths hadn't helped at all.

"I'll be okay, now that you're here," she mused aloud.

Kurt squeezed her thigh. "Maybe I should perform a more thorough physical exam." Without warning, he turned down a dirt road that wound its way to a deserted stretch of beach.

"What are you doing?" Carrie grabbed hold of the handle on the door above her as they hit a pothole. To the right, she spied a small stream that tumbled down the hillside to the beach.

"I'm fulfilling a fantasy," he said. "What do you say we see if that stream has a swimming hole?" His heated expression hinted that they wouldn't be doing much swimming.

She could think of a thousand and one things she should be doing in preparation for the wedding, but Kurt was smiling at her in a way that made her heart race and her nerve endings tingle. He drove on until they reached a small, empty field that was obviously a parking area. This afternoon, the Jeep was the only vehicle there.

"Think of this as a prelude to the honeymoon." He opened his door and headed around the car to take her hand.

He led her across the grassy field to where a thick jungle of trees, ferns and vines nearly hid the stream from view. They followed the slow-moving water along the streambed until they could no longer see the parking area. Though the ocean was still out of sight, the sound of the waves crashing on the beach blended with the rush of the stream.

"Here we go." Kurt smiled and waved toward a spot where the rocks formed a natural pool. Though the sky was overcast, the air was warm. "I'll bet on a sunny day this place is crawling with tourists. Lucky for us it's still overcast." He slipped out of his rubber thongs and pulled his shirt over his head. When he reached for the fly of his jeans, he paused and said, "Undress, Carrie. We're going skinny-dipping."

"But—" She glanced around the empty jungle. "What if somebody comes along?"

He walked over to her, ran his hands up and down her arms, took hold of the hem of her top and pulled it over her head. "The water will hide what we don't want seen," he whispered.

"But—"

"The only butt I want to think about right now is yours." He cupped her left cheek and brought her up against him. She felt his erection. He was hard and ready for her. Despite the fact that someone could come along at any moment, she felt herself melting inside, aching for fulfillment.

Within seconds he helped her out of her shorts and stripped off his pants and briefs. It took a moment for them to negotiate the mossy rocks that lined the streambed, and the fresh water cascading toward the ocean was a lot cooler than she expected. To her overly warm skin it felt downright cold.

She let out a squeal when she jumped off the rock and slipped into water up to her neck. Seconds later Kurt took her in his arms and they came together, skin to skin beneath the surface of the water. His hands traced the curves and hollows of her body. Her hands found him unerringly. Within a heartbeat he was pulsing hard and insistent in her hand. He hooked his arm around her waist and lifted her in the water so that she moved against him. She wrapped her legs around his body and felt him slide between them until he sheathed himself inside her.

The sultry air, the chill of the water fresh from the clouds on the mountaintops, the soft sigh of the leaves moving on the breeze, the call of the birds in the trees, all blended together to delight the senses and add to their erotic pleasure.

Carrie lost herself in the moment and let go of all inhibition as Kurt held tight to her waist and she moved up and down his hardened shaft. She clung to him, begging for more and more until she knew that he was near the breaking point. When she could no longer stop the rush of sensation, no longer put off her own release, she pressed her lips to his ear and whispered, "Come with me, Kurt. Come with me *now.*"

He covered her mouth with his. A kiss swallowed her cry of ecstasy. The world disappeared until there was just the two of them climaxing in the stream like primeval forest creatures, panting, sighing, reveling in one another.

Finally, replete, she laid her head on his shoulder. Her heartbeat slowed to a near-normal rate.

"That was wonderful," she sighed, pressing her cheek against his shoulder. She cupped clear water in her hand, lifted it, let it cascade down the back of her neck. She thought about how silly she'd been last night when she'd worried about warning signs and omens.

Now that Kurt was here, now that she was in his arms again, there was no doubt this is where she belonged.

"Carrie?"

"Mmm?"

"Let go, hon."

She wondered why he was whispering.

"What?"

"Let go. Slide down." He was prying her arms from around her neck. "Now."

"What's wrong?"

"Duck down so that your breasts are underwater."

She turned around and there, spread out on the bank above them, was a Cub Scout troop decked out in their navy shorts and shirts with yellow bandanas tied around their necks. Their scout leader was nowhere to be seen.

"Hey, mister," one of the boys yelled. "We know mouth-to-mouth, too, if you need any help."

"Way cool," another chimed in. "He saved her from getting drownded!"

"She sure made a lot of weird noises," added a short kid who was staring at Carrie in amazement.

She was wondering how long she could hold her breath when one of the Cubs yelled, "Mister, if that's your Jeep back there in the field, you forgot to set the parking brake. Our troop master said to tell you it rolled down into a culvert."

A RECORDING OF DON HO'S mellow voice wafted through the hotel boutique the next morning. Since her bag still hadn't arrived, Carrie decided to shop for a few more necessities.

At breakfast on their *lanai,* Kurt tried to assure her that a mini-shopping spree would help her forget about the spectacle they'd made of themselves in front of the Cub Scouts, not to mention the embarrassment of having to climb out of the pool, hurriedly dress and then wait two hours for a tow truck to come and pull the Jeep out of a drainage ditch and back up the hill.

She chose a floral bikini in hot pinks and sunny yellows, some pretty sandals, a sundress and a *pareau,* a piece of colorful rayon fabric that could be tied in numerous ways to create wraparound cover-ups. Kurt waited near the door, chatting on his cell to his father, Bogie, a retired art history teacher.

Carrie changed into the swimsuit in the boutique dressing room and wrapped the *pareau* around her. Tucking her tank top and shorts into the shopping bag, she was ready for the pool, ready to start over on Kauai. Ready to put the past two days behind her.

When she stepped out of the dressing room, Kurt

glanced over and gave her a big smile and a thumbs-up. Snapping his phone shut, he waited for her to join him.

"What did your dad say? Shouldn't they be on the flight from Denver already?"

Kurt's father and twin brother, Turk, were traveling together, making the long trek from Vermont to Hawaii.

"They've reached Denver, but their flight is delayed." He looked away a little too quickly for her peace of mind.

She'd only met his brother once. The word eccentric didn't do Turk justice. Their parents, Bogie and Trini, hadn't been expecting twins and had only chosen the one name, Kurt. When their second son was born moments later, they quickly scrambled the same four letters and came up with Turk.

Turk was as handsome as Kurt but not identical in looks. He was also an artist—but instead of choosing a traditional art form, Turk had made a name for himself crafting sculptures out of dryer lint.

When Kurt told her that his brother was one of the foremost dryer lint artists in the country, Carrie thought he was kidding until she discovered Turk had been awarded a National Endowment Grant for his artistic pursuits. The entire hamlet of Verdant, Vermont, where the Rowland boys grew up, shared in Turk's fame by contributing bushels of colorful dryer lint for his projects.

"Anything wrong?" She had the feeling Kurt was holding something back.

"Everything's fine." He nodded, but only slightly. Just enough *not* to reassure her.

"Kurt, what's going on?"

"The Denver airport is snowed in."

She felt her heart sink to her toes. Snowed in. A natural occurrence, but was it another omen? Turk was Kurt's best man—and now he was stranded in Denver. So was their dad.

"They'll *be* here, Carrie."

"There's something else you're not telling me. I can see it in your eyes."

He ran his hand over the night's growth of dark stubble on his jaw. "I'm not going to tell you unless you promise not to start in with the bad omen thing again."

Last night in bed, she'd tried to tell him a bit about the article she'd read, but his attention kept straying to her breasts and he fell asleep without hearing her out.

"Kurt, please tell me what *else* is going on," she demanded.

"My great-aunt Harriet is missing."

"Missing?"

He nodded, took her hand and led her out of the store. By now both female clerks were not even pretending to ignore them. They'd sidled up closer and were openly listening to the exchange.

He led her down a lava-rock path, through an extensive garden full of dripping crab claw heliconia and overhanging plumeria trees. When they reached a small stone bench beside the pool's cascading waterfall, he sat down and pulled her down beside him.

She stared at their bare toes lined up in their sandals. His great-aunt Harriet was eighty-nine. She lived in a retirement condo in Miami and was to have met up with Bogie and Turk in Denver and travel on to Kauai with them.

Kurt laced his fingers through hers and rubbed the back of her hand with his thumb. "They haven't heard from her since yesterday. She wasn't on her flight from Florida to Denver. They got the airlines to tell them that much. She's not answering her home phone."

"What if…" Carrie hated to say it aloud. Anything could have happened to the woman.

"Dad called her neighbor, Mr. Morganstern, and had him go check the apartment. She's not there. He saw her leave in an airport shuttle."

"You think she could have been kidnapped?"

He laughed and shook his head. "If anyone had kidnapped her, they'd have turned her loose by now. You've never met my great-aunt."

She'd seen photos, though, and Harriet looked harmless enough. "What are we going to do?"

"There's nothing we can do until we hear from her. She'll turn up."

"Aren't you in the least bit worried? She's eighty-nine, Kurt."

"She's always said age is just a number."

"Still, I'm sure your father is worried sick."

"Dad? No way. He believes the universe is in charge."

The universe is in charge. She fell silent, thinking. How could the Rowlands *not* be worried? Is this how Kurt would react if they had a child who was late getting home from school some afternoon? Would he leave it up to the *universe* to take care of Junior?

What if the universe was trying to tell them something right now?

A snowstorm in Denver. Another natural sign. *Ho'ailona.*

She thought, for a moment, she heard the drumbeat of the island echoing inside her—until she realized it was only the pounding of her own heart.

"I'd like to go back to the room," she told him. She didn't dare add that she thought she was having a heart attack.

BY THE TIME THEY reached the door to the Honeymoon *Hale,* Kurt noticed Carrie was more than a little anxious.

"What's wrong?"

She walked inside as if she hadn't heard. The huge cottage was airy, bright and pure luxury. He followed her over to the sliding doors and they walked out onto the balcony. Kurt was still astounded by the breathtaking view of the lush, tropical foliage and the walking paths that meandered past the pool down to the beach. He studied the view with an artist's eye. The colors were magnificent.

He found Carrie in the dressing area, staring at her shopping bags.

"You don't really need to wear anything." He took a step closer, bringing them together, slipped his arms around her waist and brought her against him. He loved that she was tall, that they fit together perfectly. He lowered his lips to hers, tantalized by the same electricity he'd felt the first time he'd kissed her.

She was almost smiling, still distracted. When she pulled out of his arms, alarm bells went off inside him.

"What's wrong, babe?"

She stared down at her hands, refusing to meet his eyes. He placed his hand beneath her chin and gently forced her to look up. "What is it?"

She shrugged. "The signs."

"Not this again." From the look on her face now, he wished he'd paid more attention last night.

Signs and omens, astrological forecasts, mediums

and psychics. His mother, Trini, had been a great believer in all things mystical. His twin brother was, too. But Kurt's feet were planted firmly on the ground.

"You're kidding, right? You're not *really* worried," he said.

"I *wish* I was kidding." She crossed over to the table that held a pile of books he hadn't given more than a glance until now. Books on Hawaii, local lore, myths. She shuffled through them until she found the same magazine he'd ignored on his flight. She held it up, tapped the cover.

"Ancient Hawaiians believed that nature sends us signs…*ho'ailona* they called them. The spirit world gives us warnings of troubles to come. Omens. It's up to us to heed them."

He looked at the books. "Where did you get all this stuff?"

"The hotel gift shop."

She had at least ten books on Hawaiian legends, myths, spirits, *kahuna* magic and healing. One of the things he loved about her was that she threw herself into everything, every new interest, with abandon. But all this talk of signs and omens gave him pause—surely she wouldn't resort to such a flimsy excuse to call things off.

He'd dated countless women before Carrie, but from the moment he'd laid eyes on her, he'd known deep in his soul that she was the only one who would ever claim his heart. He wanted her to be his wife. He didn't care how elaborate the ceremony, how many attended, or where it happened. He wanted to stand beside her and officially vow to love, honor and cherish her all the days of his life.

"You aren't having doubts, are you?" He steeled himself for her response.

"What?"

He'd never seen her so distracted. "Doubts. About us. About our marriage." Was she trying to come up with an excuse to cancel the wedding? He couldn't, wouldn't believe it.

She shook her head. "No! No doubts about us, but I'm wondering if this is the right time to get married. Or maybe this just isn't the right place—"

"Everyone's on the way, Carrie. Everything is set."

"I know, but the signs—"

"*What* signs?"

"My lost luggage. I didn't reserve that Jeep and yesterday it rolled into a ditch. Those Cub Scouts—" Her face was flaming with embarrassment. "Your last-minute flight delay—"

"I'm here now." He spread his arms wide. "Hey, I think it's a *good* sign that I was resourceful enough to get here even though there was no transportation available."

"There wasn't?"

"No. I had to bribe a movie-tour van to let me hop a ride."

"You're kidding."

"That's not something I'd kid about. You know what it's like to be cooped up with a bunch of Texans singing Elvis tunes at the tops of their lungs? It was only for a few minutes, but I think I may have irreparable ear damage." He knew a surge of relief when the corner of her mouth lifted in a half smile, but her smile disappeared in an instant.

"But now there's more than just the Jeep incident and my lost bag," she said. "Your dad and brother are stuck on the mainland. Your aunt is *missing*. Our wedding planner and her caterer are MIA, too. If it was just *one* thing, I might not worry, but your family is stranded and no one here returns my calls."

She shook her head, gnawed on her thumbnail for a second and then sighed. "I'm really trying not to turn into Bridezilla here, Kurt, but something *weird* is going on."

"Listen." He reached for her again and started nibbling on the exposed skin of her shoulder. Then he slipped his fingers under the strap of her tank top. "Why don't we get comfortable and discuss this in bed? Afterward, I could really use a nap." He had the strap off her shoulder when he realized her palms were pressed firmly against his chest—and not in a good way.

"Kurt…wait. There's something else I need to talk to you about…"

He pulled back. Stared down into her eyes. "I thought you wanted to—"

"I…it might be bad luck to…you know—" she waved her hand around "—keep this up…" She blushed up to her hairline.

"Bad luck to *keep what up?*"

"To make love anymore before the honeymoon. I mean, it's supposedly bad luck for the groom to see the bride on their wedding day and here we are, *sleeping* together in the same cottage. The *honeymoon* cottage. It's only two days until the wedding. Maybe this isn't such a good idea."

He glanced at the pile of books again. Kahuna *Magic, Myths and Legends of Hawaii.*

"Don't tell me that the ancient Hawaiians thought it was taboo for engaged couples to share a honeymoon cottage before the wedding."

"Are you making fun of me?"

"Certainly not. I'm worried. I put you on the plane and everything was fine. Now, less than twenty hours later, you're getting cold feet."

"I'm not getting anything of the sort. It's just that all these weird things keep happening."

"They aren't weird things. They're just *life.* You're thinking like one of those celebrities who puts a moratorium on sex before the wedding—revirginiz-ing—they call it."

"I'm not revirginizing. I just don't think we should make love before our wedding night. Is that too much to ask?"

"Do you want me to get another room?"

"We can still *sleep* together…" Her words faded away.

"But no lovemaking before the wedding?" It was ridiculous to think they shouldn't make love until the wedding. They'd shared the same living space for two years. "So sleeping side by side is okay? Or do I have to bunk on the floor?" He glanced at the pile of reference books. "Did you read that in an ancient Hawaiian rituals manual somewhere? Sleeping, yes. Hanky-panky, no."

He would have laughed if her eyes weren't so suspiciously bright with unshed tears. She was totally serious.

"I know it sounds ridiculous—" she was clinging to both his hands "—but I don't want any more bad luck. I want our wedding to come off perfectly, so lovemaking is taboo. In Hawaiian the word is *kapu*. It's only for two nights, Kurt."

"What about days?" He tried to kiss her.

"I'm serious."

He shoved his fingers through his hair, paced

across the room to put some space between them, walked back and took her hands in his.

"Carrie, honey, you know how much I love you. You know that it doesn't matter to me even if it ends up being just the two of us exchanging our vows on the beach alone. All that's important is that you be my wife. We don't need the luau or the flowers. All we need is each other and the officiate."

"*Kahuna,*" she whispered. "Rainbow said she'd booked a *kahuna*. That's a Hawaiian shaman."

"Whatever. Just so it's legal." He paused, squeezed her hands gently. They were cold as ice. "You know I love you, don't you?"

She nodded. "I do. I don't know what's wrong with me. Ordinarily I wouldn't be frightened of anything…" She let her words drift away.

"Ordinarily you'd be in complete control, just as you are in control of every other aspect of your life. Your career, your shop. You make things happen, Carrie. You're a doer. But you can't control the weather, or the airline luggage department, or the rental company's vehicle availability. Or the Cub Scouts."

When she started to open her mouth in protest, he saw the doubt in her eyes.

"Don't try to tell me a little snow on the mainland is a bad omen. It always snows in Denver in the winter," he said.

"It's almost spring."

"Last year it snowed in Denver in June."

She sighed. Her hands were finally warming up. "You're right. Maybe I am just nervous."

He reached for her, tucked her into his arms as he'd done a million times before and was relieved when her arm slipped around his waist and she melted against him.

"Aren't jitters part of being a bride?" He kissed her, thrilled when she responded like his Carrie, the Carrie who wasn't under the spell of the island lore, signs, omens and a case of nerves.

"Why don't we go for a swim?" He suggested. He needed a plunge into cold water in the worst way. "And I've got another idea. Let's book a couple's massage at the hotel spa. My treat."

"Is that a bribe?"

"You think I'd try to bribe my way into making love to you?"

"Exactly."

SOFT, SOOTHING MUSIC played in the background. The swish of overhead ceiling fans melded with the hush of trade wind breezes gently blowing through bamboo privacy shades that blocked the view of the outdoor massage area at the hotel's spa.

Two massage tables were separated just enough to

let the therapists move between them to work on Kurt and Carrie at the same time. She lay there replete, draped in soft batik fabric as the therapist expertly smoothed scented oil down both sides of her spine. Kurt lay on the opposite table.

Bright red cardinals and shama thrush sang in the nearby branches. Carrie opened her eyes and found Kurt staring into them. She smiled. If she'd been a cat, she would have purred. A male therapist was working the muscles across Kurt's shoulders.

At the end of the massage, they showered off in the spa's private couples' shower, an indoor-outdoor grotto complete with a lava-rock wall that offered the experience of showering beneath a faux waterfall without having to go through a strenuous hike to get there.

They returned to the bungalow where Kurt drifted off to take a much-needed nap.

Carrie was just about to call Rainbow again when her cell phone rang. She caught it on the first note and hurried out onto the *lanai*, closing the slider so she wouldn't disturb Kurt.

"Carrie?" It was her mother.

"Hi, Mom."

"Did you see the news? A terrible snowstorm in Denver is headed our way."

"We heard from Kurt's dad. They're waiting for

the airport to reopen. You shouldn't have any problem. Storms don't move that quickly."

"What a fiasco. It would have been so much easier if the wedding was in Chicago."

"It's not a fiasco, Mother. It's just a storm. They'll get here. You will, too." Carrie found herself sounding as positive as Kurt and smiled. He was stretched out asleep with his bare feet dangling over the end of the bed. Peering at him through the sliding doors, she was tempted to join him as soon as she hung up. Perhaps wake him with a kiss and—

"It would have been so much nicer if—"

"If I'd gotten married at the club. I know you would have preferred that, Mom, but that's not what we wanted."

"It's not what Kurt wanted, you mean."

"It's not what *I* wanted. Kurt just wants to get married."

"I'll bet he does, now that your shop is doing so well—"

"Mom?" Carrie wasn't in the mood to listen to a lecture on what she had to lose by marrying an artist. Dorothy had no idea that Kurt commanded close to seven figures for most of his murals now. "I've got to go. Someone is coming up the walk."

"Oh, well, goodbye then."

"I love you, Mom. See you day after tomorrow."

"Yes." That sigh again. "Goodbye, dear."

FROM THE *LANAI* Carrie could see a young woman walking up the stone path that led to the *hale*. She hurried through the room to get to the door before the girl knocked and disturbed Kurt.

Carrie stepped outside and quickly closed the door behind her.

"Aloha!" The ethereal-looking blonde was outfitted in a tiered gathered skirt of India gauze. The bright purple fabric was dusted with glittering sequins. Her long, fine hair swirled around her shoulders, which were tan and bare except for the thin spaghetti straps of her satin blouse. There was a ring on every one of her fingers. She didn't look a day over eighteen.

"I'm Oleo. I'm representing Rainbow Roberts of Happily Ever After Events."

Oleo as in margarine? Carrie wondered.

"I'm Carrie Evans." Carrie shook Oleo's hand. Her relief at finally connecting with someone from Happily Ever After was short-lived.

"Rainbow isn't here this month. She's in Bangkok. I'm her assistant and I'll be handling your wedding on Saturday."

"Bangkok?"

Oleo smiled. "She went for liposuction."

"To *Bangkok?*"

"Best cosmetic surgery in the world. A third of the cost." She was carrying a clipboard stuffed with sheets and bits of paper. As Oleo began to riffle through the pile wedged beneath the clip, Carrie didn't know whether to laugh or cry. Her wedding planner was in Bangkok having lipo and left a teenager in charge?

"Do you mind my asking how many weddings you've handled for Rainbow?" Carrie glanced out over the grounds of the hotel. It certainly *looked* like paradise.

Oleo wasn't ruffled in the least. "Oh, I don't know. Five weddings this week alone. I've worked for Rainbow for almost five years. "

"How old are you?" Carrie blurted out the question before she could stop herself.

Oleo blinked. "How *old* am I?"

Carrie shrugged. "I'm just curious."

"Thirty."

"Thirty?" The knot of tension behind Carrie's eyes began to ease.

"I told you they do wonders in Bangkok. Now…" Oleo glanced around. "Is there somewhere we can sit and go over things?"

"My fiancé is asleep inside. How about we go to the poolside tables?"

"Great."

"Let me slip inside and grab my folder."

A few minutes later they were seated beneath an umbrella, poring over Carrie's notes.

"I think photos of you and your husband in the outrigger canoe should be taken after the ceremony. That way if your dress should get wet, it won't matter as much. We've had brides who wanted to arrive at the ceremony by canoe and they've gotten drenched. Far better to exit that way when it won't matter if your dress gets wet afterward."

"Maybe we should cut the canoe ride altogether?"

Oleo waved that idea away with the toss of her beringed fingers. "It'll be a great ending—all the guests watching as you two are paddled off into the night. Tiki torches will be burning on both ends of the canoe. You'll just be paddled a few yards away to another cove and from there, driven back to the hotel."

"It certainly sounds like a dramatic ending."

"Unforgettable, really." Oleo sighed. "Well worth the extra two hundred dollars."

"Here is a photo of what I'd like my bouquet to look like," Carrie held up a magazine shot of ivory roses arranged in an abundant nosegay.

Oleo's lips pursed. Carrie realized Oleo might have been frowning, too, but who could tell with all the Botox injected between her brows?

"Elegra has her own sense of style."

"Elegra?"

"The florist. There's no need to show him, I mean *her,* any photos. Elegra doesn't work that way. He, I mean *she,* works by intuition alone. He...*she* meditates and the image of the arrangement comes to...her."

Carrie couldn't help but notice Oleo was having some gender issues in regard to Elegra.

"Let me guess," Carrie said. "Elegra just returned from Bangkok?"

Oleo's relief was mirrored in her glowing smile. She nodded. "Exactly. She was Erik before she went to Thailand."

An image of the staid, conservative wedding planner at Willow Creek Country Club flashed across Carrie's mind. The woman was in her fifties, tailored, composed and efficient. She and her staff had coordinated years of tasteful weddings, anniversary and birthday celebrations.

And I have Rainbow, Oleo and Elegra.

A soft hint of the trade winds blew across the poolside courtyard. Somewhere nearby, a wind chime tinkled. A chill ran down Carrie's spine.

What have I done? she wondered. Asking our families to fly thousands of miles to participate in what might very well turn out to be a sideshow. She was tempted to wake Kurt up and tell him to call his dad and brother, have them spend their time tracking down his aunt Harriet and then head back to Vermont. She still had time to stop her parents. And maybe reach Ellen Marshall, her maid of honor.

She and Kurt could fly back to L.A. and marry in a couple of weeks, after things settled down. Everything was fine the way it was anyway. They were happy. They were in love. They were devoted to one another. A promise made under the full moon was binding enough for his parents for over thirty years. Why couldn't that sort of arrangement work for him?

"Carrie?" Oleo was watching her expectantly.

"Excuse me. I was just thinking about something."

"I'm sure there's a lot on your mind."

"You have no idea."

"I was just saying that you're welcome to stop by the wedding reception I'm handling this afternoon on the beach at Kalihiwai here on the North Shore." She slipped a map out from the mass of papers on the clipboard. "The ceremony is at three. The reception is on the beach afterward. Come whenever you like."

"I'm afraid my luggage hasn't arrived yet."

"It's just aloha wear. No worries." Oleo's smile was genuine.

It was too late to cancel and find another wedding coordinator at this point. Besides, Carrie had put down a huge deposit for the flowers, the cake, the luau. Which reminded her, "I tried to find the caterer earlier."

"You did?" Oleo blinked.

Carrie shrugged. "When I couldn't get a hold of Rainbow, I drove to Anahola. The caterer's mother said she's gone *holoholo*. I hope she'll be all right by Saturday."

"That just means she's gone on a pleasurable outing," Oleo explained.

"You speak Hawaiian?"

"Everyone learns a smattering of everyday Hawaiian and a few words of pidgin English if they're here long enough."

"Leinani went all the way to the Big Island. Should I worry?"

Oleo took a deep, calming breath and closed her eyes. Carrie waited. When Oleo opened her eyes she said, "It's all good."

"The marriage certificate?"

"I have it."

"It'll be legal?"

Oleo laughed. "Perfectly legal in all fifty states. By the way, what time is it?"

Carrie noticed the young woman wasn't wearing a watch. What professional in her right mind didn't wear a watch?

"Eleven-thirty," Carrie said.

Oleo started to gather her things. "I've got to run. Lots to do before this afternoon. I'll see you there."

When Carrie walked back into the room, Kurt was awake and watching the news. The minute she crossed the threshold, he hit the power button on the remote and turned off the television, hoping she hadn't seen the screen.

"Hey, babe." He smiled and quickly tossed the remote on the chair he'd vacated. By the time he'd reached her side, he could tell something was wrong and wondered if she'd seen the news while he was sleeping.

"Where have you been?" He tried to sound as if he hadn't a care in the world.

"The wedding planner's assistant dropped by. We chatted out by the pool."

"Feeling better about things?" If anything, she'd lost all the color in her cheeks. He watched her chew on her bottom lip for a second before she finally met his eyes.

"Her name is Oleo."

"Oleo? What happened to Rainbow?" He was proud of himself for remembering the event planner's name. He'd left everything up to Carrie and now he was wondering if he shouldn't have taken a bigger part in the planning. The stress was obviously getting to her.

"Rainbow is in Bangkok getting liposuction. The florist was there recently, too. He was getting… well…let's just say he's not himself anymore."

"I'm sure they do this all the time."

"Go to Bangkok for cosmetic surgery?"

"Coordinate destination weddings."

She walked into his embrace. "Hold me, Kurt. I think I'm going nuts."

"Hey, look at me."

He placed a thumb beneath her chin, tilted her head until she was looking up at him. Her lips were the color of pastel flower petals. Her eyes lush turquoise, outlined with sable lashes. He could see that she was troubled. Her nerves communicated through her touch. It wasn't like Carrie to fall apart and the fact that she was clinging to him now had him worried. He had no idea what she would say or do when she realized what was going on back on the mainland.

"I love you," he reminded her, suddenly hoping his love was enough.

"I love you, too. With all my heart. You know that, don't you?" She reached up, brushed his hair back, smoothed her fingertips across his brow.

"I know," he said softly.

"Love was enough for your parents, wasn't it? They didn't put themselves through all of this—"

"Six guests and a wedding on the beach is not that much, is it? But it doesn't really matter to me who actually gets here in time. I want you to be my wife. Now and forever, Carrie," he whispered.

"I want you forever, too," she said softly. "I love

you. I know I'll always love you. I don't want to risk that love…not now, not ever."

"You really think we'll risk losing our love for one another by taking marriage vows?"

"My parents—"

"We are not your parents. We are not my parents, either."

She sighed. "You're right. I know how much this wedding means to you."

"It should mean everything to you, too."

He wanted her so bad it hurt. He wanted to strip her naked and take her to bed, to make love until dusk crept into the room and the stars came out one by one and filled the tropical night sky like jewels on midnight velvet. He wanted to run his hands over the smooth hills and valleys of the body he knew as well as his own. He wanted his touch to reassure her, to guide her, to encourage her to open her heart and trust in him, to trust in their love and their future together.

But he'd promised not to make love to her until the official honeymoon. As ridiculous as it seemed, he knew that she was dead serious about the *kapu*.

He had a hard-on that wouldn't quit when he stepped away from her and walked out onto the *lanai*. He hoped the colors and textures of Hanalei Bay and the mountain ridges encircling the valley would take his mind off of making love to Carrie.

But she followed him outside, wrapped her arms around him from behind and laid her cheek against his back. He could feel her warmth through his aloha shirt.

"I'm sorry," she whispered.

He turned and took her in his arms again. "I'm trying to understand."

"I know. I have a feeling Ellen would think I'm nuts. She's always said any woman in her right mind would be dragging *you* to the altar and not the other way around."

"The beach. I'm only dragging you to the beach to get married at sunset."

"Right." She smiled up at him. "By the way, we've been invited to a wedding Oleo is handling this afternoon.

"Great. We have a little time to go sightseeing first. Besides, if I don't get out of this room and away from the bed, I'm going to try to coax you into it."

"I'll get my purse. Speaking of Ellen, I need to call and see if she got away all right."

He wanted to tell her not to bother. The last thing he needed right now was for Carrie to connect with her maid of honor.

"Why don't you call her later?"

"It'll just take a second."

He wished he'd had the presence of mind to hide her cell.

"YOU'VE REACHED Ellen Marshall. Leave a message and I'll get back to you as soon as I can."

Carrie waited until she heard the beep on Ellen's phone, left a message and added, "I can't *wait* to talk to you. I *need* to talk to you. Call me ASAP."

Ellen was pragmatic, funny and had been Carrie's best friend since middle school. When Carrie first told Ellen about Kurt, her friend had flown to L.A. from Chicago to meet him. Later, Ellen told Carrie that Kurt was a keeper and if Carrie didn't marry the man, she was going to steal him for herself.

Carrie knew her friend was kidding, but Ellen's approval was very important to her. They'd been inseparable during their formative teen years and the hours Carrie had spent at the Marshall household had been wonderful reprieves away from her own home where the tension between her parents was so thick you could almost see it.

Ellen would understand her hesitation. She would listen without laughing when Carrie explained about the signs and omens. Well, Ellen might laugh, but she wouldn't make light of Carrie's concerns.

That's what friends were for.

"Ready?" Kurt was waiting by the door looking like *GQ*-goes-Hawaiian in his bright aloha shirt and *The Ultimate Guide to Kauai* book in hand.

"Ready." She dropped her cell in her purse and followed him out of the Honeymoon *Hale*. She didn't feel nearly as ready as she sounded.

"CLIMB, climb, climb, climb. Then climb some more."

Carrie stared down at the open guidebook in her hands and read the rest of the Hanalei 'Okolehau Trail hike description to Kurt.

"It says 'There are breaks in the vegetation affording grand views, but you couldn't care less because you're puffing so hard.'" She closed the book and handed it back to him.

Her rubber-soled reef walkers were covered with red dirt and mud. Sweat streaked her face as it slipped down from her hairline. Her new shorts had a smear of dirt ground into the seat where she'd hit the steep slope and slid a few inches after tripping over an exposed tree root.

Hands on hips, she shook her head and smiled at Kurt. "This is really no way to win a woman's heart."

Kurt laughed and kissed the tip of her nose. "Hey, admit it. You haven't thought about the wedding for a good thirty minutes."

"How could I? I've been fighting to keep my footing and trying to keep my heart from exploding."

She frowned at the narrow trail through a forest of star pines. It ran straight up along the top of a ridge that rose from the floor of the Hanalei Valley to far beyond the point where they'd stopped at the top of a packed red dirt trail. Beside them power lines from a huge tower swept down toward the watery taro fields below.

"Are we going all the way to the top?" Her legs were aching. She wasn't sure she could make it. In fact, she wasn't sure she wanted to try.

Kurt flipped through the pages of the guidebook. "It says here when you get to the top you'll be 'richly rewarded' with a sweeping view. You can see a fifth of the island from up there."

She didn't want to tell him she'd already seen enough of the island as it was, but just then a cloud slipped across the face of the sun, offering a respite from the heat. She took a deep breath and looked around. The view from where they were was already spectacular.

"How about I sit on that flat rock over there and wait while you go up and enjoy the view? When you come back you can tell me what you saw, okay?"

Kurt hesitated, staring uphill. "No problem. I'm ready to head back if you are."

He loved challenges. She could tell that he really wanted to go on.

"Seriously, I'll be fine. I'll sit and relax. It's so peaceful here." She took a cleansing breath and looked around. Indeed, the spot was magical. The forest floor looked as if a primeval sprite had sprinkled ferns and tiny star-shaped pine trees all over the ground.

"You sure?"

"Positive."

Kurt slipped a small bottled water out of his pack and handed it to her. "It shouldn't take me long," he promised.

"Take your time." They hadn't passed a soul on the trail. Nor had there been any cars parked in the trail-head lot beside the Hanalei River. Carrie made an attempt to brush off the large rock she'd chosen then remembered her pants were already stained. She sat down, stretched out her legs and crossed them at the ankles. She pulled her cell phone out of her pocket. There was no service on the side of the mountain.

A soft, cool breeze started the trees whispering *hush, hush.* Somewhere nearby, a thrush sang a trilling song. She tried whistling in imitation. The thrush stopped singing for a moment, then whistled back.

Carrie closed her eyes and leaned back on her hands, turning her face to the sun until the sound of twigs snapping on the trail below her brought her upright, eyes open, alert.

As if he'd materialized out of nowhere, a tall Hawaiian man with long white hair falling well past his shoulders stood before her. He wore a pair of faded shorts, a T-shirt with the image of a bone fishhook printed on it, and bare feet stained with red dirt. He seemed impervious to the pine twigs and pebbles beneath them. Beside him, a white, mixed-breed shaggy dog sat on its haunches with its tongue lolling.

Startled by the intrusion, street-smart from living in L.A., Carrie immediately got to her feet, ready to run, to scream, to defend herself. She glanced up the hill. Kurt was already out of sight, hidden by the mass of jungle growth.

"Aloha," the man said. His voice was deep, resonant, as if it came from depths outside himself and was channeled through. "Beautiful day, eh?"

"V…very." It took a second to find her voice. She glanced down at the dog then back up at the man. "I…I'm waiting for my fiancé. He's…he's just up there a little way."

She had no idea exactly where Kurt was at this point. Still within shouting distance, she hoped.

"Fiancé."

She nodded. The man hadn't moved an inch. She took a step back and realized there was nowhere to go. If she backed up any farther, she risked sliding down the steep mountainside. "Our wedding is Saturday."

"Congratulations." The man was watching her closely. Too closely. He was silent for a moment or two, his expression serious.

She had the strangest feeling, almost as if he could see into her soul. He closed his eyes, raised his palms and began to chant in a voice that carried on the trades, over the tops of the trees, down into the valley.

"He kau auane'i i ka lae 'a'a."

Goose bumps rose over Carrie's skin. The man's hands dropped to his sides again, he opened his eyes and smiled without explanation.

"Was that a blessing?"

Rainbow Roberts had arranged for a *kahuna* to perform a traditional wedding ceremony. Oleo said it was confirmed.

The man shook his head. "An old Hawaiian proverb. Watch out, lest the canoe land on a rocky reef." He reached down and scratched the dog behind its ear. The animal panted and looked up at him in adoration.

To her relief, the man glanced at the trail ahead and said, "I'd better get going."

Obsessing over the meaning of his words, Carrie barely nodded when he bid her goodbye.

"Aloha," she said, watching him head up the trail. Her knees weak, Carrie sank back down onto the rock.

Watch out lest the canoe land on a rocky reef.

Watch out.

Rocky reef.

The rocky reef of life? The canoe of marriage?

Was it a literal warning?

Is he warning us not to get into the torch-lighted canoe after the ceremony?

Or not to get married at all?

She kept glancing at her watch for another forty minutes before she saw Kurt heading back down the trail and greeted him with questions rather than a kiss.

"Did you see that big Hawaiian man?"

"I didn't see anyone." Kurt wiped his brow with the back of his arm. "The view up there was spectacular. I could see all the way to the Kilauea lighthouse. It was incredible."

"You didn't run into a Hawaiian with long white hair? And a white dog?" She glanced around him, gazed at the trail. "There must be more than one way up."

"No, and I didn't pass anyone on my way down, either."

"But…" Her heart started to pound. "But there was a man here. He spoke to me. He had a big white dog. He scared the heck out of me. It was almost as if he appeared out of nowhere—and he said something in Hawaiian."

Kurt was digging in his backpack. "There's only one way up and down. I didn't see a man or a dog." He found what he was looking for and pulled out a plastic bottle. "You need some Gatorade. I think you're dehydrated."

"I'm not *de*-anything. I saw a Hawaiian and his dog. He gave me a warning."

Kurt stopped, Gatorade in hand, and stared at her as if he'd just realized what she was saying. His voice dropped an octave. "What *kind* of a warning?"

"Cryptic, that's for sure. Something about the canoe hitting a rocky reef."

"Did he threaten you?"

Suddenly he was all testosterone, ready to defend her, ready to take on an unknown threat. The last thing she needed was him tearing off after some innocent guy who was only trying to impress a tourist.

She laid her hand on his arm. "He didn't threaten me. In fact, I'm sure it was probably nothing."

"What's a canoe got to do with anything?"

"We're leaving the reception luau in a canoe."

"We are?"

She frowned. "Maybe I should cancel it. What do you think?"

"I think you're starting to lose it."

"You're afraid *I'm* starting to *lose* it?" She shook her head. "You don't *believe* I just saw someone standing right *here?*" She pointed to the spot where the man had been. "You think I'm cracking up?" She waved her arms around. "You think maybe this wedding is driving me crazy?"

He tried to put his arm around her shoulders and draw her near.

"It's okay, babe. You've been under a lot of stress."

"Don't *babe* me." She skirted around him and started back down the trail. The slope was steep and slick. The descent was as hard as the climb.

She gave him the silent treatment all the way back to the Jeep. As soon as they were on the road back up the hill to the Hanalei Plantation, she pulled her cell phone out of her pocket. Kurt glanced over for a moment as if about to tell her something, but then turned his attention back to the road.

Three voice mails. Relieved, she saw that one was from Ellen. Two were from her mother. She dialed her maid of honor first.

"HI, CARRIE. It's Ellen. Can you believe this weather? Sheesh. The whole world is shut down. What happened to global warming anyway? I made it to Denver but nothing is moving. Don't worry, though, where there's a will, there's a way. It'll take a national disaster to keep me from getting to Kauai for your wedding."

"Now Ellen is stuck in Denver, too." Carrie stared out the front window. Kurt focused on the narrow road to the hotel.

"Hmm."

"That means your dad and Turk haven't gotten out yet." She was punching in the number to hear the next message.

"Carrie. It's your mother. You must be just frantic

by now. Thank heavens we hadn't already left for the airport. O'Hare is shut down. All of the city streets are closed. Give me a call."

"What in the world is going on over there?" She turned to Kurt as he pulled up to the valet parking stand. Her stomach did a backflip as she slid out of the Jeep and waited for him.

"Ready?" He ushered her through the lush tropical garden of the open-air lobby toward the path to their *hale*.

"Both Denver and O'Hare airports are shut down." She glanced up, saw that his expression never changed and realized he wasn't surprised in the least. She stopped dead in her tracks beside a faux waterfall.

"You knew."

When he finally met her eyes, she was certain he'd kept the truth from her.

"You already *knew* both airports are shut down. What's going on, Kurt?"

"Storm of the century."

"What?"

"That's what CNN is calling it. A freak storm of the century. It's moving across the U.S. from the northwest. Ice and snowstorms hitting with unprece-dented ferocity. Nothing's moving."

"You knew—"

"Carrie."

"You knew and you didn't even tell me. Why not?"

"I wanted us to have a few hours alone without you worrying about it."

"When did you hear?"

"While you were out at the pool with the wedding coordinator, I woke up and turned on the news."

She remembered how he'd turned the set off the moment she walked in.

None of their guests were on the way. Her parents hadn't even left their house—which in itself was actually a relief. She couldn't imagine her mom and dad camped out in the frequent-flyer lounge. Poor Ellen was no doubt stuck in the airport waiting area with the masses. Turk and Bogie were there somewhere, too.

She pictured Kurt's aunt as a frail eighty-nine-year-old in an airport somewhere, slumped over in a corner with a blanket draped over her shoulders.

Carrie couldn't help it. She moaned.

"What?" Kurt's dark eyes mirrored his concern not for his stranded guests, but for her sanity.

"Your poor aunt," she mumbled.

"Aunt Harriet is more resourceful than my dad and the dryer lint genius combined."

She almost smiled. "What are we going to do, Kurt?"

"What can we do? I'll call Turk and Bogie and see

how they're doing. You call your mom and Ellen. Then we'll change clothes and head up the road to meet Oleo and check out that wedding reception."

"That's *it?* That's your idea of *doing* something?"

"We could stand around and wring our hands, but there's really nothing we can do about the weather, is there?"

He had a point. There wasn't much they could do but wait out the storm on the mainland. *The Storm of the Century.*

Another natural occurrence.

Another omen?

"We can worry just as well on the beach sipping glasses of champagne," Kurt reasoned.

Carrie pictured the Hawaiian on the mountain trail, his piercing dark eyes, his nimbus of white hair. His white dog.

Watch out lest the canoe land on a rocky reef.

Forget about the rocky reef. Things were already bad enough. Standing there beside the faux waterfall with its cool mist on her skin, Carrie shivered. She felt adrift, buffeted by life, as if she were about to capsize.

"What are you thinking?"

She couldn't tell him she was wondering how many more warnings they could ignore before calling off the whole thing.

KURT FLIPPED the plastic key card in the lock, opened the door to the Honeymoon *Hale*. He stood back to let Carrie enter. When she skirted past without a word or a look, his heart sank. All the setbacks were getting to her and he felt helpless.

"I'm going to call Ellen and my mom," she said.

"I'll check in with Bogie and Turk."

His call took less than two minutes. Bogie had managed to nab a table in a pizza and beer bar at the airport and was content watching the sports network. Turk was off trolling for women. Kurt could just see his twin in a casual slouch, hands in his pockets, his long hair artfully falling over his left eye as he flirted with every woman in the place.

Women tended to view Turk as harmless once he started quizzing them on the make and model of their clothes dryers and asking whether or not they used fabric softener or dryer sheets.

When he hung up, Kurt heard Carrie tell Ellen goodbye. Then she tried to call her mother, but gave up.

"The phones must be down. My calls to Chicago aren't going through."

"What about Ellen? Did you reach her?"

She nodded. "She's made her way over to the private jet terminal, hoping to find a way out other than on a commercial airline."

"If anyone can do it, she can." He wished there was something he could do. Wished he'd told Carrie about the storm when he'd learned of it.

She picked up the television remote, muted the sound and flipped through the channels until she found CNN. She stared at the screen for a moment, then turned to him with a disappointed sigh.

He crossed the room, wrapped her in his arms, slipped his hand beneath her tank top, cupped her breast, felt the familiar weight and shape of it against his palm.

She closed her eyes and leaned into him. "Don't tempt me, Kurt. We don't need any more bad luck."

"Run all that by me again. I still don't get how this could be bad luck." She was warm and pliant in his arms and with a little encouragement, he knew she'd be willing.

"Even if it isn't bad luck for the bride and groom to see each other before the wedding, you should have something to look forward to on our wedding night," she whispered.

"Hey, I look forward to this every night. What's that they say about men? We have a sexual thought every twenty seconds?"

"It's more like every two, I think. Especially with you."

"So you can guess what kind of agony I'm in. It's

been a hell of a lot of seconds since we made love." He lifted his hips and pressed his erection against her thigh.

She pulled away. She wasn't smiling, but she looked a bit calmer.

"Where are you going?" He watched her long legs and the seductive sway of her hips as she walked across the room.

"To take a shower and change into my new sundress before you succeed in breaking the *kapu* and seducing me. We're going to a wedding reception to see what Oleo can do, remember?"

THEY DROVE TWENTY MINUTES out of their way before they realized they'd missed the road to Kalihiwai Beach. According to KONG radio, the trades were gusting a good twenty-five to thirty knots. Kurt parked as close as he could to where all the wedding guests were huddled inside a huge, white vinyl cabana enclosed on three sides.

The reception tent, complete with see-through plastic windows, had been set up on the sand. Ironwood pines planted on the edge of the roadside shed long, green-gray needles every time the wind blew through them. Wedding guests in colorful attire were huddled inside the tent like garments stuffed in a dry-cleaning bag.

Some gathered near a long buffet table full of

appetizer platters and a three-tiered wedding cake on display at one end.

As Carrie and Kurt made their way into the tent, Oleo spotted them and rushed over.

"Aloha, you two." She pressed her palms together and bowed, her smile wide as the horizon. Apparently she wasn't a bit concerned that the stiff breeze was about to lift one corner of the tent.

Carrie introduced Kurt. He held tight to her hand, almost as if he feared she'd go racing back to the car.

"Let me show you the *pupu* table," Oleo offered.

Kurt leaned close to Carrie's ear and whispered, "The poo poo table?"

Carrie laughed. "Appetizers. *Pupus* are finger food."

"Heavy *pupu*, we like to call this sort of spread," Oleo explained. "This isn't just light finger food. This is enough for a meal." She waved her hand over an array of sushi, delicate lettuce wraps, a mound of stuffed mushrooms, skewers of barbecued chicken strips, fruit and veggie trays.

"Did Kau Kau Katering provide all of this?" Carrie stared at the spread, incredulous that it could have come out of the small house in Anahola.

Oleo shook her head. "No. Leinani does our luau menu, which is what you've chosen. She's still on the Big Island."

Kurt leaned close. "Looks like Oleo can handle

our wedding. This is a much bigger event than we've planned."

"Considering there may not be anyone at our wedding at all," Carrie whispered.

Her concern about Oleo's abilities was the least of her worries now. There were at least a hundred guests under the big tent and everything appeared to be well organized, every detail covered. Oleo certainly couldn't be held accountable for the stiff breeze.

As they neared the serving table, Carrie noticed the cake frosting appeared to be coated with a light dusting of sand carried on the wind.

"I see you've noticed the Swarovski crystal bride and groom on top of the cake." Oleo drew them closer to the wedding confection. She pointed to the miniature couple planted atop the cake.

"These were handcrafted from a photo of the couple. Each pair is unique."

The little bride and groom were encrusted with colorful crystal gems, their feet anchored in frosting.

Kurt leaned close and whispered in Carrie's ear. "Please. Tell me you didn't."

She glanced over her shoulder and caught him smiling into her eyes. She couldn't resist a chuckle. "Of course not. We're having flowers on top of the cake. A lei of orchids. Somehow I couldn't imagine us encrusted in crystals."

Outside the tent, the real bride and groom were positioned near the water's edge, posing for photos. They were dressed exactly like their crystal clones. The young woman had chosen a traditional wedding gown with a wide tiered skirt that billowed out like a parachute. The trade wind gusts wreaked havoc with her dress, tipping it up behind her, exposing her backside.

The groom wore long linen pants, a white shirt and a yellow cummerbund that matched his bride's bouquet. He snagged her veil just as it went sailing off her head.

Sand pelted the sides of the tent with each gust. The harried bride and groom gave up on the photo-op, held hands and shielded their eyes as they sprinted toward the shelter.

Just as Carrie looked down at the cake, the crystal bride and groom toppled off and landed facedown at her feet in the sand. A chill ran down her spine.

KURT STARED AT THE FALLEN CAKE topper for a heart-beat before he turned to Carrie. All the color had drained from her face. As signs and omens went, the toppled bride and groom was a biggie. *Huge.*

Drastic times called for drastic measures, he reckoned. He had to act and act fast if there was any hope of salvaging the situation. Before Carrie could utter a word, he took a deep breath and said, "I'm beginning to think you're right."

"What?" She tore her attention away from the unfolding drama playing out in front of them. Oleo was reaching for the bejeweled bride and groom while the newlyweds came reeling into the tent.

Kurt grabbed her by the arm and dragged her across the beach to the car.

"I think the signs and omens are pretty damn clear," he told her.

"What are you saying?"

"I'm finally convinced you're right. *Somebody,* the universe, the island, the ancient spirits, *whatever,* something is trying to warn us not to go through with this. I think the only recourse we have is to call off the wedding until we figure out what's really going on here."

THEY DROVE BACK to the hotel in silence as Carric wrestled with the realization that Kurt had finally seen the light. When he suggested they have drinks in the hotel lounge, she agreed. They were shown to a table overlooking the magnificent view of Hanalei Bay and Mount Makana in the distance.

On the far side of the open-air room, a trio entertained guests with a medley of Hawaiian songs. Accompanied by the tinkle of ice in glasses and the hushed conversations going on at various tables scattered around the terrace, the singers' mellow voices sometimes faded beneath the occasional whir of the blender behind the bar.

Still adjusting to Kurt's announcement on the beach, Carrie tried to focus on what he was saying.

"I mean, when you first mentioned signs and omens, I have to admit I thought you were just having bridal jitters, but obviously, that's not the case. I see that now. When those figurines fell off the cake, my eyes were opened."

Carrie's stomach was too queasy to enjoy the frothy white *chichi* the waitress set before her. She pulled the violet vanda orchid off the rim of the glass, took a sip of the coconut and vodka whipped drink, then ignored it.

"It's not as if we're going to disappoint our families," Kurt was saying. "They aren't even here. We'll probably lose our deposits for the tables and tent and caterer—" he shrugged "—but I can afford to take the hit." He reached for her hand across the table. "Better safe than sorry, right?"

As she sat listening to this new Kurt, the Kurt who had campaigned for her to say yes for years, the Kurt who wanted to be married more than anything in the world, all she could think of was…*the wedding is off…the wedding is off.*

After everything that had happened, after all the signs and warnings, she should have been relieved, but now all she felt was empty. She'd been planning their wedding for months and now it was suddenly over. To have it end so abruptly—

"I probably should call Oleo and tell her," she said.

"No problem. I'll handle it. You've done all the planning. It's the least I can do."

She listened as he went on about his determination to research Hawaiian lore. There definitely was something going on, he said, and he wanted to learn as much about it as he could.

"I'm so sorry, Carrie. I'm sorry it took me so long to become convinced canceling is for the best." He finished his mai tai in record time and added, "Something bigger than us is at work here." Then he noticed her untouched drink. "Are you going to drink that?"

She shook her head. "No, I…"

He reached for the tall glass and polished off her *chichi* in record time. She'd never seen him have more than a couple beers or a minimal amount of wine at dinner.

"Come on," he said, taking the lead and pushing away from the table. "I'll walk you back to the *hale*."

He walked around her chair, waited for her to stand. His charm, his smile, his old-world manners were part of the reason she fell for him. All the way back to the *hale,* she felt the warmth of his palm as his hand rode possessively at her waist.

When they reached the door, she realized now that the wedding was officially off, it would be safe to lift her self-imposed ban on lovemaking. She needed him more than ever. Needed his reassurance that their love could stand this and any test. She needed to lose herself in him. In their love for each other.

Outside the front door, she turned and wrapped her arms around his neck. He kissed her long and hot and for a moment she forgot she was no longer going to be his bride on Saturday.

Images of Kurt carrying her over the threshold of the Honeymoon *Hale* and then repeating the custom when they returned home to their L.A. loft filled her with melancholy. When the kiss ended, she cupped his cheek and whispered, "I love you."

"I love you, too, babe." Kurt reached around her to open the door. Once inside, he walked straight to the table where she'd left her books.

Kurt riffled through them, picked up three or four and asked, "Mind if I borrow these?"

"Of course not." She watched him head to the closet. He pulled out his travel bag, set it on the bed and then began to take his clothes out of the low chest of drawers.

"What are you doing?" Her heart nearly fell to her toes.

"Packing." He didn't look at her.

"Why?"

The wedding is off.

Could he have *possibly* meant their relationship was over, too?

"The signs were pretty clear, Carrie, and we ignored them. We don't need any more bad luck, do we? Why tempt fate any more than we already have?"

She watched him toss in the last of his things and then he laid the books atop his clothes. He zipped the bag shut, set it on the floor and pulled up the handle.

"You're *leaving* me?"

He walked over and kissed the tip of her nose. "Of course not."

"Then what's going on?" She indicated the bag with a wave of her hand.

"I'm getting my own room. We don't want to upset the Hawaiian spirits any more than we have already, do we?"

IN THE HAZY TWILIGHT of half sleep and the gray hour before dawn, Carrie woke up alone. She lay nestled in bed watching the sunlight gain strength as dawn illuminated the room. Without Kurt beside her, a heavy emptiness pervaded the cottage and she realized his presence filled her life in ways she hadn't realized until now. She felt hollow without him. A future without Kurt was unthinkable.

Just then, her cell phone went off, and she leaped out of bed and tore across the room to grab it. She found her phone on the table near the remaining books. Hoping it was him, her heart faltered when she read Ellen's number on the screen. Still, she needed to talk to her closest friend in the worst way.

"Carrie?" Ellen sounded as if she were right next door. "How are you doing?"

"I'm fine," she lied.

"You sounded down when you answered."

"There's a lot going on here. Everyone is stuck in airports. My parents decided not to even leave the house. I hate to have put you out like this—"

"Oh, Carrie! Don't worry about me. I've met the most fabulous guy. I was trying to pick up any kind of flight the minute this storm lifts—it is moving on by the way—and it just so happens his private jet is headed to Maui. He offered to fly me to Kauai. We got to talking and he's the *greatest* guy. Single. Good-looking. And he flies his own jet! All this has happened because of you, so don't worry about me."

Ellen barely paused to take a breath before she asked, "So what about Saturday? Are you ready?"

Carrie took a deep breath and decided to quickly fill her in on the details. She ran through the events of the past three days, right up to the minute the Swarovski crystal couple took a dive and hit the sand.

Ellen had begun chuckling about the time Carrie mentioned the word *holoholo* and by now she was wheezing with laughter, so much so that she couldn't speak.

Carrie added, "And now the wedding's off."

There was an abrupt, sobering silence on the other end of the connection.

"Kurt agreed to this?" Ellen asked.

"It was his idea."

"You're kidding, right? He's the one who so wanted to get married all along."

"He moved out and got his own room." Carrie still couldn't believe it. She glanced around the silent *hale*. Outside, a lone couple was strolling along the beach. That should be us, she thought.

"He got his own room? So as not to upset the gods, or what?"

"Yeah. Something like that. I'd suggested a ban on sex until the wedding night—"

Ellen started laughing again but not for long. "Possibly one of the dumbest ideas you've ever had, Carrie."

Carrie rolled her eyes. "Oddly enough, it seemed perfectly logical at the time. I was willing to try anything." Even now she wasn't so certain that Kurt's change of heart wasn't the last and final sign.

"What are you going to do?"

"Any suggestions?"

"Where's Kurt right now?"

"In his own cottage."

"Kurt is the best thing that ever happened to you. You make damn sure that wedding comes off on Saturday, Carrie. If I don't get there, we'll all celebrate when you get back. Besides, I might make it for the reception," Ellen said.

"I'm still convinced the wedding was doomed," Carrie admitted.

"Unconvince yourself. Most of all, unconvince him."

"He didn't believe me for days and now, suddenly, he's a complete convert. What if I'm wrong? What if there are no signs, no omens? What if it was just my fear and nerves and now Kurt's called it off."

"Convince him that you should go through with it."

"What if I can't?" Carrie wasn't so sure she was ready to change her mind about things, let alone his.

"Do what comes naturally. Resort to a method as old as time. Seduce him."

SEDUCE HIM.

Kurt loved her. The proposal, the wedding, had been his idea from the start. There should be no need to seduce him if it really was safe to hold the ceremony.

What surprised her the most was how very much the

idea of putting the wedding off until some unknown date and time depressed her—and how terrible it had been waking up without him this morning.

Carrie slipped into her new swimsuit, tied the bright *pareau* around her waist and paused before the mirror in the dressing area. She left her hair loose, skimming her shoulders. A touch of peach lip gloss and she was ready.

As she walked down the path toward Kurt's smaller cottage, she plucked a plumeria blossom off a nearby tree and tucked it behind her ear.

He was outside on his *lanai,* a cup of coffee on the table. Feet up, casual in a swimsuit and no shirt, he was browsing through one of the mythology books.

Inexplicably nervous, Carrie smoothed down her hair and carefully picked her way across the flat stone path to his *lanai.* When he saw her he looked up and smiled.

When he started to stand, she waved him back into his seat and then bent to kiss him hello.

"Have you been up a while?"

"No, I slept like a baby. Just thought I'd read a bit."

She wished he'd set the book down and hold her. She sat on the arm of his chair, practically draping herself across him as she slipped her arm across his shoulders. Her breast was a fraction of an inch from his cheek. He didn't seem to notice.

Instead he asked, "Remember that guy you saw on the trail? White hair? White dog?"

She nodded. "Of course."

"The one I didn't see," he added.

"You still don't believe me."

He tapped the cover of a book. "Oh, but I do now. Madam Pele, Goddess of Fire, is known to appear in the form of an old woman with long white hair—"

"But I saw a man—"

"She also appears as...*a white dog.*" His brows went up. "A white *dog,* Carrie. Like the one that apparently appeared to you and then disappeared on the trail."

"But, you surely don't think—"

He set the book aside, spread his hands and shrugged. "What other explanation could there be?"

She frowned, thinking. "Well, the man could have taken another trail."

"I didn't see another trail. You are convinced the island was trying to warn us not to marry. I think you're right."

She thought about the dog, innocent-looking enough, tongue lolling. One would think that Madam Pele, Goddess of Fire, would have more going on behind the eyes—

"I'm pretty sure now that was just a dog," she

said. "But…I've been thinking, maybe if we hadn't chosen Kauai, if we'd opted for the country club or L.A. or somewhere else, things might have come off without a hitch."

"Hitch. Glitch. Whatever. We shouldn't chance it. Right?"

She thought about this morning, about waking up alone. Remembered how excited he'd been about the wedding, how anxious he was to be married—which reminded her to ask, "Did you call Oleo and cancel yet?" She held her breath.

"I spoke to her, yes. Last night."

Her voice sank to a near whisper. "Oh."

"Why?"

"I thought maybe I should call myself and explain," Carrie said.

"She completely understood," he added. "And she wished us luck."

When Kurt stood and started gathering up the books, Carrie realized he hadn't given her more than a cursory glance since she arrived. Under normal circumstances, he'd have pulled her into his arms for a welcoming kiss the instant he saw her. She adjusted her *pareau,* shoving it lower on her hips. When that failed to draw his attention, she got up and walked over to the door of his cottage.

"Maybe we should take a walk on the beach," she

suggested, leaning provocatively against the wall, her back arched, one arm casually thrown over her head. She hoped he would respond to the invitation in her eyes.

"How about a massage later?" she tempted. "My treat this time."

Kurt glanced at his watch. "Sorry, babe. I went for a run earlier this morning and met a great guy named Gavin Kapono, an art teacher from Kapa'a High School. I saw him outlining a mural on the wall near the luau pavilion and introduced myself. You know something? He even recognized my name.

"Some of his students are going to be here working on a mural this weekend. I told him about the at-risk kids I work with in L.A. and we realized we have a lot in common. Gavin invited me to play a round of golf at Princeville before he meets his students here this afternoon."

Finally he reached for her, but only held her long enough to give her a quick kiss on the cheek. "You don't mind, do you?"

KURT WOULD NEVER FORGET the look on Carrie's face for as long as he lived. Shock, puzzlement, frustration—a stew of emotions clouded her deep blue eyes when he told her that he'd rather play golf than take her up on her massage invitation.

He didn't think turning the tables on her would be this painful, but when she'd perched herself on the arm of his chair and leaned against him, it had taken all his willpower not to pull her across his lap.

He'd been up all night, pacing, hoping he'd done the right thing, wondering how   because of one short article in an in-flight magazine—she'd gone off on such a tangent. After looking through the reading material she'd amassed, he had to admit Hawaiian legend was definitely steeped in mystery, magic and tragedy.

At first he'd worried Carrie was using the signs and omens the article mentioned as an excuse to call off the wedding, but now he saw how it had been fairly easy to become convinced the island spirits were conspiring against them.

It had taken him two years to convince her that he loved her and that they should get married. He'd never lost sight of his goal. All he could do now was hold out until she realized that their love was stronger than any setbacks, that nothing should or could stand in the way of their future happiness together.

"OKAY, KIDS, put your palms together and wiggle your thumbs so it looks like a fish swimming in the water."

Carrie paused near the pool to watch a Hawaiian woman with smiling eyes teach a half dozen tourists' kids a simple hula. A few minutes later she reached her *hale,* opened the door and saw her suitcase sitting in the middle of the floor. A note from the airlines was attached.

Sorry for the delay. Mahalo for your understanding.

The minute she opened the bag, her wedding gown was revealed. She caressed the ivory silk with her fingertips, held it against her and studied herself in the mirror. It was simple, yet as elegant and sophisticated as she remembered. Seeing it against the backdrop of tropical decor and the azure water in view beyond the *lanai,* she realized it wasn't the perfect choice anymore. She sat down on the edge of the bed, holding the gown in her lap.

Kurt was right. Their wedding wasn't about all the trimmings or the party. It wasn't about her gown, or their guests, or the location. It was an outward symbol of their love and it shouldn't matter where or when it took place so long as it did take place. Their wedding was about them. It was the beginning of a lifetime of love and commitment.

She carefully hung the gown in the closet and then her cell rang. Her heart jumped, but it wasn't Kurt calling from the golf course. This time it was her mother.

"We're definitely not going to make it, dear. I'm so sorry." Her mother didn't sound as sorry as Carrie felt. "Has anyone from Kurt's family arrived?"

"As far as we know, his dad and brother are still in Denver."

"I hear Denver might reopen, but nothing is for certain. O'Hare is still closed. I hate to say I told you so, honey—"

Then *don't* say it, Carrie thought.

"—but I was afraid this was a bad idea from the get-go." Then Dorothy added, "I called the club and luckily there's been a reception cancellation in July. I asked them to hold it for you until I could get back to them, but if we're planning to book, they need to know now."

Chicago in July. Carrie pictured herself a melted puddle of ivory silk. A formal reception at the country club was far from the simple sunset-on-the-beach wedding she'd planned.

She glanced across the room at her suitcase. Her mother just said Denver airport was about to reopen. Maybe another bad omen was reversing itself.

"Call and tell them we won't be booking a wedding or a reception at the club."

"Do you plan to go through with this without anyone there?"

Suddenly everything became perfectly clear to Carrie.

"Kurt and I are here. That's what this is all about. Us. Our love for each other." Carrie waited, but her mother was silent on the other end of the line. "I'll call and let you know how things are going on Saturday, Mom. As far as I'm concerned, the wedding is on."

"You're sure about this, dear?"

"I am," she said, amazed and suddenly more certain than she'd ever been about anything. "Everything is going to work out the way it's supposed to."

She hung up, found her wedding folder and called Oleo but was only able to leave a voice mail. She leafed through the notes and numbers and found the name of the *kahuna* scheduled to marry them.

Ekau Ka'awai didn't advertise, but Oleo assured her that all Rainbow's clients raved about him. Carrie found his name listed in the white pages. She took a deep breath and punched in his number.

"Aloha." His voice was deep and sure. She explained that he was supposed to have been officiating at her wedding, but that it had been canceled and she wanted to rebook him.

"I don't have my calendar in front of me," he told her. "Give me your name and I'll see what's up. What happened that you thought you had to cancel?"

"There were just too many things going wrong," she explained.

"You two not getting along?"

"Oh, it's not that. It's just—"

"Jitters?"

"No, at least I don't think so. I don't get jitters. Except—"

"Except what?"

"So many things kept happening over the last few days. Things I took to be omens of bad luck. *Ho...ho'ailona,* I believe you call them."

"*Ho* what?"

"*Ho'ailona?*" She struggled to pronounce the word correctly. "Signs and omens."

She heard a pause and then he said, "*Hua ho'ailona.* Where did you hear this term?"

"I read about it in an in flight magazine article and started researching—"

"Hawaiian words have more than one meaning. There are hundreds of words for rain alone. *Ho'ailona* not only refers to signs and omens, but it can also stand for a trophy or an emblem of victory."

"But...this past week, it seemed as if nature was transpiring against us. The storm on the mainland. My guests stranded. My fiancé's aunt is missing. I was given the wrong rental car. My bag was lost."

"*Was* lost."

"Yes. They found it."

"And the weather?"

She glanced at the television where the *Weather Channel* was on mute.

"Clearing."

"And the guests? The missing auntie?"

"We haven't heard yet. My parents aren't coming now. And there's a possibility—"

"Anything is possible if you believe in it enough."

"I know." She did know. She had believed in herself enough to make a success of her shop. She believed in Kurt, in his talent. She believed in their love, his commitment to her and hers to him.

"A triumph. A trophy," she whispered. A wedding was certainly the outward symbol of a union that was meant to survive the test of time. Promises made and vows of love that would last for an eternity. *A triumph.*

Suddenly she needed to talk to Kurt in the worst way.

"Thank you so much for your time, Mr. Ka'awai."

"No worries. Get back to me when you're sure."

KURT SHOT THE WORST GOLF round of his life. It was impossible to focus with his future riding on the hope that turning the tables on Carrie would bring her to her senses.

It wasn't until he and Gavin Kapono finished up and stopped by the nineteenth hole for a beer and some chili dogs that he finally called her.

She picked up on his first ring. He tried to sound nonchalant.

"We just finished up," he told her. "What are you doing?"

"Wandering around the hotel shops. How was golf?" She didn't sound at all sad about the canceled wedding.

"Golf was great," he lied.

"Will you be back soon?"

"About an hour, I guess." He wanted to see her right now, but thought he better not rush back yet. "Anything up?"

"I miss you, that's all."

"I miss you, too, Carrie." He noticed Gavin was nodding and smiling his way. "See you in a bit," he added before he hung up.

"What's so funny?" he asked the art teacher.

"You got it bad, man. You got it bad. I hope your plan works."

"If it backfires, I could be flying home without a wife or a fiancée."

"I just hope you're better at convincing your girl to marry you than you are at golf."

"FLIGHTS ARE FINALLY LEAVING Denver airport. The airlines are trying to handle the backup and the backlash from angry customers stranded for more than twenty-four hours…"

After Carrie raced back from the hotel boutique with her hands full of shopping bags, the first thing she did was turn on the *Weather Channel*. When she heard Denver was reopened, she actually laughed out loud and thought, *an omen. A very good omen indeed.*

She started pulling things out of the bags—she'd found just about everything she thought she'd need this afternoon—and ordered the rest from room service. There was a long *pareau* of transparent red fabric shot through with gold thread, a wisp of black thong bikini that was probably illegal on a family-oriented beach, and some Tahitian noni massage oil.

Too modest to wear the thong in public, she slipped into the terry robe provided by the hotel. Then she packed the see-through *pareau* along with the massage lotion in the shopping bag and headed out of the *hale*.

When she arrived at Kurt's room, she thankfully discovered he'd left the door to his *lanai* wide-open. Room service had already delivered the ice bucket and the bottle of champagne she'd ordered along with a tropical fruit platter and an assortment of chocolate brownies and macadamia nuts.

She checked the time then draped herself across Kurt's bed and arranged the crimson fabric across her nearly nude body. She turned on the television and proceeded to wait for him to walk in.

Forty minutes later, the ice in the bucket was nearly melted when she heard Kurt's key card slide into the lock. She had a cramp in her neck from resting her head on her hand while she watched TV, but managed to rearrange herself into a seductive pose.

Kurt stopped just inside the door. His eyes widened. His gaze slid over her body, her barely covered breasts, the rise of her hip, the hint of thong bikini beneath the red and gold fabric.

"What's going on?" He glanced at the table laden with delicacies and swallowed.

"I missed you."

"I wasn't gone *that* long."

"Try that again."

"I missed you, too." He hadn't taken a step toward the bed.

"Make love to me, Kurt."

He swallowed hard. "Taboo, remember? Or *kapu*." He crossed his forearms in the shape of an X and held them up in front of his face. "*Kapu!* No make love."

She tried not to laugh. "I've done a little reading myself. Since I'm the one who issued the *kapu*, I can lift it."

"You sure you want to? We might be asking for more trouble."

"You haven't seen the news. Denver airport is open. *And,* my bag arrived. Our luck is changing."

He glanced at his watch. "Listen, Gavin wants me to meet the kids working on the mural and give them some advice."

She couldn't believe it. "But—"

Just then, someone started pounding on the door and a high-pitched voice rang out, "Kurt? Kurt, open up!"

"Damn," he mumbled, quickly grabbing the end of the bedspread and tossing it over Carrie, covering all but her head and shoulders.

"Who is it?" She grabbed the bedspread and pressed it to her breasts as she struggled to sit up against the pillows.

"It's my great-aunt Harriet." Kurt shoved his hands through his hair as he headed for the door.

"Kurt, wait!" Carrie called out, but it was too late. He opened the door.

A spark plug of a woman in a pith helmet, khaki jodhpurs and camp shirt came breezing in. She looked as if she'd taken a wrong turn and stepped out of a Victorian novel set in deepest, darkest Africa.

"Aha!" She pointed at Carrie, suddenly sounding like Stanley discovering Livingston. "The blushing bride, I presume!"

Aunt Harriet scanned the room, spotted the champagne and brownies and made her way to the table.

Grabbing the biggest brownie on the platter, she plopped into a chair and turned to Kurt.

"Pop the cork on that champagne, dear. Have I got a story for you."

"SO THERE I WAS, in Florida, aware that if I flew to meet your father and Turk in Denver, I'd never get here. I got online, rerouted my trip and went through Dallas and L.A. instead. I decided to spend a night there with an old friend and thus, I had some fun and avoided the *Storm of the Century.*" Harriet shouted "storm of the century" like an overzealous television newscaster.

Kurt jumped up off the end of the bed. "Great story, Aunt Harriet. I told Carrie we didn't have to worry about you."

He glanced at Carrie. She was gaping at his aunt and he was sorry he hadn't told her that his family was a bit more eccentric than he'd led her to believe.

"Well," he said, standing over Harriet as she helped herself to another brownie, "I'm sure you'll want to get settled in your own room."

"I'm fine here," she said, sipping on a glass of champagne. "Like to get to know your bride a bit better."

"Actually I was just telling Carrie that I'm late for an appointment. I'm sure you'd enjoy meeting a local artist and his class, though."

"I am sure I'd like to take off these hiking boots and kick back here with Carrie."

When she refused to budge on her own, Kurt took his aunt by the elbow and hefted her off the chair. He refilled her champagne glass, handed it back and said, "Come along with me, Harriet. Carrie was just saying how tired she is. She's looking forward to a nap."

"Nap? Gave those up years ago. Sleeping is just practicing to die."

He glanced over his shoulder at Carrie and mouthed, "I'll be back in a few minutes. Stay right there."

Carrie nodded. "Nice meeting you, Aunt Harriet. I'll see you in a little while."

She heard Harriet ask as Kurt ushered her out, "Why is she in bed in the middle of the day?"

The door closed behind them with a bang. Sweltering beneath the spread, Carrie threw it off her and got up. She poured a glass of champagne for herself and went into the dressing area to check out her thong in the mirror, wondering how much Harriet had seen before Kurt covered her up. The darn thing was riding up something awful.

Just as she flicked on the light, she noticed a slip of paper lying on the counter. It was written in Kurt's handwriting. The heading at the top immediately drew her attention.

Goal: Wedding by Saturday.

Things to Do:

1. Keep goal in sight.
2. Don't weaken. Prior planning prevents poor performance.
3. Don't give in to temptation until Carrie comes to her senses.

Carrie stared at Kurt's notes to himself. Obviously he hadn't believed they'd been given any signs or omens at all. He'd been humoring her, hoping she would "come to her senses."

Carrie read his note to himself again and realized she'd played right into his hands. At least he didn't yet realize he'd accomplished his goal with such ease.

Two could play at this game, she thought.

She set the paper down exactly where he'd left it. She slipped on her robe, grabbed her shopping bag with the massage oil and *pareau* safely tucked inside, and hurried back to the Honeymoon *Hale.*

Twenty minutes later, Kurt knocked at her door. She took her sweet time answering and effectively blocked the opening with her body.

"Aren't you going to let me in?"

"Actually I really do feel like taking a nap. Power of suggestion, I guess." She shrugged and tossed her hair back over her shoulder.

He reached for her. She let him slip his hand between the lapels of the terry robe, let him run his thumb over the edge of her breast before she pulled back. She heard him groan in frustration.

"You mentioned something about lifting the *kapu,*" he reminded her. His eyes were half lidded, his lashes dark and thick. She took a deep breath and reminded herself that he'd tricked her into thinking that he believed her, that he shared her concerns and that he'd called off the wedding because of them.

She leaned close, ran her finger across his lips and whispered, "I changed my mind."

"But, Aunt Harriet's here. That's a good omen. It's a sign that things are turning in our favor."

She thought of the chubby woman in the pith helmet inhaling brownies and washing them down with champagne. "Possibly, but you've read the Hawaiian lore. I'm just not sure her arrival is proof enough."

"Your luggage has been returned. Denver airport is open."

He looked so darn hopeful she almost gave in.

"Sorry, honey." She reached out to cup his chin, pulled him close and planted a long, slow kiss on his lips. "Why don't you call me later? I'll meet you and Harriet for dinner at the Plantation Café."

"You're sure?"

"Positive."

The minute the door closed, she got on her cell and left a voice mail for Oleo.

Afraid she'd get no response she added, "Call me back. It's a matter of life or death."

Then she changed out of her thong and into a comfortable summer sundress. She found Bogie's and Turk's cell numbers in her wedding folder and left them both voice mails. Then she dialed Ellen and ended up leaving a voice mail for her, too.

Her phone rang a few seconds later.

"Life or *death?* What on earth is happening?" Oleo wanted to know.

"I had to get you to call me back somehow."

"Kurt specifically asked me not to call you. He said he was handling things from now on."

"Actually I'm back in charge, so no need to call him."

"I'm glad you're feeling better. Is the wedding on or off?"

Feeling better? "What did Kurt tell you, exactly?"

"That I wasn't to talk to you at all. He said you ate something that gave you a bad case of King Kamehameha's revenge, that he didn't want you disturbed. I was to put everything on hold and check in with him tomorrow morning."

"Very interesting." Carrie talked to Oleo for a good twenty minutes and then hung up.

SATURDAY MORNING, Carrie skipped breakfast and walked on the beach alone thinking about last night's dinner. She needn't have worried about keeping Kurt at arm's length. Aunt Harriet had talked the whole time, regaling them with details about a recent wine-tasting trip to Italy and France with the Gad-A-Bouts, a group of senior travelers from her condo complex in Miami. By the time Kurt walked Carrie back to the bungalow, she truly did have the headache she claimed was plaguing her.

She almost confessed to having found his note, but decided turnabout was fair play and sent him off with a good-night kiss, although she slipped out onto her *lanai* to watch him walk away.

After a leisurely morning walk on the beach, she returned to the central courtyard area of the hotel where guests were dining on macadamia nut waffles in the open-air restaurant and kids were already splashing in the pool.

She spotted Kurt across the courtyard with Gavin Kapono and his art students, who were working on their mural. She drew close enough to watch, choosing a seat in a shady corner of the outdoor poolside bar that was not yet open. From her vantage point, she could see Kurt, but he couldn't see her.

The mural depicted a scene straight from precontact Hawaii—a traditional Hawaiian village with terraced fields and huts thatched in *pili* grass nestled on the shores of Hanalei Bay. Outrigger sailing canoes sailed into the bay. Waterfalls streamed down the mountainsides. Wisps of clouds wreathed the peaks.

She listened as Kurt spoke to the teens, inspiring them to be great, to dream big dreams. When he told them how important it was to set goals, write them down and never lose sight of them, she couldn't help but smile.

She watched Kurt pick up a brush and begin to sketch a couple standing near the water's edge—a man and woman holding hands, gazing out at the setting sun. The figures were Hawaiian in stature and features, but in her heart she knew without a doubt that he was thinking of the two of them, portraying a timeless scene of a couple committed to one another—a couple whose love would stand the test of time.

As she watched him work his magic with brush and paint, she realized more than ever what she'd known since the night their eyes first met across a crowded hotel lobby. Their love was not about a wedding ceremony, not about gifts or banquets or the guests who would have wished them well.

Their love was not about an hour or a day. It was about a lifetime together.

KURT WATCHED the Kapa'a High School teens paint, offering suggestions when asked. Mostly he enjoyed listening to their easy banter and commenting on the color choices they made.

He'd spent most of the past two days in a cold sweat. He hadn't been able to reach Oleo and finally, her florist phoned him to say that Oleo had to go to the other side of the island and could no longer keep things on hold. She said she was fed up. The wedding was canceled.

He hadn't heard from his dad and brother, and, as far as he knew, Ellen Marshall hadn't contacted Carrie, either. This morning, when he discovered Carrie wasn't in the *hale,* he spent the early morning hours staring out at the bay convinced he'd handled things in the worst possible way. Around ten, he'd wandered out to the central pool area to join Gavin's class, which was better than moping alone on his *lanai*.

He felt someone come up beside him and knew without looking that it was the woman he loved. He turned to her and his heartbeat spiked as it always did whenever he saw Carrie.

"Hi." He leaned in for a chaste kiss and then introduced her to Gavin and the students. The girls checked out Carrie's capri pants and tank top. The boys simply checked out Carrie until Gavin reminded them all to get back to work. She admired the students' work and then they told the art teacher goodbye. Kurt led her over to the bar where he ordered two mango-guava juice drinks.

"To you," he said, raising his glass in a toast. "I love you."

She took a sip, refused to meet his eyes. "I love you, too."

He slipped his hand beneath her chin, raised her face until their eyes met.

"This was supposed to be our wedding day."

"Yes," she whispered. "It was."

"It's not too late to—"

She cut him off. "I was thinking—"

"What were you thinking?"

"That we should have dinner out on the beach tonight. Right here, at the hotel. They'll set it up for us. Just the two of us. It would be so romantic—"

Romantic. But not a wedding.

He'd played the wrong hand. His heart sank.

"Listen, Carrie, I have a confession to make."

"What could you possibly have to confess?" She reached up and ran her fingers through his hair.

"I wasn't ever really convinced the island was conspiring against us. This whole thing about warning signs and omens is just nuts. I went along with you, hoping that you'd come to realize nothing should stand in our way. Instead I should have persuaded you to marry me in front of a judge before all this escalated. Now I've messed things up with Oleo, and she canceled on me. With any luck, she might be able to pull something together. We'll get married and celebrate back on the mainland. In L.A., in Chicago, in Vermont. All three places if you'd like."

Her eyes widened in shock. "You *never* believed in the signs and omens? You were just *pretending* to go along with me?" She was no longer smiling.

"I thought fighting fire with fire was the way to go. That if I left you alone to really think about it, if I called it off, you'd come around and realize nothing should stand in the way of our future together."

"You thought pretending to go along with me, that letting me believe you were actually sensitive to my fears, would somehow help me ignore the signs and change my mind?"

"I never, ever meant to hurt you."

"But even if your little scheme worked and I *had* changed my mind, it's too late now."

"So you're still convinced we shouldn't go through with the wedding?" He reached for her hand, relieved to see that at least she was still wearing her engagement ring.

"When the time is right, we'll be married." She smiled into his eyes and shrugged. "Will you have dinner with me on the beach tonight?"

"Anything you want." He tried to hide the fact that

his heart was breaking. He'd be kicking himself all the way back across the Pacific.

"I'll go talk to the concierge." She finished her juice and smiled up at him sweetly. "At least we'll be alone together on the beach at sunset—unless you want to invite your aunt to join us."

"I'd rather it be just the two of us," he assured her.

As he watched her walk away, his dream of marrying Carrie tonight faded like the fleeting colors of a rainbow, and he knew he had no one but himself to blame.

MUSIC DRIFTED OUT of the lounge and across the hotel terrace. The haunting lyrics of a 1950s love song embraced Carrie and Kurt as they strolled hand in hand down the winding path to the beach below the plantation hotel. He couldn't help but notice that many of the guests dining at the outdoor café watched as they passed by.

When Carrie had opened the door to the Honeymoon *Hale* to greet him, her loveliness took his breath away. She was wearing a long white cotton gown with a deep ruffled hem. The print was a white-on-white hibiscus pattern and unlike a traditional muumuu, the gown was fitted to outline her figure. Her hair was down, the way he liked it.

"You're beautiful," he whispered.

She smiled and lifted her skirt to reveal her white sandals. "Thank you. I found this muumuu in the boutique and couldn't resist taking home a memory."

"If I'd known you were going to wear it, I'd have worn something less casual." He had on swim trunks and an aloha shirt, hoping they might take a moonlit dip after their al fresco dinner. He thought about slipping the white cotton gown off her shoulders and watching her sleek body slip nude through the shimmering water.

"You look great," she told him. "Perfect."

Halfway down the path, the trail curved along the hillside. They'd reached a secluded section where the beach directly below them was still hidden by the overgrown foliage. Carrie stopped walking and Kurt took the opportunity to pull her into his arms.

She melted into his embrace, slipped her arms around his shoulders and kissed him with a searing passion that had nothing to do with the heat of the tropics.

"Sunset is in an hour," she whispered breathlessly when the kiss ended. "The hotel promised tiki torches, white linens, the works for our little dinner. I really think we should be heading down."

He tried to smile. The weather had been clear and sunny all day. There was a light breeze to keep things just cool enough. Sunset promised to be stunning.

Hand in hand, they continued down the path to the beach. When they cleared the final bend, Kurt stopped in his tracks.

A scene reminiscent of a fairy tale appeared on the beach below. A peaked tent, much smaller than the one they'd seen at the disastrous beach wedding, had been set up in the center of the cove. Every tent pole was decorated with a huge spray of tropical blooms. A few round tables draped with white linen were scattered beneath the canopy. Floral centerpieces with tropical flowers in bright yellow, red and orange graced each table. Tiki torches surrounded the area. His heart sank.

"Looks like someone is getting married." Even he could hear how pathetically disappointed he was, but it was his own fault their wedding wasn't happening tonight.

He scanned the rest of the cove, wondering where the hotel might have set up their intimate dinner for two. It was bad enough their wedding had been canceled—now he'd have to watch some other lucky couple celebrate their wedding day.

His gaze swept the beach and trailed back to the center of the reception tent where there was something oddly familiar about a short, stout woman in billowing white linen pants and an oversize shirt standing drinking champagne.

"That looks like Aunt Harriet." It would be just like her to wrangle an invitation to someone else's wedding.

When Carrie didn't respond, he realized her hand was trembling inside his own. He turned to her and noticed bright, unshed tears swimming in her blue eyes.

"Are you all right?" he whispered.

"That *is* your Aunt Harriet."

"Party crashing, no doubt."

"I don't think so." Carrie smiled, blinking back tears.

"What's wrong?"

"Look again."

He did and there, beside his great-aunt, stood his dad, Bogie. Not far away, Turk was chatting with a petite blonde—who just happened to be Oleo. As he watched, dumbfounded, a golf cart equipped with sand tires came rolling down the beach. The Island Grinds Kau Kau Katering logo was painted on the side of the cart.

Two Hawaiian women were seated in front and the back of the cart was piled high with boxes, dishes and serving trays. In the lagoon that fronted the hotel beach, an outrigger canoe decorated with ti leaves and tiki torches was just touching the sand. Five Hawaiian men jumped out and beached the canoe.

"What's going on?" Kurt shook his head in confusion.

Carrie squeezed his hand. "Will you marry me, Kurt? Will you stand beside me as I promise to love and cherish you all the days of my life? Will you make me the same vow?"

For the first time in his life, he found himself close to tears. Suddenly the scene on the beach was forgotten and there was just the two of them.

"Of course, I will. Now and forever."

Someone on the beach shouted, "There they are!"

Everyone started clapping. The outrigger paddlers picked up a ukulele and a guitar and began to sing in Hawaiian. One of the women on the golf cart danced the hula on the sand.

"Looks like they're starting without us." Carrie laughed and clung to his hand as they ran down the path to the beach.

WHEN THEY REACHED the canopy, it was Carrie's turn to be speechless as Ellen Marshall appeared on the arm of a tall, handsome man she introduced as her knight in shining armor. He had whisked her out of the Denver airport on his private jet before the commercial planes were cleared to leave.

"I didn't know you'd be here!" Carrie cried. The last she'd heard from Ellen, her friend was still in Denver.

"I told you I wouldn't miss this for the world," Ellen said.

"I can't believe it." Carrie hugged Ellen again.

"When I checked in, the woman at the front desk let me in on what was happening and told me I'd better hurry or I'd miss the wedding. We rushed right down," Ellen assured her.

"So everyone knew but me?" Kurt was still beside Carrie, though busy shaking his brother's hand and accepting congratulations from his dad, Turk and Oleo.

Carrie nodded. "Everyone. I'm amazed no one let the cat out of the bag. Oleo was pretty upset about having to pretend to cancel on you."

Just then a woman who had to be six foot four handed her a tropical bridal bouquet made up of pink anthuriums, orchids, touches of tuberose and fern.

"I'm Elegra, the florist. I hope you like it." The woman wore an off-the-shoulder print gown and towered over everyone on the beach.

"It's absolutely stunning. Truly inspired," Carrie told her. "Thank you so much."

Carrie paused to take in the scene again. Her breath caught when she recognized the Hawaiian man she'd seen on the hiking trail. He was standing at the water's edge, same long white hair, same white dog at his side.

"Oh, no. What's he doing here?" she whispered.

Oleo followed her gaze. "Him? That's Ekau Ka'awai, the *kahuna*."

Carrie turned to Kurt and they both started laughing at the same time.

"I guess it's a sign," she said.

"I guess it's an omen," he added.

Oleo nodded to Turk and suddenly, Kurt's brother whisked him away from Carrie and led the groom across the sand. Together, they stood beside the *kahuna*.

The musicians started to play the Hawaiian Wedding Song. Elegra handed Ellen a wreath of flowers to place on Carrie's head and then adjusted the hem of her gown. Without urging, everyone fell into place, encircling Ekau, Kurt and Turk near the shoreline. Bogie offered Carrie his arm and escorted her to Kurt. Ellen followed close behind.

Then as the sun began to sink into the turquoise water and the sky fired with a pink and orange glow, Carrie smiled up into Kurt's eyes.

"I promise to love and cherish you all the days of my life," she whispered.

He held her hands in his and vowed the same.

When a wispy passing cloud sprinkled them with a light mist and a rainbow danced on the rays of the setting sun, Ekau Ka'auwai announced, "May you be blessed by *'ehu,* the Hawaiian mist, and *anuenue,* the rainbow, all the days of your lives." Then the *kahuna* winked and told all those gathered around the newlyweds, "In Hawaii, a rainbow is a very, *very* good sign."

BITING THE APPLE

Jo Leigh

❧ ❧ ❧

To Marsha, for thinking of me

Dear Reader,

One of the questions I'm asked most often is "Where do you get your ideas?" Most of the time I'm not sure. But with "Biting the Apple," I know exactly where the idea came from—my own love story!

Like Trish and Mark, I'd been madly in love when I was much younger, but we couldn't make things work. My dreams carried me all over the country, and his dreams kept him in L.A. But I never forgot him, and frankly, never stopped loving him. Flash forward twenty years (!) and who should walk back into my life? You got it. The man I'd loved forever found me, and we've been together ever since. In fact, we got married three years ago at a romance writers' conference!

I cried during the entire ceremony. Not delicate little tears glistening on my cheek, oh no. I sobbed so hard I could barely say, "I do." And yet, it's still my favorite day ever.

Enjoy!

Jo Leigh

CHAPTER ONE

WITH GRAVEL CRUNCHING beneath her boots, Trish Avalon focused on the scent of blooming acacias as she walked to her listing mailbox at the edge of her driveway. The mesquite trees her grandfather had planted years ago gave her shade from the warm spring sun and hid most of the barren landscape surrounding the ranch.

Some ranch. There were no cattle, no horses, no crops. Just the big old house filled with memories and ache. Since her mother's recent passing, Trish had been getting the place ready for sale. It wasn't a quick job, given that her folks had been pack rats. Neat pack rats, she'd give them that, but neither one ever threw a darn thing away.

Just this morning she'd found a stash of mementos from her childhood. Baby shoes, clothes, toys. Report cards and gym trophies she hadn't thought about in years.

The packing would have gone faster if she hadn't

taken that job at the drugstore. It was worth it, though, as she hadn't had to dip into her savings. The only thing she hoarded was money. Money that would get her out of Briscoe, Texas, and into New York City.

She pulled the large stack of mail from the box and closed its rusty mouth, swearing as she did each day that she'd grease the hinges. But then she'd walk inside and by the time she finished with the mail, something else would catch her attention and she wouldn't remember about the mailbox until she opened it the next time.

Once back at the house, she went straight to the big oak dining table where she dropped the stack of mail and then to the kitchen for more coffee.

Armed with the hazelnut brew she liked, Trish sat down to face the seemingly unending task of taking care of her parents' affairs. Her father had died a year ago next month, and her mother had taken sick shortly thereafter. Most everything had been set aside in Trish's life at that point—including her newspaper job in Dallas.

But soon, she'd have the place ready for the market, and the proceeds, if the house sold, would be another big step toward her dream. Unfortunately the real-estate market in Briscoe was about as brisk as the bone-dry Briscoe river.

Bills, social security, advertisements, catalogs, a

sip of coffee, more catalogs—then her heart went wild as she looked at the big white envelope that had been forwarded from Dallas. It had one fancy word in the upper left corner—Hush.

There was no address underneath because none was needed. There was only one Hush, at least for Trish. Hush hotel in Manhattan. The sexy, sophisticated, expensive, unbelievably hip Hush hotel, which, just under a year ago, had launched a contest to debut their brand-new wedding services.

Trish, who never let an opportunity pass her by, had entered the contest with a video essay. But she couldn't have won, could she? No. Impossible. No one from Briscoe ever won a thing. Not the lottery, not the spelling bee, not even one football championship, ever.

Still, she couldn't stop her hands from shaking as she opened the envelope. There were a bunch of brochures, but her gaze was firmly on the letter. And there it was. The word that made the rest of the universe fade away.

Congratulations!

She'd won. *She'd* won.

Her gaze shot up to top of the page, just to make sure it was really, truly Trish Avalon they'd written to, not some other woman.

She smiled as she read the full letter. The judges,

including the incredible Piper Devon who owned the hotel, had selected her video out of thousands of entries. Thousands! Two first-class tickets to JFK airport, then a penthouse suite in Hush. Eight other tickets would be hers to give to family and friends, although those would be coach. There would be a wedding dress created exclusively for her by one of the world's top designers. Flowers. A wedding dinner catered by the hotel's chef. A week's exclusive use of a hotel limousine. Spa treatments. A makeover. Wedding pictures and a video by someone she'd never heard of, but who apparently was quite famous. Free meals. Free drinks. Free tickets to a Broadway show. Free everything a girl could want for that special, special day.

It was all perfect, extraordinary. Unbelievable. A week in New York. A whole week, free of charge, where she'd be able to go to every single newspaper and magazine and personally hand in her résumé. She'd be able to meet with editors face-to-face. To show them her clippings, her enthusiasm, her determination.

She was being handed her entire future in a silver-wrapped package, special delivery, no postage due. Nothing would ever be the same. Nothing.

All she had to do was one tiny thing. She'd have to get engaged.

BY THE TIME Mark Reynolds got back to the house, he felt like he'd been ridden hard and put away wet. Working the ranch did that to a man, and even though it ached where Gypsy had stepped on his foot, he still wouldn't trade it for anything.

He threw his hat on the coatrack then stretched his neck as he headed for his dad's office. Mark stood at the door as he watched his old man type at his computer, his bifocals perched on the end of his nose, his music, classical as always, playing softly in the background.

Mark didn't say anything. He knew better than to disturb his father when he was writing. It had shocked the hell out of Mark when his father had decided to turn the running of the ranch over to his sons. He wanted no more to do with it after a lifetime of working sunrise to sunset. The ranch was worth something now, a lot actually. The horses Bill Reynolds had bred had become champion stock, but Bill had had enough. He wanted to write his life story, then he wanted to write a book about Briscoe, then some fiction, just to change things up.

Mark, as the oldest, had happily taken over, glad that his father had found something that gave him satisfaction. It was difficult to understand, though. Mark loved the ranch. He liked the hard work, the toughness of the country, the breeding program. He, like his father, had found his calling.

His kid brother, Chris, on the other hand…

Chris wasn't home from school yet, or at least not home from practice. The boy still bitched like hell when he had to come home each evening to chores, but Mark felt responsible for turning Chris into a man to be proud of, and a large part of that was teaching him to take his responsibilities seriously.

Leaving his dad to his typing, Mark went to the kitchen. He stood by the sink for a long time, trying to get the grime from underneath his fingernails. He needed to put some dinner together, too. Chris would eat crap all night if left to his own devices, and Dad forgot to eat if he wasn't reminded, so even though Mark didn't like to cook, he'd learned how. He wasn't going to win any prizes, but he wasn't hopeless, either.

As he dried his hands, he saw the light flashing on the answering machine. Only one message. The second he heard the voice, he knew who it was. What he couldn't figure out was why Trish Avalon wanted not just to see him, but to spring for dinner tomorrow night at the Blue Cloud, the best restaurant in Briscoe.

He played the message once more, trying to buy a clue, but she just sounded like Trish.

He went to the coffeemaker on the counter, poured himself a mug from this morning's pot, then stuck it in the microwave. As the seconds ticked away, he thought about the last time he'd seen Trish. It had been at her mother's funeral. Despite the six years that had passed since they'd been an item, he still had feelings for her. Not the kind he'd had back then, but he considered her a friend. They'd had a long talk that night, after all the other mourners had gone home, about what it was to lose a parent so early in life.

The conversation and her tears had flowed freely, but that was the last time he'd talked to her.

She was probably lonely, that's all. Come right down to it, he was pretty lonely himself. He might love the ranch, but his bed was still empty at the end of the day.

He picked up the phone and dialed her number.

THE BLUE CLOUD wasn't half as woo-woo as the name sounded. It was actually a very nice restaurant that would have been happier and more appreciated in Austin, but Trish was pleased it was in the middle of what was laughingly referred to as downtown Briscoe.

Mark had gotten there early and she joined him just as the waitress, Jennifer, put down his beer. Trish ordered a white wine, then took a moment to look at the guy who'd been her very first love.

He'd gotten better after high school, and he'd been a major babe then. Of course, they'd known each other since first-grade and it had taken a summer apart and a major influx of hormones for her to see Mark as anything but the kid who sometimes let her see his math homework.

Once the discovery was made, however, she had a whole new appreciation for what the ranching life could do for a man's body. He was everything a cowboy should be—tall, lean of hips, broad of shoulders. His eyes were as blue as the Texas sky and his hands... She sighed as her gaze settled on those amazing hands. Long fingers, kind of rough, but always clean. A person wouldn't guess they could be gentle, but they were.

"Hey, is something wrong?"

She looked up, embarrassed that she'd gone into the ozone while he was sitting across the table from her. Usually she did that in the privacy of her bedroom, but she just smiled. "Not a thing."

"So why the dinner? Is everything going all right over at your mom's place?"

"I'm still packing. I swear, I don't understand how two sensible people could get so attached to *things*. They didn't get rid of anything."

"I remember. But they probably just thought they were being frugal."

"Yeah, well, there's frugal and then there's nuts."

"Your folks weren't nuts."

She sighed as Jennifer came back with her wine. "You two ready to order?"

"I'll have the rib eye," Mark said.

Trish, like Mark and all the other locals, no longer had to study the menu. The special was always printed on the chalkboard out front. The rest of the menu never did seem to change. "I'll have the salmon."

"Good enough." Jennifer, who'd been a couple of years behind them at school, saved her best smile for Mark, but then that wasn't anything unusual, either.

Mark was the most eligible bachelor in Briscoe, but he was also the most reclusive. Not that he was mysterious or even shy. He just did the work of three men, which didn't leave much time for socializing. It had been an issue between them in high school— she couldn't imagine what it was like now. Trish wasn't sure, but she didn't think he'd gone out with anyone, at least not seriously, since they'd broken up at the end of their senior year.

"So why did you ask me here?"

"Yeah, well, it's gonna take a bit of explaining."

"But you're not in trouble."

"No. Unless you call being stuck in Briscoe trouble."

Mark gave her a grin that took her straight to the back of his '74 pickup after the game. Any game. They always ended up on Tripper Road, under the big trees, making out with such desperation. She could still remember the butterflies she always got whenever Mark touched her. She just hoped he thought of her as kindly. "I have a favor to ask you."

"Go ahead."

She'd worn a white T-shirt to dinner, after an hour of debate, one that was low cut and showed off her boobs. Then she'd chosen her skinny jeans, the ones she had to lie down in to zip up. Along with her high-heeled boots, she was about as sexy as she could get, which wasn't saying a whole lot. Her boobs had decided long ago to give up trying to grow, and her waist was more like a boy's than it should have been. She wasn't butt-ugly or anything, but she was no beauty. She'd never been all that clear why Mark had liked her back in the day. She'd just learned to accept it for the miracle it was, and move on.

But tonight, for this particular favor, she'd wanted to be a knockout. It didn't seem fair that he could look so handsome in his everyday clothes, and she'd had to spend half a day getting ready.

"Trish? The favor?"

"Right. Okay, well, you know how I've been trying to save up to move to New York."

"Yeah, I know."

"Of course you do. I just wanted to reiterate that my dream hasn't changed one bit since forever. Getting the job in Dallas just made me want it more. I need to be in New York, Mark. I belong there."

"How do you know that when you've never been?"

"I feel it. I always have. If I didn't know better, I'd swear I had New York in my blood."

Mark shook his head slowly, his dark hair shaggy and sexy as all get-out. "I know you mean it, but I don't get it. I thought you liked that job in Dallas."

"It was fine, honest. But writing community news for a Dallas suburb paper isn't quite the same as writing for the *New York Times.*"

"You could apply at the *Dallas Morning News.*"

"Mark, no matter how much art and culture Dallas has, it'll never be New York."

"It's a long way to go for your dreams."

"It's not the moon. New York is just a few hours away these days."

"It's likely to be as strange as the moon."

"Maybe, but then maybe it will be everything I've dreamed of. Everything I've worked for."

He gave her a considered nod. "How can I help?"

"I'm really glad you asked," she said. She swallowed once, then looked him straight in the eye. "I need you to be my fiancé."

CHAPTER TWO

"YOUR WHAT?"

"My fiancé. Intended. You know," Trish said, "fiancé."

Mark looked at her for a long minute waiting for the punch line. Only Trish didn't even crack a smile. "What the hell are you talking about?"

"Okay, there's this hotel in Manhattan, it's called Hush, and they're starting this brand-new wedding service called Weddings by Desire and to promote it they had this big contest where they asked everyone to send in a videotape of why they should be the winner and when I was in Dallas I used the video equipment at the paper and made my own tape, which I sent in." She took a breath, but only one. "I never expected to win, of course, because nobody I've ever known has won anything, well, not anything important so I wasn't expecting anything but then today I got a package in the mail forwarded from Dallas and I won."

He waited to see if there was more. Trish took a

sip of her drink then stared at him expectantly, as if she hadn't just said the craziest thing he'd ever heard from a grown woman's mouth. "Were you engaged when you made your videotape?"

"I didn't think I'd win, so, well, that didn't seem to be important. At the time."

"If you didn't expect to win, why did you—"

"I enter everything. No, that's not true. I don't enter for trips to Hawaii or Paris or for anything I couldn't sell, but the prize was a week, Mark. A whole week in New York. First-class airfare. A hotel suite. A limousine. Everything I'll need to get my dream job. I figure I'll send out résumés first, then do the follow-up interviews when I actually get there."

"You've figured that out, have you?"

"I know, it doesn't seem like enough time, but it is, because if I get a second interview I'll just stay there. I'll find a cheap hotel and I won't eat much. I've got enough saved to do that. Just not enough to do it all."

He took a big swig of his beer, questions tumbling all over themselves in his brain. The first was, "Why do you need me?"

"The prize is a wedding. A big wedding at the hotel. They're doing everything, too, including eight coach tickets for friends and family to come attend the nuptials."

The questions now all had exclamation points

attached. "For real? A real wedding? With a preacher and a license and all that?"

"Well," she said, drawing out the word as she stared at her hand on her wineglass. "Yeah, it would mean getting married, but only for a little while."

"How little?"

"A couple of weeks, max. Then we'll get it annulled, and voilà."

"Trish, honey. You're nuts."

"I know. But I also know this is a once-in-a-lifetime thing. If I don't go, I'll regret it forever. I'll always wonder."

"You never expected to win, so don't you have an alternative plan?"

"Sure," she said, but he could tell she'd lost interest in Plan B the second she'd opened that envelope. "Although it'll take me a long, long time to save up enough money to go."

He was surprised to find Jennifer next to the table waiting for them to move their arms for their dinner plates. Normally he could smell a nice rib eye from across the room, but Trish had found the ultimate distraction in her little request.

"Thanks," he said.

"Sure thing, Mark. You want anything else? Steak sauce? Another beer?"

"I'll be needing another beer, Jennifer. Thank you."

Trish didn't say a word. Nor did she look at her plate or have more to drink. She just stared at him and damned if he didn't feel like Scrooge on Christmas morning. But come on. *Married?*

"When's the last time you took a vacation, Mark Reynolds?"

"I'll admit," he said, cutting into his dinner, "it's been a while, but I can assure you, if I was to go on a vacation, the last place I would go is New York."

"They have interesting things in New York. Even you could fill up seven measly days."

He chewed on her proposition along with his steak, wanting to help a friend out, but damn. He would suffer through a week of New York if he had to, but getting married? She'd think he was an old-fashioned idiot if he told her how much the idea of a sham marriage bothered him. Unlike most folks in the country who traded in wives like returnable pop bottles, he actually believed in the institution. There'd been a time, a long time, when he'd figured he and Trish would be heading down that very road. It had been her New York dreams that had split them up.

He'd felt like hell about that for a good year after they graduated, but then he'd mellowed. No, he hadn't found anyone that he'd liked quite as much as he'd liked Trish, but then he hadn't really looked, had he?

He glanced up from his steak into eyes that used to haunt him. Sometimes still did.

"If there was anyone else to ask, I would."

"What about Dallas? You didn't meet any guys there?"

"Not any I could trust. Not like you."

Trust how? To not take advantage of her in the fancy suite? He wasn't so sure about that. They'd never had a problem between the sheets. In fact, the notion of sharing a suite was the only tempting thing about her favor. But he had a feeling she'd need him more for hand-holding than anything else. He admired her spirit, and if anyone could get a job at a big New York paper in a week, it would be Trish. Even so, the odds were pretty damn slim.

Hell, maybe he should go. He didn't love the idea, and he hadn't loved Trish for a long time, but he liked her and he'd feel like hell if she crashed and burned with some joker who didn't understand that her dreams had carried her through all life's hardships. Failing in New York was going to send her into a tailspin.

On the other hand—

"Oh, thank God," Trish said, then she dug into her dinner as if she hadn't eaten in a week.

"Wait a minute. I never said—"

"Oh, honey, I could see it the moment you decided

to say yes. Of course I knew you would. And trust me. I'll make sure you have the best time ever."

He let out a long, slow breath. "Chris is going to have to agree to take on the ranch. Dad's going to have to pitch in, too."

"Oh, no." Trish shook her head, making her hair shimmer. "They'll be coming to New York, too. Well, for three days. Free airfare, free hotel. It's going to be wonderful for both of them. Imagine, Chris getting his first real taste of a big city. Your father going to the heart of publishing country."

Mark frowned. "The ranch—"

"Mark Reynolds," Trish said, putting down her silverware. "Just because you're not happy unless you're spending every waking second working on that ranch is no reason to punish your family. It's a wonderful opportunity for both of them. You can always get Nate and Tom to take over for a few days. Heaven knows they can both use the work."

"But—"

"Please, Mark. I'm convinced this is the opportunity of a lifetime and not just for me. I'm going to ask Ellen, Penny Foster and a couple of friends from Dallas to come along. And you could ask Darryl, right? He's always up for a lark."

Mark took another bite of steak as he tried to think of a nice way to back out of the whole deal. But what she said about his dad, about Chris, made him give her a very reluctant nod. Maybe it wasn't the worst thing in the world to show his family a good time. And the ranch wouldn't fall apart in a week.

Trish smiled delightedly. "We leave in three weeks. On the fourth. Bring that nice suit you wore to Mamma's funeral, okay? And those good shirts you got in Austin."

"I'm not your husband yet. And even when I am, I won't be, so don't you start up."

She gave him a look that made him think of his happiest days. Days that had been filled with her laughter, her sweet scent.

"You're surely going to heaven for this, sweet Mark. It's honestly the kindest, most thoughtful—"

"Yeah, yeah," he said, interrupting the flow of bull. "I'm a freakin' saint."

Her mouth opened wide, and so did her eyes. "I hope not. Did I mention that the Hush hotel suites all come complete with a cabinet full of toys? And I'm not talking about jump ropes."

It took him a full minute for that tidbit to gel, for his imagination to go from a slow walk to a full gallop. It didn't help much that Trish was laughing loud enough to make everyone in the place look their way. Or that he was blushing hot enough to start a bonfire.

HIS SECOND THOUGHTS started the moment he stepped out of the restaurant. They didn't let up all the way home, and after he'd done his final chores he had a list a mile long of why it was a stupid idea and how he wasn't going to do it, no sir.

As he finished brushing his teeth he made the mistake of remembering something he'd tried to forget. The way Trish looked in the wee hours of the morning. Her slim body naked and tan, her dark hair wild and curly on the pillow. That mouth of hers slightly open as if ready for his kiss.

"Shit," he said as he crawled into his empty bed. "Nothing but trouble with a capital T."

BY THE TIME they were ready to take off for the airport, Trish had listened patiently to each and every one of Mark's doubts and complaints. She'd tried her best to appear thoughtful. Concerned. But she knew in her heart that he'd never back out. Not for anything.

If only Mark wasn't so damned in love with Briscoe. She'd tried to tell him there was a great big world out there, but he'd never wanted to hear it.

That's what made this trip so special. It wasn't just about her dream, although that was huge. It was also about getting Mark to step outside his comfort zone. Who knows, maybe he'd even like New York. Maybe…

No, she couldn't go there. Her destiny was in the Big Apple, but she had no doubt that Mark wasn't meant for that particular city. Maybe Austin or even Dallas, but he'd be miserable living in Manhattan.

They'd been right to break it off after high school. Yes, they had been best friends as well as lovers, but being a best friend meant supporting each other, no matter what the dream. Mark wanted his ranch to prosper. He wanted Briscoe to prosper, and she had no doubt that in the years to come, he'd be a strong influence in all areas of the county's interests. That's why he'd bought the property across from the courthouse and was part owner of the general store. He had a stake in Briscoe.

Mark had plans, all right. None of which appealed to her, unfortunately.

She was meant for the big city. She didn't even care if she had to start out writing obituaries or as a research assistant. Eventually, just as Mark would have his prize ranch, she'd have her prize job. Investigative reporter for the *New York Times*. It might take years, but all things worth having were worth waiting for.

CHAPTER THREE

AFTER THE BELLMAN LEFT. After the concierge left. After they'd been shown how to work the high-definition TV, the remotes that opened and shut everything, including the drapes, and after they'd been informed that the champagne, and everything else in the incredibly well-stocked minibar was theirs for the taking, Mark stood before the open armoire not quite believing his own eyes.

"I told you I wasn't talkin' jump ropes," Trish said from behind him.

"Uh-huh."

"Did you look at the itinerary?"

"Nope."

"Mark? Are you okay?"

He blinked. "I recognize a few things," he said. "I know where they go and what they do. But I swear to God, Trish, there are things in here that frankly scare the hell out of me."

She laughed as she put her arm around his shoulders. "Don't sweat it, sweetie. Just consider it part of the New York experience. Something to tell Darryl while you two are having a cold one."

He looked at her, not surprised in the least that she was in such a good mood despite their horrible travel day. It had taken forever to get through the airport. First-class was nice, but he'd never been comfortable flying. Add to that his serious misgivings about this whole deal, and he'd had better days.

Not so, Trish. She was giddy with wonder and excitement. He just wished he could enjoy her happiness more. He'd never thought of her as foolish, and no, he didn't know for a fact that this whole trip was an exercise in foolishness. Maybe she would get her dream job. He wanted that for her, despite the fact that her success would mean he'd probably never see her again.

"You have to admit, this is one damn fine hotel room," she said. "I'm going to take a bath in that huge tub tonight, when it's dark and I can see all the city lights."

"Uh-huh."

"We have dinner reservations at Amuse Bouche at seven."

"Uh— Amuse what?"

"Amuse Bouche. It means a delight for the mouth. Like a tiny appetizer. Jeez, you don't get out much, do you?"

He turned toward her to give her a look. She dismissed him with a laugh. "I had to look it up. It's supposed to be a fabulous restaurant."

"That gives us two hours?"

"Yep."

He headed back into the living room, away from the giant bed and the scary armoire. The couch seemed big enough, but he wondered if it opened into a bed. Nope.

"Not a chance," Trish said. She was standing in the bedroom doorway, her arms crossed over her chest. She looked pretty, despite the time change and the jet lag. "You're not sleeping on the couch."

"Well, I'm not gonna let you—"

"I have no intention of sleeping anywhere but the bed. Did you see the size of that sucker? We could sleep four in there, easy. We'll share."

He took a step back as the thought, the idea, the picture of them in bed together combined with all that stuff in the armoire hit him a low and powerful blow. "Uh…"

She smiled as if she was fully aware of the effect her casual comment was having on his body and mind, but then she took pity on him. "Relax. We're not going to do a thing that makes either of us uncomfortable. This is supposed to be a vacation. The kind with no worries. We'll make it work, okay?"

Mark sat down on the couch, not all that sure they

could make it work. Yes, he'd known they were going to share a suite, but he hadn't let himself think about the sleeping part. He'd made sure not to have expectations, and more than that, he didn't want Trish thinking she was obliged. He just wished he hadn't taken a look in that armoire.

What the hell had happened to him? Used to be, especially when he and Trish were together, he didn't need an excuse to get her into bed. Or permission. Or a bed.

He wasn't even that old. Okay, twenty-five wasn't seventeen, but hell, why had his thoughts centered around not taking advantage of her? She was a grown woman. She could make her own decisions, be they to share a bed or move halfway across the country to find some kind of magical dream job that would probably end up making her miserable.

"Mark?"

He looked up to find Trish standing right in front of him. "Yeah?"

"Are you okay?"

"Jet lag."

"Uh-huh."

He tried to smile.

"Why don't you go on and use that incredible shower, then take a nap. I'll make sure you don't sleep too long."

"What about you?"

"I can't stand it. I have to get out there. I have to see at least some of the city before I go nuts."

"Good idea. Wouldn't want you to go nuts."

She bent over and kissed him on the cheek, but she didn't stand up right away. Instead with her soft perfume giving him a gentle nudge and her long brown hair tickling his ear she whispered, "Thank you, Mark. You're my hero."

TRISH GOT IN the elevator and found herself next to a very famous rock star. Not that she could remember his name, but she knew she'd seen him on the cover of magazines. She'd had no idea that he was that skinny. Whoa, dude had no ass, but he did have hair plugs.

Boy howdy, was this not Briscoe.

At the lobby, the rock star pulled out a cigarette and a lighter, closing his fist tightly around them before stepping out. There were no paparazzi waiting, only the beautiful deco lobby and the artwork that was sexy and sophisticated at the same time.

As Trish walked toward the door, she paused at the bar, which wasn't terribly busy at five-thirty, but those who were there were dressed as if they'd stepped out of the pages of a fashion magazine.

Trish had thought she looked nice for the trip. Dark jeans, white blouse, her best leather boots.

Those girls, those women, made her feel like the hick she was. But was determined not to be.

She headed for her first real walk in New York, and the moment she stepped outside a frisson skittered through her body. If she'd had a hat, she probably would have done the whole Mary Tyler Moore thing. Instead she smiled. Grinned like a loon. Not one of the hurrying pedestrians spared her a second look, which was just what she expected.

Someday soon she'd be like them. Walking fast, eyes straight ahead, important things, stories, interviews, just ahead. She'd be on her way to the little corner market where she'd pick up a quick salad and maybe some wine, then to her apartment. It would be tiny, and she'd probably have a roommate, someone she'd met at the paper, and it would be three floors up, but she'd love it. Because it would be The Road, and she'd have made it happen. She'd be out of Briscoe and she'd never look back.

Her head turned then, and looked straight up the hotel building, its brownstone exterior giving no hint to the glamour inside. Or the man in the honeymoon suite.

She'd miss him. But that was nothing new. She'd been missing Mark for years.

She headed down the street, staring into store windows, gasping at landmarks. She had no idea where she was going even though she'd been perusing maps of Manhattan since the day she'd opened the letter from Hush.

She hadn't quite counted on so much of her time being taken by the wedding plans. Or the fact that the entire event, not just the wedding itself, would be followed by the press.

That last bit wasn't so bad. In fact, she planned on making some friends during the next week, and who knows what could happen from there?

It was still light outside and there was a nice breeze lifting her hair from her neck. The scent of hot dogs, of fresh baked bread, of trash and perfume and apples, made her deliriously happy, helping her find the rhythm of the city, to walk fearlessly across streets even when the light was still red.

Why, why did Mark dislike big cities so much? He'd only been to Dallas that one time, and besides, Dallas was in Texas, so that didn't count.

Tomorrow, she'd find the time to take him out. Straight to the Chrysler Building. No one could look at that building and not fall in love. With New York. And then she'd take him to eat. Not at some fancy restaurant but to Papaya King for a hot dog. Mark loved dogs, and everything she'd read about Papaya King said they were the best.

Just thinking about it made her walk faster, made everything around her seem glamorous and fascinating. Or maybe everything was already wonderful, but the idea of sharing it with Mark…

She slowed as she passed a man lying on the sidewalk. He wore a heavy, filthy coat and his hair was matted and thick on his head. A brimming trash bag sat next to him, his filth-encrusted hand resting on it possessively. His shoes didn't match.

No one saw him. No one even broke stride.

She supposed that after a while, after she'd lived in the big city for a few months, it wouldn't faze her, either. She wasn't quite sure how to feel about that.

MARK WAS DRESSED when she got back to the suite. His hair, dark brown and shiny, had been combed a little too neatly, his jaw was shaved smooth and his eyes, a mix of green and blue that changed with the weather, looked bright and dark as he stood in front of the floor-to-ceiling windows.

"You look nice," she said.

He looked down at his pressed jeans, his polished boots and his cowboy shirt, the one that had the blue piping. His shoulders lifted in a modest shrug, which she knew for a fact was true. He didn't think he was anything special, not in the looks department. How a smart man could be so dumb was a mystery. She thought of that rock star in the elevator. On his best day he couldn't have held a candle to Mark. Every girl in Briscoe had swooned over him, but back in the day, he'd only had eyes for her.

She hadn't been the prettiest girl in their small high school. Not a cheerleader or class president or anything fancy. Just the editor of the school paper and at graduation, she'd been the valedictorian. Even so, Mark had always told her she looked great. He'd even called her beautiful once. That had been quite a night.

"Did you like it?"

"It's pretty amazing."

"I imagine it is." He walked over to the minibar and pulled out a beer. "You think I should?"

"I have to shower and change, so sure. It won't interfere with dinner."

"I was thinking about taking a look at that high-def TV."

"Have at it."

He grinned the smile that had made her melt. "I figure after tonight, I won't have time to do much TV watching. Did you get a look at that schedule?"

"We'll find time. I promise." She met him as he walked toward the couch and touched his arm. She'd meant to kiss him. Nothing big, nothing that would shake things up, but she felt suddenly shy and awkward.

She'd talked so big just an hour ago. Now she realized just how much of that was bluff. The toys in that armoire scared her to pieces. The only walk on the wild side she'd taken was to get herself a mail-order vibrator. "I won't be long," she said, hoping he didn't hear the slight crack in her voice.

"Take your time. There's like fifty channels of ESPN."

"Be still my heart."

He grinned. "You're gonna love that shower."

"I intend to love every minute of this miracle."

Mark looked out the window and whispered the same words. On his tongue it sounded like a joke.

CHAPTER FOUR

BY THE TIME TRISH came out of the bedroom, Mark had lost interest in the baseball game despite the fact he could see the individual blades of grass growing on the field. He couldn't stop thinking about after dinner. After dinner when they came back here. To the bedroom.

The last time he'd made love with Trish had been prom night. They'd gone to a real nice bed-and-breakfast over in Calloway. The rest of the class had gone to El Paso. But that night, for them, had been as painful as it was sweet. They had decided that they wouldn't sleep together again, or even hang out over the summer. Trish was convinced their relationship was like an addiction and the only way to end it was cold turkey.

It had been the worst summer he'd ever spent. Getting over Trish had been brutal. He'd thrown himself into working the ranch. Each day he'd get up with the sun then wear himself out so hard that he could barely eat dinner at sunset. He'd fall into bed, exhausted, only to dream about her.

It had taken a long time to cure himself of his addiction to her. Did he want to go through that mess again? What if Trish was like heroin? What if one night was all it would take to pull him back in?

The bedroom door opened, and there she was looking fresh and pretty as a bluebonnet. She'd left her hair down the way he liked it best. The dress she wore was tight in just the right places, and the purple, well, she'd always looked good in purple.

"You look beautiful," he said.

She reacted the way she had since day one. Her head tilted down and to the side, her cheeks pinked up and she whispered a "thanks" that she didn't believe.

He'd never understood why she felt so shy about her looks. She wasn't the most traditional beauty out there, but he liked that. He didn't want a cookie-cutter gal. He wanted—

He stood up, stopping himself before he took that thought too far. "We're gonna be late if we don't get out of here now."

Trish went to the door. "Let's hit it."

As he walked her to the elevator, he fought hard not to touch her, then remembered they were supposed to be engaged so wouldn't not touching her look suspicious? Well, he could wait until they were in the lobby, then it was a short walk to the restaurant, and that would take care of things for the short-term.

He still had no idea what he was going to do about after dinner.

"Hey," he said, "knowing you, you've looked up what's what at this restaurant."

She nodded. "I have."

"What should I order?"

"I don't think there's a thing on there you wouldn't like. They even have big, thick steaks. And onion rings."

"Okay, then. With a name like Amuse Bouche, I was afraid they were gonna force-feed me couscous."

The elevator arrived, empty.

"Have you ever had couscous?"

"No."

"Then how do you know you won't like it?"

"Same way you knew you'd love New York."

She smiled at him, and instead of giving him a jab for being a smart-ass, there was a sudden tenderness in her eyes that made him check out the elevator buttons.

He breathed again when they stopped on the twelfth floor to let in a couple of very tall, thin women. By the time they reached the lobby, they'd picked up four more passengers, men who seemed very interested in the skinny chicks. He didn't get it. But then, he didn't get most of what passed for the modern world. Not that he didn't keep up, at least to some degree. He read the big news magazines, subscribed to newsfeeds along with his grain and cattle reports. But he'd been one step behind his whole life. It wasn't going to change anytime soon.

Bucking up, he took Trish's hand as they headed for dinner. Damn if it didn't feel as natural as breathing.

She was just right. They fit together. That's why it had been so hard when they were torn apart.

"I'm nervous," she said. "It's just dinner, and I've been to really great restaurants in Dallas, but my stomach is all jittery."

"You're gonna be the classiest woman in the place," he said. "And I'll try hard not to spit on the floor or get into a brawl."

Her laughter lightened everything. "Yeah, that's just what I was worried about." She bumped his shoulder with her own.

"Anyway, tonight's just about food. The hard part starts tomorrow."

"I know," she said. "I have to sit down with that itinerary first thing and figure out when I can make some appointments. And I want to take you out. There's so much to see."

"We'll find the time," he said, although he'd already seen enough of Manhattan on his ride from the airport. Thousands of people, thousands of cars, taxis, buses, no one paying a bit of attention to any of the others, just racing to get where they were going.

The door to Amuse Bouche was high and elegant, the room itself a smooth mix of sleek and rich. There were flowers and screens and there wasn't anyone seated who wasn't dressed to the nines.

He gave his name to a woman in a short skirt, and that changed everything. The woman's eyes widened, there was a signal to someone behind her, then they were taken to a table in a private corner. A table set for four.

Once he'd held Trish's chair, another woman joined them. She, like so many of the women he'd seen at the hotel, was slender, attractive and put together as if she was prepared to be on television. Her blond hair was pulled up on top of her head, she wore pearls around her neck and a blue suit. Despite all that, she looked young, in her early twenties. Although maybe she just had real good New York doctors.

He stood as introductions were made. Gwen Holmes was her name, and she was the new director of Weddings by Desire.

"I'm not going to intrude for long, I promise," she said. Then she turned to the hostess. "You can bring the champagne now, Lilly."

Mark held the chair for Gwen Holmes, then he sat opposite Trish. She seemed as surprised as he felt.

"I wanted to go over the schedule for tomorrow. Answer questions. Prepare you a little."

"Prepare us for what?" he asked.

"There will be cameras. Quite a few of them, in fact."

"Where?"

"Pretty much everywhere," Gwen said. "As much as I'd love to tell you we're throwing this shindig because we're just sweetie pies, the truth is, we're launching a very expensive enterprise and you're our major promotion. Your pictures are going to be in lots of magazines, on television, maybe on billboards. First thing tomorrow, we'll be signing releases. You're going to sign away all rights to your images, and for the event itself. That was in our letter, but I wanted to bring it up one more time. It can be intimidating."

The champagne arrived, and Mark hoped Trish liked the stuff more than he did. He was a man of simple tastes. Beer. Home. A good truck. A good—

"We understand," Trish said, "and believe me, this is the most exciting thing in the world. For both of us."

Her gaze met his, and she lifted her glass toward him, more to agree on the conspiracy than to celebrate their upcoming nuptials.

"There's no problem with the releases," Trish continued as she turned to look at Gwen.

"Great. Then, after we get all that boring stuff out of the way, we'll be off to Harry Winston to pick out the rings."

Mark put his glass down as he checked up on

Trish. Rings were something concrete. They stood for a lot, and he knew for a fact Trish took great stock in that particular symbol. Sure enough, color came up on her cheeks and she turned away from him.

He'd had a suspicion that all this wasn't as casual as she'd like him to believe, and this proved it.

TRISH SMILED as Gwen said her goodbyes, but the smile faded as she turned back to Mark. He'd been mostly quiet as Gwen had covered all they had to do tomorrow. It would be one of their busiest days. Fittings for both of them after the rings, which they'd been told would take an hour, and that they would need to pick the rings from those taken out of the case. They were lovely rings, she'd assured them, all of them worth a great deal of money. But they weren't to window-shop.

It all seemed so real now. She was going to marry Mark. They would be husband and wife. Only, not for keeps.

Her guilt punched her square in the stomach. These very nice people were spending a great deal of money on a sham. When she knew they were alone, she leaned toward Mark. "Maybe this wasn't such a good idea," she said. "Maybe we should back out now, before they spend any more money on us."

The candle on the table made Mark's eyes seem

green tonight. He was everything safe and comfort-able, and yet she felt the censure in his gaze. Or maybe that was her own guilt she was staring at.

"You have to make that decision, Trish. I'm here for you. Not for them. I'm sure they're going to get everything they'd hoped for. Great publicity for their new service. For what it's worth, I don't think they'll give one damn about us after we're gone. They'll be moving on to the next publicity stunt."

"Okay, let's take them out of the equation. Am I doing something despicable? The truth now."

"No, it's not despicable. It's not the single most noble gesture I've ever seen, but I know you're not doing it to screw them."

"I'm going to send the rings back," she said, hating this. Not an hour ago, she'd been so pleased with herself. She'd been nothing but thrilled that she'd come up with this glorious plan, and now she doubted everything.

"I'll do whatever you like, Trish. I'll even pay for the tickets home. It's your call."

She sipped the champagne, amazed that she liked it so much. It was probably hugely expensive. Yet another thing that wasn't really her.

On the other hand, this was it. Her shot. So she'd used some ingenuity, that wasn't a bad thing was it? Mark was right—Weddings by Desire was going to get everything they'd hoped for out of this stunt. What happened after didn't matter. They hadn't stipulated how long the marriage had to last.

"Trish?"

She jerked, realizing the waiter was standing next to the table holding a menu out to her. "Sorry," she said.

"No problem. Take your time."

They were alone again in a snap, but neither of them opened the menus.

"Honey, what do you want?"

He'd called her honey. He hadn't done that in a long time, and the word shimmied up her spine and landed in a part of her heart she had ignored since—

"It's okay to want what you want," he said. "It's okay to go after it with everything you've got. Just don't kid yourself about what you're doing and why."

"But what do you think?"

"You're asking the wrong guy. I've found my place. I don't know what I'd be willing to do if that was taken from me. I do know I'd go far. Real far."

She nodded even though she wasn't completely convinced. Although something told her this was the kind of go-getter attitude that would make her a great reporter.

"You're right about one thing," he said.

"What's that?"

"The steak and onion rings sound perfect."

She smiled as she opened her own menu. She read each item, not skipping anything, even the soups, which were her least favorite. It all sounded incredible. In fact, everything about this place was incredible.

Her gaze moved up to look at Mark once more. It still broke her heart that they couldn't find some way to make it work. The one thing he'd always been clear about was that he wanted to marry someone who would love the ranch as much as he did. That wasn't her.

She would order the sea urchin panna cotta and the wild striped bass. She'd finish this champagne. And she wouldn't think about what they were going to do in the suite until they hit the elevator.

Yeah, right.

CHAPTER FIVE

HE WASN'T THE ONLY ONE worried about the next few hours. Mark watched Trish play with her dessert, some custard thing with chocolate cutouts that, if she were back home, she'd have finished in record time.

He'd tried to lighten things up, and for a while, it had worked. The food was about the best he'd ever had, and it always cracked him up to hear Trish moan each time she took a bite. It wasn't quite the same as her moaning in the bedroom, but close.

And the bedroom was close now, too. Unless she changed her mind about an early night and decided to go off into the city. Half of him wanted her to do just that. The upper half.

"This is how I want to die," she said.

"Huh?"

"I want to eat this until I explode. I want this to be the last thing to touch my tongue."

"I'm glad you like it."

"Are you sure you don't want a taste?"

He laughed. "Look at you."

Confused, she did. Then she smiled as she saw that her left arm was on the table, shielding her dessert from any possible encroachment. "Well, I was going to suggest you order your own."

He leaned back, enjoying this. Her. "Order another. Order two."

She shook her head. "If I wasn't getting that fitting tomorrow…"

"I have to wear a tuxedo, huh?"

"Yep."

"They're not gonna try and do a makeover or anything, right? I won't have to meet those *Queer Eye* guys?"

"Sweetie, there's nothing those boys could do to make you prettier than you are right now."

He lifted an eyebrow. "All right, what favor do you need now?"

"I'm not buttering you up. You know perfectly well how gorgeous you are, so don't even try to pretend."

"Gorgeous?" He rolled his eyes. "How much of that champagne did you drink?"

"Enough. And, sadly, I've had enough of dessert, too."

Her plate was empty. Not even a crumb left as evidence. "I'm sure they could whip you up another in no time."

"Get me out of here before I sin," she said, pushing her plate toward the middle of the table.

"What are we supposed to do about the bill?"

"It's on Hush, but I think we need to leave the tip."

"Okay," he said, pushing his chair back. "How much?"

"Except for the champagne," Trish said, lowering her voice, "I got a rough estimate. I'd say fifty bucks."

He winced as he realized that fifty was just tip money, but put the bills on the table. This was New York, after all. He'd expected no less.

THE ELEVATOR RIDE had been brief, the walk to the suite was over before she could blink, and now they were standing in the living room, and she didn't know what the hell to do.

Mark brushed her shoulder as he went to the giant window. "Get a load of this," he said.

Was she really so stressed over the sleeping arrangements that she'd forgotten to look at the city? She joined him, staring out across an ocean of lights. None of the movies or pictures she'd seen had come close to this view. It took her breath straight away. She had to turn a bit, but there it was—her favorite building in the whole world, the Chrysler Building. It was stunning at night. The stuff of dreams.

"I can see where a person could grow to like this view," Mark said.

"Really?"

He nodded. "It's really something. It almost makes up for the lack of stars."

"The stars are there."

"I know, but it would still be tough to lay back and stare up into a pale, empty sky."

"We're on top of the world, Mark. Can't that come close?"

He reached out and took her hand in his. "Don't let me spoil your fun. This is what you've always wanted. A shot at the biggest city in the world. A chance to kick ass with the big kids."

"You're right. And you know what?"

"What?"

"I haven't a clue what I'm doing."

"All great stories start that way, didn't you know?"

She looked at him instead of at the skyline. "How can you have so much confidence in me?"

"I've known you since we were six."

"And you've seen most of the bonehead things I've done since then."

"Everybody does bonehead things. You don't let them stop you."

She lifted his hand to her lips. "Thank you."

"You have to stop saying that. We're friends. This is what friends do."

"Bullshit. I have other friends. They aren't here."

"You were just too chicken to ask them."

"Yeah. They were all too smart to fall for my line of bull."

"Hey, weren't you supposed to be soaking in that great big tub?"

"Why, yes," she said, dropping his hand, suddenly afraid she'd made him uncomfortable. "I do believe it's calling."

"I'm gonna tackle that TV set again," he said.

"You don't need to use the bathroom?"

"I can wait. You soak as long as you want."

She nodded, then headed toward the bedroom. Once there, she got all her bathroom goodies together, then got out the slinky pink nightie she'd bought just before they'd left. But after a long study, she put it back in the drawer and took her old sleep T, the one she'd had forever, and carried that with her.

Mark didn't know it, but the shirt used to belong to him. She'd stolen it from his mother's clothesline and hadn't felt an ounce of guilt. It was the most comfortable thing she owned, and she needed all the comfort she could muster tonight.

Give her a few years in this city, and she'd wager she wouldn't have a moment of doubt.

As she turned on the water in the tub, she wondered if that was a good thing or a bad thing.

MARK CLICKED OFF his cell phone, wondering what he was going to find when he got back home. His father had said everything was fine, that Chris was doing his chores and that the horses were well cared for. That Nate and Tom were happy to have the work. But in these last few years, his father's idea of taking care of the ranch and Mark's own had become real different.

Used to be, his dad was all over every aspect of the ranch, and there wasn't one detail that was left to chance. Then he'd gotten that idea about writing and suddenly the little things hadn't meant so much.

They still mattered to Mark.

Not that he didn't want his father to be happy, to do what he wanted to with his life, but things sure would have been a lot easier with all three men on board.

Finally, after a good couple of years of internal battles, Mark had made peace with the fact that he could only control one person—himself.

He looked at the bedroom door, wishing again that things could have worked out with Trish. She was so many things he wanted in a wife, in a partner. But she hated Briscoe and the ranching life.

With a sigh, he closed his eyes and leaned his head back on the cool leather couch. The muffled sounds of a soccer game were just indistinct enough to ignore. He smiled as he thought about Trish eating dessert.

HE WOKE WITH A START as the bedroom door opened. It took him a few seconds to get his bearings, but then he saw her, saw what she had on and whatever willpower he'd had dissolved in a heartbeat.

She had on his old T-shirt. The one that had gone missing years ago. He'd shrugged off the loss because it was just an old thing, nothing special. It was special now.

"How was your bath?"

"Incredible."

"I'm glad."

"You can get in there now. Sorry I took so long."

He clicked off the television and put the remote on the couch. When he stood, he thought about her in the bathtub, her slick wet skin, the way her breasts would bead at the nipple. He nodded at her. "So that's where that old thing got to."

She smiled shyly, then ineffectually tugged the shirt down her thighs. "I was young."

"It looks a hell of a lot better on you than it did on me."

She headed his way and he couldn't help his wandering gaze. Barefoot, she didn't make a sound as she walked. He probably wouldn't have heard her anyway, not with the way his heart was pounding. Her legs were amazing. He could have watched her walk around the world. And the T-shirt, faded blue, short, a picture of a local rock band he hadn't thought of in years barely perceptible after a thousand washes, was just thin enough that he could make out the soft shimmy of her breasts.

She'd pinned her hair up on top of her head in some kind of wonderful mess. All the makeup from earlier had been banished, leaving her pure and sweet.

They were only inches apart now, and his hand went to the curve of her neck. The touch was like the very first touch. Softness beyond belief that made him curse his callused fingers. "Beautiful," he whispered.

The way she looked at him then stole the rest of his breath.

"Tell you what," she said, kind of breathless herself. "Let's not think about anything but right here, right now."

He tried to tell her that was fine with him, but his words got stuck as he looked at her mouth.

"There are so many things I've forgotten," she said. "But I haven't forgotten one thing about you. Not the way you kiss, or the way you touch me. I—"

He couldn't stand it one more minute. His lips came down on hers for a kiss that filled a long-empty well. Slowly, slowly, he remembered her. Her taste.

The way she teased him with the tip of her tongue. How it felt like honey and velvet, how it made him ache to taste every single inch of her.

She moaned, and his already hardening cock stiffened more. And when she pulled him close against her, with just that old worn T-shirt between them, he ached that old familiar ache.

With a strength he didn't know he possessed he pulled away from her. "I'd better…"

She nodded. "Right."

"So, I'll see you…?"

"Yeah."

He left quickly, before he threw her on the couch. Despite the insistence behind his fly, he needed to be a gentleman, at least on the outside.

The bathroom made him laugh out loud. Her stuff was on every counter. Makeup stuff, hair stuff, more makeup, lotions. Good God, he had no idea she used all this goop. But, being a lady, she'd left him about ten square inches near the sink where his small black case looked lost in a forest of girly gewgaws.

It was tempting to brush his teeth and run, but he forced himself to get into the shower, which was some damn fine shower. He even washed his hair. Then he dried off, brushed his teeth, checked himself out in case he'd forgotten something vital.

With a big white towel around his waist, he headed

for the door, his step slowing as he got closer. A sudden shot of nerves filled him with questions, mostly about what the hell he thought he was doing.

Then he opened the door, stepped into the bedroom. Looked at the woman on the bed.

There were no questions left. No doubts. Not even a single thought. Just need.

CHAPTER SIX

HOLY CRAP.

Trish swallowed hard as she watched Mark walk toward the bed, his towel slung low on his hips, his chest worthy of magazine covers, his hair slicked back and his face, oh man, his face was the sexiest thing she'd ever seen. Mostly because he was looking at her as if she was the sexiest thing *he'd* ever seen.

She was glad she'd put the condoms on the night table. Glad she hadn't worn a thing under her T-shirt. Grateful beyond words for winning a prize that let her be with Mark.

He got to the side of the bed and his gaze moved slowly from her toes to her eyes. The hunger was in him. In her. As she struggled to breathe she remembered being with him in all kinds of sensory detail. Her body tingled with anticipation.

When he let the towel drop, the old memories vanished. Nothing existed except this moment. His unbelievable body. The way his slow grin made her shiver.

"I think I'll take back that T-shirt now," he said, his voice thick and low.

She sat, then rose up on her knees. With him watching every gesture, she took the hem of the T-shirt in her hands and lifted.

Slowly.

His eyes were something to behold as he followed her hands. Inch by inch, she exposed her body to him. Over her hips, her tummy. A hesitation just below her breasts. Then up. Hard nipples, goose bumps everywhere. Quickly now over her head.

She tossed the shirt off the side of the bed and dared him with a smile.

He put one knee, then the next on the bed. Close. His heat touched her first, then his rough fingers skimmed her breasts. Gently, with a patience she didn't share, he painted her skin. Down her sides, across her belly, a whisper across her thighs.

All the while he looked into her eyes. A connection, one she'd thought lost forever, reestablished itself between them. Her first lover. The only one who'd ever mattered.

"I want—"

"I know," she said. There was time enough for everything, but not enough hours in the world to do all she wanted with him. So much to taste, to feel.

He moved closer and his sweet peppermint breath

brushed her lips and they parted. His kiss, when it finally came, made her knees weak. Made her want to cry.

He pulled her into his arms, and even though it was awkward, her still on her knees and all, when she got there, it was home. It was the best place. Better than a hundred New Yorks.

For a long time, she kissed him back as her hands learned his body all over again. He'd changed. He'd always been well built, beautiful in fact, but now his shoulders were so broad, so perfectly muscled. His ass, well, against all reason, that had gotten better, too.

She felt him hard and ready against her hip, her tummy, but that would be the delicious dessert after her banquet of touch, of taste, of scent. God, he smelled like her dreams. Nothing on earth smelled exactly like Mark. She had carried the scent through the years, through the distances that separated them.

He pulled away from her lips but only to lay her down on the soft sheets. She looked up at him as he reached behind, admiring his chest. The dark hair that ran from his breastbone in a V all the way down past his flat belly where it met the hair around his erection.

Without conscious thought, she reached out to touch him there. Even before her fingers met flesh, he jumped in anticipation. He hissed through clenched teeth as she ran her finger down his length. A groan as she took him fully in hand.

She looked up to watch as his head fell back, as his chest swelled with held breath all from the slow pump of her hand.

No one fit her like Mark. No one made her feel like this. How many nights had she wondered if she'd ever feel like this again?

"Honey, you have to let me go."

"Why?"

"Because it's gonna be over before it's even begun."

She released him, embarrassed to admit she'd thought he meant something completely different. But no mind. He was moving again, coming to meet her on the bed, his head joining hers on the pillow.

"This is looking like trouble," he whispered as he ran his hand down her arm.

"No troubles tonight. Nothing but wonderful."

"Right," he said. "Nothing but you."

She traced his lips with her fingertip. "I've missed you."

He nodded as his hand went from the safety of her hip to the heat between her legs.

She gasped. Trembled. Without her consent, her eyes closed.

As the waves of sensation swept her away, she forgot that this was a game, a time outside of time.

And then she forgot she wasn't really his.

MORNING CAME with a phone call. Mark struggled to find the damn thing on the nightstand and when he finally got it up to his ear, his greeting was less than cordial.

It was Gwen, from last night, and she set them off in a world of hurry. A room service call first, then showers, then dressing. Trish doing that voodoo stuff with the makeup and the hair, so when she walked out of the bathroom she looked so good he wanted to go straight back to bed.

A cup of coffee and a Danish later, and it was time to run. First, to the fittings, where he lost Trish and found himself standing on a pedestal as a man took every kind of measurement it was possible to take. No, that's not true. No one wanted to know his hat size.

He had to try on a bunch of different tuxedo jackets as three women eyed him like a side of beef. They picked the winner, then it was a few more measurements then away to a room full of cameras and microphones.

He was seated on a tan wing chair facing an identical chair that was filled with one reporter after another. They all asked the same questions, even if they worded them differently.

"How did you and Trish meet?"

"In kindergarten. We were both six."

"When did you fall in love?"

"That would be in high school."

"What's Briscoe like?"

And on and on. What surprised him was that he didn't have to lie but a couple of times. He wasn't thrilled about the wedding. He hadn't proposed to Trish. So on those two, he became a shy cowboy and hemmed and hawed, and they moved on. He just kept waiting for it to be over.

That took another two hours.

THE FITTING was finally over and Trish felt as if her feet were going to explode. They'd put her in heels that were just small enough to hurt after the first five minutes, then made her try on a bunch of dresses, all of them more gorgeous than she could believe, and when they finally chose the winning number (a strapless gown with a shirred satin bodice, a full tulle skirt and a little flower on the waist) that made her feel as if she were the most beautiful bride in the world as well as the biggest fraud.

Despite standing in front of a huge three-way mirror, she managed to not quite look at herself as she was tugged and measured and photographed.

All the while, her thoughts kept slipping back to the night. To Mark. To how he'd taken her to the moon and the stars and how she'd never wanted to come back.

It was never going to work between them, so why did she continue to torture herself over it? A New

York kind of gal would do exactly what she was doing only without the regret. Without the guilt. And definitely without the wishful thinking.

Tomorrow morning was her first interview. It was with the *New York Post,* and while she would prefer to write for the *Times,* she wasn't going to bitch if she nailed it. The *Post* would be a huge coup, and instead of daydreaming about a cowboy that couldn't be hers, she should be rehearsing her interview answers.

She wasn't stupid. She knew she would have serious competition, but dammit, she also knew she was good. Her enthusiasm was unlimited, her willingness to work hard was a given, and no one, no one could want it more than she did.

"Arms up."

She lifted. They fitted. One thing for sure, these women weren't shy. One of them physically reached inside the gown and moved her boob. Now that was what she was talking about.

She wanted to be a boob-mover. Not literally, of course, but still. She wanted to face her tasks without sentimentality. Without concern for anything but getting the job done perfectly.

"Arms down."

She relaxed, only to be scolded for slouching.

"How much longer, do you think?"

"Not too long now."

That from seamstress number two. There had been no names asked, none given. Everyone in the room seemed focused and too busy for such pleasantries.

Trish kept her mouth shut and did as they asked, but she couldn't help thinking that if this had really been her wedding, she'd have wondered if she was missing out on something pretty darned important.

HARRY WINSTON was next, but first, more photographs. Not at the wedding gown shop but back at the hotel. On the roof. In a garden that was one of the most beautiful Trish had ever seen.

They'd put up a tent thingy right next to the elevator and when she walked inside it, she saw three racks of clothes—two women's, one men's. Most of the clothes were casual and Western. Jeans, boots and hats, but when she got closer, she saw they weren't the kind of Western she could buy in Briscoe. These were fashion pieces with big designer names on them. They were all her size, and she wondered if it would be incredibly gauche to ask if she could keep them.

Yeah, probably.

Along with Gwen, a stylist named Ricky was there and the first thing he did was put every ounce of his attention on Mark.

"Well, this is going to be a much more pleasant afternoon than I'd imagined. Turn around, big boy."

Mark gave her the Evil Look of Death as he turned for the man, and Trish thought of his makeover phobia. If she had to step in, she would.

"Let's go with the jeans you're wearing, and…" He drew the word out as he riffled through the men's shirts. He pulled out four, all of them similarly cut with not that much ornamentation. "The boots are fine." Ricky narrowed his gaze. "Did you bring your own hat, cowboy?"

The muscle in Mark's jaw twitched. "It's in the room."

"Well, hurry up and get it. I have a feeling I'll like it better than the ones I brought."

Mark obeyed, getting out of the tent as if it were on fire.

Trish wondered if he'd come back. But she didn't have long to ponder Mark's troubles. Ricky descended on her with an eye toward making her into someone else.

"Those jeans do nothing for your behind, honey." He pulled a couple of dark pairs off the rack. "These should help. And that blouse is too big. You want something that will hug your curves. Show a little hoochie."

She wasn't sure what hoochie he meant, but she was sure she'd find out.

What really got to her was when he told her to

change. Not behind a curtain, either. He wanted her to change right there in the middle of the tent.

"This is show business, honey. And believe me, you don't have a thing I haven't seen before."

"Well, I haven't shown it before, so you just turn your butt around."

With raised eyebrows, he looked at Gwen then back at her. But he turned.

She put on a Western shirt that was two sizes too small, a pair of jeans that cut off her circulation and boots that made her poor feet squeal.

The hoochie, it turned out, was boob cleavage and lots of it. So much, she had to wonder if the pictures they were taking would end up in *Playboy.*

But she just let Ricky do his thing. Thankfully he didn't stick his hand down her blouse. But that was the only thing to be thankful for.

Until Mark came back.

He wasn't wearing his cowboy hat. Instead he'd put on the hat he'd bought for his cousin Dill. Who was eight.

She laughed so hard she almost busted a button.

Ricky was not amused.

CHAPTER SEVEN

HARRY WINSTON WAS ONE hell of a jewelry store. After walking through the most intricate wrought-iron and gold-plated gate Mark had ever seen to a foyer so fancy it had a chandelier that was covered with flowers and gold and then the black and gold carpet, not to mention the cases of jewels that had to be worth more millions than he could ever imagine, he, Trish, Gwen and about a half dozen reporters were led into a private room.

Grateful to be sitting down so he had less chance of breaking something that would cost the ranch, Mark sat back as the jeweler, a really well dressed woman with white hair and a huge rock on her hand, pulled out a large velvet box. There were half a dozen engagement rings, all with matching his-and-hers wedding bands.

Mark didn't know all that much about diamonds, but he knew big. These were big diamonds. No cubic zirconium in this place. Just the real thing. Diamonds in gold, in white gold, in platinum. Round ones, ovals, pears, squares.

But the thing that captured his attention wasn't the glitter on velvet, it was Trish.

He knew right away that this was going to be tough for her. Some mysterious female gene had been switched on. Her face, always pretty, now seemed somehow softer, more vulnerable. It wouldn't shock him if he saw a tear or two—no, wait. Her jaw clenched, she sniffed away the sentiment, and steeled her shoulders. She was not going to be carried away by diamond dreams. This was not the real thing, and she best not forget it.

He hoped, for her sake, she could carry it off. Him? He was screwed.

Last night had taken him straight to the bad place. Or was it the good place? Whatever. He just knew that saying goodbye to Trish was going to be hard as hell. Harder than the last time, because this time, he knew it wasn't going to be easy to replace her. Easy? It was impossible.

"Each of these exquisite pieces are original designs by our master craftsmen. The diamonds are all GIA certified, one carat or greater, VVS1, which means there are only minute inclusions, and, as you can see, they vary in color and cut. Feel free to try them on, and ask any questions you may have."

Trish nodded as her gaze toyed with staring directly at the diamonds. Finally her hand reached out, hovered for a few seconds, then plucked one of the rings from the velvet.

If he wasn't mistaken, she trembled just a bit as she slipped the thing on. When it was home, she looked at him.

He wanted to take her out of this place. Not because she was cheating, but because she deserved so much more. Not an advertising ploy, not a cubic zirconium marriage. Hell, even if it was to someone else, Trish should have the real deal.

"What do you think?" she asked.

He tore himself away from her gaze to look at her hand. It seemed small, pale. Her nails weren't done up and there was a tiny mole just below and to the right of her thumb.

Before he could stop himself he leaned over and took her in a kiss. He wanted her to know, to understand that this, the dress, the photographs, the jewelry meant nothing. They were all so much dust. But that shy blush, the way she'd offered her long, warm neck to his lips. The sounds she made when she was *almost* there.

At the sound of a discreetly cleared throat, he pulled away from her, hoping she'd gotten his message. Hoping he wasn't going to want to stop breathing when she said goodbye.

HOURS LATER, after more photos, more wardrobe changes, more makeup lessons and just more, they were finally back at the hotel, alone in the room. Her, Mark and the ring. Rings. One stunningly beautiful one-carat round brilliant in a platinum four-pronged setting that looked better than anything she'd ever had on her hand.

All she wanted to do was take it off. Bury it in one of those rosebushes on the roof.

She was in the bathroom, sitting on the edge of the tub. Wondering what Mark was doing out there. Expecting things? Of course he was. Why wouldn't he? Last night had been amazing. Sonnets could have been written about last night.

Such a huge mistake.

Not just the sex or the ring but the whole thing. What had she been thinking? She could have hired someone to be her fiancé. It would have been clean, neat. She would have sent the rings back a couple of weeks after the annulment, and voilà. No harm, no foul. Weddings by Desire would have gotten their money's worth, she would have gotten her job and no one would have been hurt. Especially not her.

She rocked back, thinking about the kiss at Harry Winston. Mark had caught her completely by surprise, and while it had been the sweetest gesture ever, it had made her heart hurt so badly she'd nearly…

In truth, she hadn't been on the verge of running.

Her feet hadn't moved, she hadn't tried to take the ring off. She'd felt bad, that's all. And for none of the right reasons.

Why had she asked Mark to do this for her? What had she expected would happen? Had she chosen him simply because she knew she could get him to agree? Or had she wanted things to change between them?

Did she still love Mark?

A soft tap on the door reminded her that the suite only had the one bathroom. "I'll be right out."

"Okay, thanks."

She went to the sink and looked at her face. After all they'd done to her today, makeup-wise, she wasn't surprised to find her skin blotchy and her eyes red-rimmed. Nice.

After a few splashes of cool water, she dried off and met Mark in the bedroom. "It's all yours."

"Actually, I'm set, I was just worried that something was wrong."

"Just tired. Anxious about tomorrow."

"The *Post,* huh?" He was sitting on the bed, his legs crossed at the ankles, a couple of the big pillows behind his back.

All she wanted to do was curl up next to him. Feel those strong arms around her shoulders. Hear his heartbeat beneath that cowboy shirt. Instead she went to one of the chairs by the window. "It's not the *Times,* but fantastic, nonetheless. I think I'd be a pretty good fit there."

"They're gonna love you."

"I just need to give them the right impression. I learned a lot from interviewing at the Dallas paper. If I'm on my game, I truly think I have a shot."

"Then let's make sure you're on your game. How about room service tonight, then an early bedtime. You need the rest."

She had to swallow a sudden rush of tears. That alone proved that she was way too tired. "I promised to take you around the city tonight."

"The city will still be there."

"Let's look at the menu, then."

He nodded, and his eyes told her he knew she was a lot more than exhausted. She didn't have to make a decision about making love because he'd done it for her. For *her*. Was it any wonder she had these... feelings?

Maybe it was still love. But love wasn't always enough, was it?

HE'D GONE to the top-floor pool and had a swim, had breakfast, read the paper, paced the room, tried to watch TV, then paced some more and still Trish hadn't gotten back from her interview.

He hoped it had gone well for her, that the people at

the *Post* were smart enough to see that she was a once-in-a-lifetime find. Of course, her success would mean...

He put the brakes on his thoughts. Even if it didn't work out with the *Post,* Trish was still going to move out of Briscoe. So why not wish her the best?

He'd thought a lot about last night. He hadn't gotten much sleep despite his exhaustion. He'd wanted so badly to touch her. To make love with her. But he'd kept his hands to himself. Literally. After he knew she was soundly asleep, he'd taken a second shower. It had been quick because he'd been hard and ready from the moment he'd seen her in that old T-shirt.

Even that hadn't stopped the ache. Maybe it had just been too long since he'd been so attracted to a woman. But probably it was because she was Trish.

He crossed the room to the minibar but nothing had changed since the last time he'd rooted through the contents. Just as he shut the fridge door, the suite door opened. He knew instantly that the interview hadn't gone well.

"Hey," she said, her accent, which she'd worked hard to lose, was clear in that one word. That only happened when her guard was down.

"Hey."

She dropped her purse on one of the end tables followed by her jacket. She looked cool and professional even without it. A pale green silky blouse and dark green pants gave her the sophistication she aimed for without all that morose black New York women seemed to like so much.

"Well, that sucked."

He joined her, choosing the leather club chair across from her so he could see her face. "What happened?"

"I waited along with a half dozen other eager young hicks. Filled out forms. Waited some more. Then we were all brought into this conference room where a junior, junior assistant, some guy named Frank who I swear was maybe seventeen, asked each of us where we'd graduated, where we'd worked and why we should get the job. The job, mind you, was as a research toady. Nothing glamorous, lousy pay. We had about a minute to answer. Frank didn't even listen. He told us we'd be contacted if they wanted us to move to the next level. That was it."

"Did he say when you'd be contacted?"

"No. And I won't be. I was about as invisible as I could be. The only shot I had was to get into a dialog with someone."

"Sounds to me like you have an even chance with everyone else there."

"Not really. There were two people that had a lot more experience. The rest of us were just hicks from nowhere."

"I'm sorry it wasn't better, but hell, it's only one

interview. You have the *Times* and that other paper, right?"

She nodded. "Right. Well, I'd better get it in gear." She looked at her watch, the one that had belonged to her mother. "Gwen will be calling any minute, and I've got to get something to eat."

"Want me to call room service?"

She thought about it for a moment. "Nope. I think I'd like to get out of the hotel. I'll call Gwen instead and find out the schedule. After that, I want to find a real New York deli. I'm in the mood for a bagel and a schmear."

He laughed, hearing her say that with her Briscoe accent in full gear. "Oy," he said.

Trish smiled. "I don't think we can pass, bubba."

He crossed over to the couch and gave her a kiss on the cheek. "No, I don't think we can."

When he started to move away, Trish caught his arm, met his gaze. "Thanks for the support."

"I want the best for you. I always have."

She opened her mouth, but didn't speak. Instead she let him go and ducked under his arm in her haste to get to the bedroom.

He watched the closed door for a long while. Wishing…

CHAPTER EIGHT

THE NIGHT STRETCHED before Trish like a giant red carpet to the city. After another round of wedding interviews and a lunch that was great, but wasn't the deli she'd longed for, she, Mark and the engagement ring were finally on their own.

"What do you want to see first?"

Mark leaned back on his heels as he watched the traffic roll by on Madison Avenue. "Darlin', I have no clue."

"Well, haven't you ever wanted to see anything in New York? Rockefeller Center? Times Square? The Rainbow Room?"

He looked at her then and his slow smile pulled her right back to their first year of high school. Mark had been just Mark since they were six. Nothing special, not the most annoying of the local boys, but a bit of a show-off. Then she'd gone to Briscoe High wearing a sassy short skirt and a twelve dollar blouse from Nordstrom's Rack. Not to mention Clinique eye makeup and lip gloss. She'd thought she was so hot, eggs would fry on her butt.

She'd walked into first period English and neighbor Mark turned in his chair. His gaze had roamed from her Payless Shoes to her Glamour Cuts hair, and he'd smiled. *That* smile.

It was all over but the formal announcements.

Here she was on the brink of her brand-new life, ready to take on Manhattan and still, as always, her heart skipped two beats, the butterflies swam in her tummy and she just plain melted. The disappointment from the nonexistent newspaper interview had transformed itself into a fierce desire to show them. Her confusion about roping Mark into the extravaganza of this wedding had become muted as he'd so clearly gotten into the spirit of the fun during the wedding chores.

If only she wasn't so drawn to him. If she'd met someone else, or if he'd done some horrible thing to her. But no. He was still that boy that had made her sigh in Mrs. Carrel's first-period class.

"How about we walk a while. I've been sitting too much. I'm getting used to it."

She pointed past his shoulder. "That way is Times Square."

"Times Square it is."

He turned, reached back and took her hand in his. "Give me the nickel tour," he said.

"I don't know enough about the city to do that."

"Sure you do. Tell me what you love about it. What draws you here above all other places."

They walked at a leisurely pace, which seemed slow compared to those rushing past them. Everyone seemed to be late for something. Trish, on the other hand, wanted the world to slow, to stop. Holding Mark's hand, thinking about how to explain her love for the city. It was heaven.

"Well?"

"Movies," she said. "Woody Allen had a large part in my first stirrings of love for New York. But he wasn't the only one. Every time I saw pictures of Manhattan I got all excited. It was as if I'd already been there, as if it was where I belonged, if I could only get there."

"I think you'd have to go pretty far to find a place less like Briscoe."

"That had something to do with it," she said. They stopped at a crosswalk and marveled at the games the pedestrians played, daring taxicabs and black limos to run them down like bowling pins.

"I don't mind traveling," he said, "but it's getting home that I like the best."

She shoved his shoulder with her own. "Liar. You hate leaving your ranch."

Mark shook his head. "I don't hate it, but I do

worry. Dad has other interests these days, and we both know that if Chris could, he'd spend all day playing video games."

"How's your dad's book coming?"

"I have no idea. He won't let me read it till it's done."

"Still. Good for him. It's really never too late, is it? Not for the big dreams." They slowed their pace as they waded through a crowd of people exiting a tour bus. As she caught sight of all the cameras around all those necks, she mentally kicked herself for not bringing hers along.

"I suppose you're right," Mark said. "It's weird, though, that I never knew he wanted to write. He never said anything."

"He probably told your mom." She looked over at Mark and was surprised at the sadness she saw there. "What's wrong?"

"Nothing."

"Mark, it's me."

He smiled at her. "I thought my father would love the ranch until he kicked the bucket."

"I'm sure he does love the ranch."

"Not so's you'd notice."

"Now he has you. He trusts you to take care of things."

"But—" He loosened his grip on her hand but she just held on more tightly.

"But what? The man's worked hard his whole life. He deserves a chance to branch out. Not everyone is like you, Mark, not even your hero."

"My hero?"

"I know how much you care about your dad. How you've tried to model yourself after him. It's a great compliment to him that you've turned out so well. But don't begrudge him because he did his job."

Mark shook his head as they stopped at the corner of Times Square. For a long time, he just looked at the lights, at the giant TV screens and the Broadway marquees. He seemed awfully interested in the pizza joint across the street, and Trish realized she was hungry, too. But pizza wasn't on her menu.

"Come on," she said, tugging on his hand. "I want to take you to dinner."

Trish had memorized the address, but had no idea how far the place was from where they were, so they hailed a cab. It took about twenty-five minutes to arrive, and after she paid the driver, they got out at East 86th Street. At Papaya King. Supposedly one of the best hot dog joints in the world.

"This is where we're having dinner?" he asked, grinning to beat the band.

"I also know how you feel about hot dogs."

Mark looked at the joint, which was really just a big old hot dog stand painted brilliant greens and yellows. There was a line, of course, but everyone in it seemed to be in a pretty happy mood, a good sign.

OF COURSE TRISH had brought him to eat hot dogs in New York. He'd loved dogs since childhood, and he was the nutcase at barbecues who passed up the sirloin steaks and even the Texas beef ribs only to eat a half dozen hot dogs, complete with mustard, relish and onions. As everyone liked to tell him so often, it was a sickness.

She dragged him into the line and she was so tickled with herself she was practically hopping from foot to foot. Damn, she was adorable when she got like this. It was one of the things he liked most about Trish, that she could be such an unabashed kid. She didn't give a damn what anyone else thought. Even the cliques of Briscoe, which were downright evil.

He was helpless, of course. He had to kiss her. And when he did, not even hot dogs stood a chance. He pulled her into his arms and in front of God and all the people in line, he made sure she was well and truly kissed.

She fell into him, as if her bones had gone soft. He was all too eager to hold her. To keep her close. To taste her and feel her.

But the hot dog line would wait for no man or woman. They broke it up and moved along, but he didn't let go of her. His arm was around her waist and hers was around his. It was just like old times when she slipped her hand into his back pocket.

He enjoyed his Papaya King hot dogs and his mango pineapple juice. But it was nothing compared to how much he enjoyed the company.

"WHAT WERE YOUR responsibilities at the *Star-Telegram?*"

Trish stopped herself from adjusting her jacket again and looked squarely at Tom Finster, the man interviewing her at the *New York Times*. "I was an editorial assistant for the Lifestyle editor. I was responsible for compiling column material for weddings, birth announcements, the calendar of events and the obituaries. I also wrote some feature articles, which you'll see in my portfolio."

He had the portfolio in front of him. Open. But he didn't even glance at it. Or her. Mostly he was watching his computer monitor.

"What makes you think you're right for the *Times?*"

"I've studied the paper for years. I know each section well, I know the styles and points of view of all your columnists. I've done my homework about the city, about the paper and about the people. I've got an old-fashioned work ethic, and I believe in doing the best possible job no matter what the task.

I'm accurate, I know about the printing cycles, and I'm not afraid of hard work."

"Uh-huh," he said, showing no more interest in her than he would a pesky fly on the window pane.

It was nothing less than torture. Her dreams smashing against indifference and shattering into a million tiny pieces. He wasn't going to hire her. It wouldn't have mattered what she'd said, either.

She knew the newspapers in New York were competitive, but she'd never have guessed she'd have been so outclassed. Her old boss at the *Star* had tried to warn her, but had she listened? She was so sure she could convince these people to take a chance on her....

It didn't mean she was going to quit. There were smaller papers in the city. If she had to, she'd apply at each one. Somehow, she'd find a way to stay here, to keep the dream going.

Only the dream had lost its vibrancy. It had turned from color to black and white, and at the moment, she wasn't sure she had it in her to repaint.

Finster typed for a moment, then turned to her. "You have a nice résumé, but I'll be honest with you. To get into this paper, you'd need a lot more experience. Go back to Dallas and get some years under your belt. Get your feet wet in the national and international sections."

Trish sat straighter. "I appreciate your honesty,

Mr. Finster. You've given me a strong direction and that means a lot."

He actually smiled. "This is the most competitive market on the planet. Good isn't enough. Excellent isn't, either. You have to walk in here a star."

She stood and held out her hand. "I'll be back."

"I bet you will," he said as he gave her back her portfolio.

She headed out of the old building, debating stealing a little more time to get a good look at the offices, at the bullpen, but she was needed back at Hush. The final wedding dress fitting was today, and then they were going to tape some TV promos. Gwen had nearly had a heart attack when she found out Trish would miss two hours.

At least Mr. Finster had turned out to be a mensch. She grinned. A mensch. She wondered if there was another soul in Briscoe, Texas, who knew the word, let alone what it meant. No, she was meant for bigger things. If it took a few more years to get there, so be it.

But on her way back to the hotel, the city looked different to her. The color here had changed, too. Or maybe it was just that her eyes had lost their stars.

MARK TRIED TO KEEP his mind on the reporter and not worry so much about Trish's interview, but it was tough. The woman, name of Patty, was from some tabloid, something he'd never heard of. She was dressed in some weird outfit that he supposed was the height of fashion, but man it looked uncomfortable. Especially the shoes. Those heels had to be at least four inches tall.

"One last question?"

Mark nodded. "Whatever you need, ma'am."

Patty smiled at him as if he were some kind of treat she got out of a cereal box. "You are just the most adorable man. Anyway, tell me a little more about your first trip to New York. What's the most exciting thing you've seen?"

He didn't have to give that one much thought. "The look on Trish's face when she put on the engagement ring."

Patty sighed. "One thing's for sure. They certainly picked the couple who were most in love. It gives me hope. Of course, finding a guy like you in New York is damn near impossible."

"Why's that? I'm not all that different, even if I do come from Texas."

She laughed, then, and he wasn't such a hick that he didn't get the joke. She didn't even bother to explain. All she did was pat him on the shoulder as she teetered out of the bar in her high-heeled shoes.

CHAPTER NINE

"WHAT AREN'T YOU TELLING ME?"

Trish looked away knowing it was stupid and useless to try to fool Mark. He above all people knew when she was upset. He read her so well. No one, not even her own mother, had ever been as attuned to her. Sometimes, she loved that. Right now, not really.

"Talk to me, girl."

They were finally back in the suite after a very, very long day. It was just past midnight, and they both needed to get a good night's sleep.

Tomorrow was the wedding.

Mark's Dad and his brother had come in yesterday along with Darryl and Trish's friends. Not that they'd had a moment to talk, but Hush was certainly treating them well.

"Is it about tomorrow?"

"Partly," she said, resigned to spilling all the beans. If she was going to talk, she might as well have something to wet her throat. She went to the fridge and pulled out a diet soda for her and held up a beer for him.

"I'll take a soda, if there's one that's not that diet crap."

She got him his favorite and went back into the living room. Her gaze skidded to the panoramic view of the city and for the very first time, it didn't make her breath catch.

"Alrighty then," he said, leaning back in the club chair. "Which part about tomorrow is making you so upset?"

"Just the wedding part," she said, only partly kidding.

"I know. It's a big deal," he said, as if he hadn't caught that it was a joke.

Okay, so maybe it wasn't a joke. Maybe she just wanted it to be.

Mark popped the top of his soda. "You know, I've come to the conclusion that we were the perfect two people to have won this prize."

She paused with her drink halfway to her mouth. "Oh?"

He nodded. Took a swig of pop. "We've given them more than they had any reason to expect. We haven't complained, we've been forthright in all the interviews. Hell, you think a young couple who were truly in this for the wedding would have been so accommodating? Couldn't happen."

"Why on earth not?"

"Because getting married for keeps is a very emotional experience. It's for life. It matters. No matter what, you're signing on to go the distance with that one other person. That ring has to be significant, and that doesn't come with a hefty price tag. No matter how beautiful those rings were, they weren't from the heart."

As if she'd been kicked out of her chair by a giant boot, she was on her feet, soda sloshing out of her can, finger pointed straight at his face. "You know what? You're stubborn as a mule, Mark Reynolds. Even when it makes sense to get some damn help on your ranch, help that wouldn't hurt your bottom line a bit, you dig your heels in and work until you get sick. How many times have you had pneumonia?"

He opened his mouth, but she just stepped closer. "You think everyone who doesn't think like you do is not just wrong, but stupid. Don't even try to deny it, because I've been with you after a night at the Renegade, and you've sliced and diced those good ol' boys into mincemeat."

Again, he opened his mouth.

"You never give your brother a break. He's a kid, dammit, and he has a right to choose his own life. Sure he can help on the ranch, it's good for him to have the discipline, but don't discount his dreams. He has a right to them, too."

"Are you finished?"

"I'm not sure yet."

"Let me know," he said, as calm as you please.

She wanted to yell some more, and the truth was there was more to yell about. Mark was no saint, and he was no angel. He brooded and was quick to leap on other people's mistakes.

But he was also the most amazing man in the whole damn world.

She burst into tears, great big wet tears, and she ran into the bedroom, slamming the door shut behind her.

A minute later, she heard him open it. Shocking, because she was still wailing like a banshee. She should have locked the damn door.

He sat on the edge of the bed. Quietly. Patiently. She didn't want him to see her like this. Not because she was crying, but because she could feel all that TV makeup running down her cheeks.

Oh, the hell with that. He'd seen her look her worst. She'd seen him, too. They'd been through it all together. No, not all.

"You need some tissues?"

She sniffed and nodded. The bed rose a little, then dipped when he came back. She held her hand out and he stuffed it. Several minutes later, she finished mopping up her face, and while she knew her eyes were swollen and her skin a perfect mess, she faced him.

"I'm not ready," she said.

"For what?"

"For New York. For the *Times* or the *Post* or any of them. I'm a small-town girl with a dream too big for my britches."

"Not forever. You'll get the experience and then you'll come back."

She shifted on the bed until she was sitting closer to Mark. "I don't know if I want to," she said, her voice an embarrassed whisper.

His hand touched hers. "It's okay. You get to change your dreams, Trish. You have a right to do that."

"I just don't know what I want," she said. "It's always been so clear. All of it. The job, the apartment, the travel. I'd dreamed it in every detail. And now, all I feel like is the biggest fool in the whole world. I screwed up, Mark. So, so badly."

He stood and pulled her up with him. "Let's you and I go to bed. You tell me every little thing that's got you worried. In the morning, things will be a lot clearer."

She nodded, drained of every bit of energy, and headed to the bathroom. She needed a shower. She needed to sleep. She wished she were anywhere but here.

SLEEP WOULDN'T COME. Trish had no idea what time it was, but it was way late. She was going to look like crap tomorrow, which was just perfect.

She looked over at Mark in the moonlight. He'd been asleep for a while. Of course, that was her fault, too. He'd wanted to talk. She tried, but in the end, she just couldn't. She'd already confessed to being a fool. She hadn't the strength to fill in the details.

So, what now? What next?

She fiddled with her engagement ring. Her fake engagement ring. Tomorrow she would add a fake wedding band and sign fake wedding papers, and kiss her fake husband in front of hundreds of strangers.

Did it get any better than this?

She laughed at her own joke because really what were her options? She couldn't stop the proceedings at this stage of the game. That truly would be unethical, even beyond her shaky moral code.

She didn't used to have the shakes when it came to stuff like this. She used to be proud of her accomplishments and her behavior.

Not only had her dreams gone up in smoke, but her self-image was way too close to the ashes.

Mark turned over, and she got real quiet, afraid she would wake him with her screaming thoughts. Too late. His head came up from the pillow.

"Go back to sleep," she whispered.

He shook his head, then scooted closer. "You need something?" he asked, his voice all growly. "Water?"

"No. I'm fine."

"Somehow I doubt that."

With a sigh, she met him halfway on the bed, resting her head on his chest. "I'm so screwed."

He laughed, but in a nice way. "There's nothing you can do about any of it tonight, Trish. You might as well get some rest."

"I've tried. It's hopeless."

There was a long stretch of silence where the only thing she heard was his breathing. Then his hand pushed back the hair from her forehead in the gentlest caress. "Maybe I can help."

For a moment she thought he was going to sing her a lullaby or something. He disabused that notion as he pulled her up to meet him in a kiss.

She hesitated, but not for long. He hadn't been sleeping so long that he had morning breath, but she had the feeling she wouldn't have cared if he had. She needed this. Needed him.

He couldn't hate her too much if he could kiss her like this, could he? Maybe he wasn't embarrassed for her. Or filled with pity.

No, she was the only one feeling those things.

"Hush," he whispered, pulling away only a smidgen. "Don't you worry about a thing, honey. I've got you."

Touching his naked chest, feeling the warmth of his skin and his comfort, she fell into his embrace leaving behind her doubts and fears and judgments.

True to his word, he never once let her go. With a slow tenderness, he made love to her. With her. So thoroughly that there wasn't an inch of her body that didn't thrum with pleasure. From her lips to her toes, he showed her how he felt about her. Despite everything.

He whispered the words that had come to be theirs alone. Words that on another man's tongue would have sounded absurd. But theirs was a shared history of silliness, of sounds whose familiarity made them special.

Even though that old T-shirt was on the ground somewhere outside the bed, she felt wrapped in him no matter where his hands were. No matter how his teasing tongue made her plead.

When it was time to catch her breath, to cool her body down after the most perfect climax ever, he was still there.

"You still with me?" he said, his voice low and intimate.

"Uh-huh."

"Good, because there's something I want you to think about. You remember when we were growing up, there was the Briscoe County newspaper?"

She nodded against his chest. "It was what, four pages?"

"On a good day. But anyway, Jeb Smith still has all the equipment in storage. It's pretty dated, but it wouldn't take all that much to get the paper up and running again, especially now that computers can do so much of the work.

"Maybe, instead of going back to Dallas, you could consider becoming a publisher. Briscoe County has grown. There's lots of folks who could use a weekly paper. And if you were the publisher, you could make that paper into anything you wanted it to be. That would give you lots of experience, wouldn't it? I mean, you could write the stories, do the copy editing, editorialize, all of it. And when you're ready, you could come back and have something real and fine to show these New Yorkers. Anyway, it's something to think about, right? An option."

"Right," she said. "An option."

He kissed the top of her head. "Go to sleep. There's plenty of time to decide what you're going to do."

She nodded again, her body limp and so tired she could barely move her head. But her thoughts? A whole different story.

CHAPTER TEN

THE ROOFTOP GARDEN at Hush had been transformed. The flowers bloomed in a sea of brilliant colors and fragrances. In the center of the roof Weddings by Desire had gone all out to create a magical space. There was a rose-covered arbor, a string quartet, champagne at the ready and chairs and room for everyone, including the press. The decorations were all pastel and soft and blended with the flowers seamlessly.

Trish wasn't able to enjoy the scenery for long, however. Gwen hurried her away into the bridal room, adjacent to the swimming pool. Hush had taken equal care there, providing the bride-to-be and the wedding party with ample space to dress, do makeup and hair—there was even a gorgeous chaise for the bride to rest on, should the need arise.

Trish would have preferred a bed and about six more hours of sleep, but her adrenaline was sufficient to keep her awake. That and the espressos she was sucking down.

She was led to the beauty station where two women and a man were at the ready. One for hair, one for makeup, one for nails. Sinking down in the barber chair, Trish tried to relax. She had an entire hour scheduled here, then it was on with the dress, then on with the show.

The team situated themselves so they could all work at once, and Trish gave herself over to the primping. But instead of the calming meditation she'd meant to do, she thought again about what came next. Not just here, at Hush, either. She knew this was a defining moment. That what she decided here would determine the course of the rest of her life.

MARK DIDN'T HAVE TO BE at the hotel for another forty-five minutes, so he let the waiter pour him another cup of coffee. His father, his brother and his best friend Darryl had joined him for breakfast in a little coffee shop two doors down from Hush.

"So what do you think?" he asked.

His father shrugged. "It's a good place to visit, but I wouldn't want to live here."

Mark turned to Chris.

"I like it. There's so effin' much to do here. All night long, man. I saw a Chinese restaurant that's open until five in the morning. Jeez."

"It ain't bad," Darryl said. "But I miss home."

Mark sipped his coffee, debating the wisdom of finishing the last Danish. Better not.

"So," his Dad said, "this wedding thing. You and Trish. It's all for show."

"That's right. But we can't tell anyone that."

"You have your license, right? And there's going to be a real justice of the peace up there?"

"The marriage will be legitimate. Just short-lived."

"Why's that again?"

Mark sighed. "Dad, I told you. Trish wants to live here. In the city. She wants to work for a major paper. I can't wait to get back to the ranch."

"That's fine and dandy, but pretty inconsequential. Do you love her?"

Mark did not want to have this conversation. It was hard enough to face the day feeling the way he did. "Can we talk about something else? Please?"

"Sure, we can talk about anything you like. But the problem isn't going away. You need to tell her."

"What, that she needs to give up her dreams and become a rancher? She hates Briscoe. She hates ranching. It's not gonna happen."

"How do you know, if you don't ask her?"

"She knows her options." Including the one he'd offered up last night. Not that he would tell his father, but he'd pulled out the only ace he'd had. That Briscoe paper idea had been his last, desperate plea.

Trish hadn't brought it up once this morning. Not a word. It was time to let it go.

"I see her point," Chris said. "If I didn't have to, I wouldn't go back to the ranch. Not a chance."

It hurt to hear his brother's words, but they weren't a surprise. Mark remembered what Trish had said about allowing Chris to have his own dreams. "What do you want?" he asked. "Is there something specific? After college, I mean?"

Chris looked startled. "Well, yeah."

Even their father was paying attention now.

"I want to fly."

"Fly what?"

Chris's cheeks were flushed and he looked as if he was exposing a dirty secret. "Helicopters. I want to join the Air Force and get my license. And when I get out of the service, I want to be a life flight pilot for a hospital."

Mark sat back in his chair, dumbfounded. "How long have you been thinking about this?"

"Since I was twelve."

"Why didn't you say anything?"

He gave Mark a look that was like a punch in the stomach. "You didn't want to hear it. I know you love the ranch, dude, but it's not for me. It never has been."

"Yeah," Mark said quietly. "It doesn't have to be for you. I'd still prefer you go to college."

Chris nodded. "I'm planning on it."

Mark got the check from the center of the table. He left the money along with a New York-size tip. "I've got to get ready. See you guys up on the roof. And, Darryl, don't you dare have a beer until the wedding's over."

"Jeez, man. I may be a hick, but I'm not a dummy."

Mark hit his friend on the back of the head, but he smiled as he did it.

"Still time to tell her you love her," his dad said.

"Dad, she knows."

"Does she? Really?"

Mark didn't answer. But he pondered the question all the way back to the suite.

THE STRING QUARTET started playing the wedding march, and it was all Trish could do not to throw up. She was standing at the edge of the garden, Gwen at her side. From here, she could see it all. The gorgeous decorations, the stunning flowers, her friends Stephanie and Larissa from Dallas, Penny who she'd known since third-grade and her maid of honor, Ellen. Across the aisle sat Mark's dad and Chris. Even Darryl looked good in his tux. And, of course, the media. There were three television cameras, a whole gaggle of photographers and reporters. Piper Devon, Hush's famous owner, was there, too, looking stunning in a pale pink dress.

It was someone's dream wedding. Just not hers.

It should have been. Mark, in his perfect tuxedo complete with a rose in the lapel, was everything she'd ever wanted in a husband. Best friend, confidant, lover. But the life he could offer her, had offered her…what of that? Was it possible for her to find happiness, the forever kind, in Briscoe? Could she find the satisfaction she'd yearned for on a horse ranch? Running a newspaper that would be more focused on the grain reports than the situation in Washington?

Gwen touched her arm. It was her cue, and she had rehearsed this moment enough that she knew just how slow to walk, just how hard to smile.

If only her heart wasn't breaking into a million pieces. If only the ring on her finger meant what it was supposed to mean, instead of a glittery, brilliant lie.

Each step brought her closer to the shambles her life had become. She'd finally, early this morning in the fabulous shower, come to terms with the end of her dream. New York wasn't for her. Not now. Maybe never.

So what would she put in its place?

Dallas, where she could get her old job back, where she could continue to learn and develop as a journalist? Where she could start dating again, looking to find a man like Mark?

She felt the cameras on her, heard the delicate

strings as they wafted over the garden. The justice of the peace looked serene and happy in his best Sunday suit. Everyone around her seemed so pleased. So thrilled to be part of this momentous occasion.

Even Mark. God, the way he looked at her! Despite every one of her sins, her conceits, her schemes, everything about him, especially his eyes, spoke of his love for her.

Too quickly, she was at his side. He smiled at her and with great care, lifted the veil from her eyes.

The justice cleared his throat. "Dearly beloved—"

"Wait."

Mark looked at her sharply. The justice seemed insulted. And she could feel Gwen's panic from five feet away.

"Wait," she said again because she had to. The veil had been lifted, all right, and with a clarity that made the rooftop shimmer, she turned to Mark. "We need to talk."

He nodded once, took her hand and led her back down the aisle. All the way to the quietest part of the garden. All the way past the furious clicking of cameras.

The quartet had stalled, but by the time they were alone, they were playing Pachelbel's Canon.

"What's wrong, honey?"

"Everything," she said, not at all sure how to go about this. "You've been... I..."

"Take your time. There's no rush."

She took a deep breath. "Do you love me?"

He nodded. "I have since that first day of high school."

"Do you love me enough not to resent me when there's so much to be done on the ranch? When you're out there in the middle of winter and I'm away on a story? Do you love me that much?"

"Someone told me once that I was as stubborn as a mule. That I could hire help when I needed it. I think that piece of advice was worth taking."

"You've always wanted someone by your side. A helpmate."

"That's true. But help comes in a bunch of different ways."

"You have to be sure about this, cowboy, because what I'm saying here is that I love you. I love you so much it would be a sin against everything that's holy to walk away. But I'd rather cut off my own arm than give you a life of resentment and disappointment."

His slow smile—*that* slow smile—changed everything. "Honey, you're who I choose. Is that clear enough?"

She smiled right back. "Wow. That's very, very clear."

"Are you gonna be okay with the Briscoe County paper?"

"Yeah. I am. As long as you're there. As long as we can be together."

He looked over his shoulder at the stunned and impatient crowd, then back into her eyes. "Trish Avalon, will you be my wife? For keeps?"

She flung her arms around his neck, whacking him in the head with her bouquet. After a kiss that made her toes curl and her heart happy, she met his gaze and said, "I do."

A VENETIAN AFFAIR

Jackie Braun

ॐ ॐ ॐ

For Mark. I'd marry you all over again.

Dear Reader,

We've all met men who are shameless flirts. Maxwell Kinnick is just such a man. Or is he? As my heroine soon discovers, much more is percolating beneath his charming exterior. In fact, you could say Max uses flirting as a defense mechanism, especially when it comes to his lovely business partner, Dayle Alexander.

But real relationships take total honesty, something that neither Max nor Dayle is quite ready to offer... until fate forces their hand.

I hope you enjoy what happens when Max and Dayle find themselves alone in lovely Venice planning Dayle's wedding to another man—and both secretly wondering if maybe a different groom should be saying "I do."

Best wishes,

Jackie Braun

CHAPTER ONE

DAYLE ALEXANDER LEANED against the doorjamb to Maxwell Kinnick's office and watched him fuss with his tie. He was standing in profile to her, using his reflection in the glass of a display case to rework the Windsor knot. He had a meeting with a client in half an hour. Dayle's bet was that the client was female.

"New tie?" she inquired.

He glanced over and grinned, not embarrassed in the least to be caught preening. They had known one another a dozen years and had been business partners for eight. If Dayle knew one thing about the man, it was that he took great care with his appearance and appreciated fine things. The silk tie and tailored suit he wore were proof of that.

"I picked it up in Milan last week." His smile turned wicked. "Same place I bought those red panties for you. Have you worn them yet?"

The man was a shameless flirt. Benign but shameless. And this was an old game.

"Maybe," she offered.

"I'll take that as a yes." He turned his head slightly and regarded her out of one eye. "So, how do they look on?"

"You'll have to ask Ryan," she replied, referring to her longtime boyfriend.

Max placed a hand over his heart, his expression shifting from wily to wounded. "You're killing me, Dayle. You know that, right? Absolutely killing me."

Unfazed by his dramatic proclamation, she nodded. "It's all part of my evil plot to take over the business."

Together they owned Globetrotter Sales, an import-export company that Max had started from nothing more than a dozen years earlier. The company had been in its infancy when Dayle had hired in as his assistant. The pay had been so-so, the hours horrendous, especially since she'd been trying to squeeze in business classes at New York University at the time. But she'd been glad for the job and eager to be totally self-sufficient after a particularly nasty divorce. Before that, she had been a coddled and overprotected only child.

Four years after hiring in, their business relationship had changed. Dayle had a good eye for investments, one reason she had amassed a tidy sum in her stock portfolio. While she didn't believe in taking big risks, she did believe in exploring opportunities.

She'd seen expanding Globetrotter's as one such opportunity. Initially Max had specialized in high-end imports. Dayle had written up a business proposal suggesting that he consider more midrange options and add exports. She'd included an analysis of expenditures and then she had boldly suggested they use her nest egg to fund the expansion.

Max had taken an agonizingly long time to study the proposal. Afterward, he'd said, "That would make you my partner."

"Exactly." She'd held her breath.

"I've never had a partner before."

His reply hadn't been quite yes. Even so, Dayle had stretched out her hand. "Well, now you do. Deal?"

Even after all these years she could clearly recall the slow smile that had spread over Max's face and the heat that, for some reason, had suffused her own. He hadn't taken her hand to shake it. Instead he'd used it to pull her forward, into his arms. Then he'd kissed her full on the mouth.

"Deal," he'd murmured afterward.

At the time, she'd been shocked—not just by the intimate nature of the kiss, but by the high-voltage current of desire that had zipped through her body during it. After her disastrous, four-year marriage the last thing Dayle had wanted was to become involved with a man, but she had been—and she remained—

especially determined to steer clear of handsome charmers like Max. He was too smooth, too ready with a compliment. And his effect on her pulse—even before that kiss—had been a little too reminiscent of the effect her good-looking, good-for-nothing ex had had.

Still, she hadn't backed down about becoming Max's partner, even if she had made it clear that business was the only thing she had in mind. They'd worked side by side, putting in many long days and weekends to expand Globetrotter's. Afterward, they'd moved their headquarters to its current trendy location in a revitalized Lower Manhattan neighborhood.

Dayle saw to the details and kept an eye on the fine print, searching out goods and products to be shipped abroad or brought into the United States. Max continued to work the sales end. The man was a natural at cutting deals and getting people to sign on the dotted line, and he loved to travel, spending more time outside of New York than he did in it. Their partnership was perfect in many ways, and though the man still flirted outrageously with her, even bringing back red silk unmentionables whenever he went on trips abroad, he'd never kissed Dayle on the mouth again.

Max buttoned his coat now and faced her. "How do I look?"

Drop-dead gorgeous was the phrase that came to

mind, but as Dayle levered away from the jamb, she merely shrugged. "How do you always look?"

"Come on, sweetheart," he coaxed, his voice turning low and liquid. "Just this once, say it."

He looked like something out of an old Hollywood movie. The jacket fit his broad shoulders perfectly. She'd never met a man who wore clothes half as well, and that included her boyfriend. Whether dressed down in jeans or decked out in designer suits, Max always looked sophisticated, elegant and decidedly debonair. Old Hollywood, she thought again, but she shook her head.

"You'll get no compliments from me, Kinnick. I don't believe in feeding your already enormous ego."

"You know what they say. Big ego…"

She felt her lips twitch, but forced her expression to remain stern. "You're lucky we're partners or this conversation would constitute sexual harassment."

"Only if the advances were unwanted and the work environment was deemed hostile." He took a step toward her. "Nothing hostile here."

"Move any closer and that could change."

Max merely laughed. "When are you going to dump Ryan and admit that you're madly in love with me?"

"Oh, about the same time you decide you can commit to one woman and one woman only." Dayle did smile now. "In other words, it's not going to happen."

"Variety is the spice of life. You should try it."

"You should try monogamy."

"I am monogamous. I don't believe in cheating." This he said emphatically.

Dayle might have wondered about that, but he'd moved closer, bringing the seductive scent of his cologne with him. It curled around her like a lover's embrace. She exhaled sharply.

"You don't have to cheat, Max. Your relationships have the shelf-life of a carton of milk." She crossed her arms over her chest. "It's called commitment phobia."

Her pronouncement didn't bother him in the least. He tapped the tip of her nose with his index finger, and then ran his knuckles lightly over the curve of her cheek. It took all of her willpower not to tremble.

"You know, a woman who's been dating a man for years and has neither moved in with him nor set a wedding date really shouldn't lecture someone else on commitment."

She cleared her throat, reminded of the reason she'd stepped into his office. "Funny you should mention that."

For just a moment, she swore Max's easy smile faltered. But then his lips curved, his dark eyes lighting. "Don't tell me you're finally going to put that poor bastard out of his misery and cuff him with the old ball and chain?"

"I've accepted his proposal of marriage, yes."

"You say tomato…" He shrugged. "Congratulations, sweetheart. So, may I kiss the bride?" He didn't wait for an answer. He leaned forward and bussed her cheek.

"Thank you."

"So, when did this come about?" he asked.

"Over the weekend."

He studied her, eyes narrowing just a little. "It's Thursday and you're just now getting around to telling me? Worried that you might change your mind? Or worried that I might *help* you change it?"

She didn't like his conclusions, especially since the former held a nugget of truth. Dayle wanted to be over the moon with excitement about her decision. Instead she felt…what was the emotion? Not resignation. No, certainly not that. Realistic? Marrying Ryan made sense, especially now. She supposed that was to be expected since their relationship was based more on pragmatism than passion.

"I'm not going to change my mind." She said it resolutely, for her own benefit as well as for Max's, before turning to leave. He fell into step beside her.

"Well, don't keep me in suspense. When is the big day?" He draped an arm around her shoulders as they walked to her office, which was right next to his.

"The last Saturday in June." She casually removed

his arm and scooted around to the opposite side of her desk, putting five feet of solid oak between them.

"This June?" He pursed his lips in dismay. "That gives you less than six months to make plans."

Dayle laughed. "You sound like my mother." And, oh, was Lorna McAvoy displeased with the situation, even though she was ecstatic that after years of fence-sitting Dayle had finally begun to make plans for a wedding. "When I told her, she pitched a fit. She's determined that I should have a big, splashy affair since I eloped when I married Craig."

That had been back when Dayle was young and stupid. She'd been eighteen and so blind, trusting her husband completely when just months into their marriage he had begun to work late. Then weekend meetings started taking him out of town, but she still hadn't caught on. It was only after she came across a credit card statement that she realized he'd not only been cheating on her but charging everything from hotel rooms and fancy dinners to expensive jewelry to their jointly held card. By the time their marriage was legally dissolved she'd been brokenhearted and broke, wounded but far wiser. She wouldn't make the mistake of marrying a flirt a second time. Ryan— solid, stable and dependable—was anything but a ladies' man.

"You're her only daughter. That's all but a sin."

Dayle fought the urge to roll her eyes. Her mother had adored Max from the moment they'd met and no wonder given the way he catered to Lorna's strongly stated opinions.

"I'm thirty-six years old and I've been to the altar once."

"Even if the bride won't be blushing, she deserves a day filled with style and romance."

Dayle liked the idea of both, but said, "I think those can be managed on a smaller scale than what my mother has in mind."

She picked up the jade-handled letter opener he'd brought her from Taipei and began opening the day's mail.

"Lorna only wants the best for you."

"Don't take her side, Max, or, swear to God, I'll have to hurt you." She pointed the opener's sharp end in his direction.

"Promises, promises."

His gaze turned sensual and the smile he offered would have done Lucifer proud. As it was, it sent the familiar burn of sparks shooting up Dayle's spine. She'd never managed to become completely immune to such sparks, but she wasn't about to let them determine her future, let alone sabotage it a second time.

Max started for the door. "Off to my meeting. It's likely to run late." Dark brows bobbed meaningfully.

"I won't be seeing you again until tomorrow morning…or·perhaps the afternoon."

She set the letter opener aside. "Actually, Max, I was wondering if you would have dinner with me this evening."

He stopped, clearly surprised by the invitation. They didn't socialize outside of work, even though they sometimes attended events thrown by clients or other business-related functions. Ryan always escorted Dayle. She no longer tried to remember the names of the women who accompanied Max.

"You're asking me out? Feeling caged already, hmm?"

"This is serious. I need to talk to you about something important. It's about us and the future," she blurted.

The easy smile slipped. For a moment, something enigmatic took its place. "Does that mean Ryan won't be accompanying you?"

"No. This is between you and me."

"How can I resist when you put it like that? Do you have a place in mind?" he asked.

"I was just thinking of something casual so I won't feel out of place in my work clothes." She smoothed down the front of the navy blazer she wore over a silk blouse and wool trousers.

She should have known Max would object. "Go

home and change into something eye-catching. I'll pick you up at your apartment and we'll dine at Daniel."

She whistled through her teeth and for good reason. A meal at the premiere French restaurant was going to set him back a few hundred dollars at least. Too intrigued by the possibility to dismiss it out of hand, she asked, "Do you think you can get reservations on such short notice? I've heard you should make them at least a month in advance."

"I know someone who knows someone." He shrugged. "What do you say? We can toast your nuptials, maybe check out the private dining room as a possible wedding location."

She should decline and suggest another, less pricy restaurant. She opted for a compromise. "We'll go dutch and I'll meet you there. Is seven okay?"

He rubbed his chin thoughtfully. "I think I can wrap things up with Janiece by then."

"Janiece?"

"The glass artist in SoHo who stopped by the office last week. Tall and blond with a very firm... handshake."

She found it impossible not to chuckle. "God, you're incorrigible, Max. Truly incorrigible."

"That's only because I try." He winked and was gone.

CHAPTER TWO

MAX JINGLED THE CHANGE in his front trouser pocket as he walked through the doors at Daniel. Nervous, that's how he felt and had for the better part of the afternoon.

Ever since talking to Dayle.

Max wasn't the nervous sort, which made his present state all the more perplexing. He preferred knowing what was coming and usually he did, but he couldn't see around this particular corner. He blamed Dayle for that. Despite her utter predictability, she was the only woman who'd ever managed to confound him—and on a regular basis no less.

Glancing at his watch, he realized it was five minutes past the time they had agreed upon. Punctuality had never been his strong suit, especially outside of work. What surprised him, though, was when the mâitre d' told him that Dayle hadn't arrived yet. Promptness was the woman's middle name. Where was she?

He ordered a cocktail and sipped it as he waited at their table, hoping the vodka martini would sand down the roughest edges of his apprehension. What did she want to talk about? She'd nearly KO'd him with the announcement of her engagement earlier in the day. He hadn't seen that particular punch coming, even if she had been dating Ryan for years. Max had just managed to find his footing again when she'd suggested that they meet for dinner so that they could discuss the future.

It was never a good thing when a woman said she wanted to chat and then used the F-word. He gave his cocktail a stir.

Max had made it a hard and fast rule not to discuss anything past the next twenty-four hours with females. If they seemed bent on going beyond that, he derailed the conversation with sex. A good, drawn-out, make-'em weep orgasm was all but guaranteed to numb the mind and force a woman to forget all about such trivialities as where a relationship was heading.

But seduction wouldn't work this time. This was Dayle. She wasn't a woman to be wooed, won and then gently dispatched before too much entanglement ensued. She was his partner, his friend, his better half…in business.

He spied her then, winding her way through the white linen-topped tables. Business was forgotten. She'd taken his suggestion and had changed her clothes. And, oh, what a change.

Dayle rarely wore skirts to the office—a pity in Max's mind since she had a first-class pair of legs. Her legs, among other things, made an appearance tonight thanks to a clingy black slip of a dress that showcased her every curve. As a connoisseur of the female anatomy, Max liked what he saw. Indeed, he liked it a little too much if the uncomfortable fit of his jockey shorts at the moment was any indication. He reached for his martini and reminded himself that not only was she his business partner, but she was now engaged to be married. He'd meant it when he said he didn't cheat. Nor did he believe in getting involved with those who did.

When she reached the table, Max stood and offered a smile that was just this side of leering because he knew that was what she expected. With a dismissive nod to the maître d', he took both of Dayle's hands in his. Holding her an arm's length away, he murmured, "Well, look at you."

Barefoot, Dayle stood nearly five-ten, so in her three-inch-high, pencil-thin heels they were the same height. Some men might be intimidated by that. He'd always found it a turn-on.

"Hello, Max."

"Hello. Are you sure you want to marry Ryan?" he asked.

She blinked. "Wh-why do you ask?"

He let his gaze meander downward. "Because that little black dress you're wearing is telling me otherwise."

"You're hearing things again," she replied on a laugh, turning her head and leaning in for his kiss.

Max's lips brushed her cheek and he forced himself to back away when he felt tempted to move a little lower and to the left. He'd kissed her on the mouth only once, and years ago now, but he knew better than to do it again, even in this crowded, upscale restaurant where things couldn't progress to anything that could remotely be deemed sensual.

"You do look lovely." He pulled out her chair and, when she was seated, dropped a kiss on her nape, which her upswept hair had left exposed. She turned, eyes the color of amethysts opening wide. "Couldn't resist. You have a very nibble-worthy neck," he said with an apologetic shrug before coming around to take his place.

"Sorry I'm late."

"Don't be. You made quite an entrance." And he meant it. Heads had turned; heads belonging to men. Max had felt both smug and proprietary when she'd come to him.

"That wasn't my intention," she said, looking dismayed.

Of course it wasn't. Dayle wasn't the kind of

woman who resorted to pretense. It was one of her qualities that Max admired. One of the many.

"It's not like you to be late. I was worried." He didn't realize how true the words were until they were out. Sitting there alone, waiting, he had been concerned and not just about the future she'd said she wanted to discuss.

"Really?" In the soft light of the dining room her fair, flawless skin glowed. Most of the women he knew were tanned, whether from idle time spent in the sun somewhere or at a salon. Not Dayle. She was decidedly pale. And perfect.

As his fingers tightened on the stem of his martini glass he vowed with intentional overstatement, "Practically beside myself. I was ready to call out the National Guard."

"Well, thank God you showed some restraint. The truth is I couldn't decide what to wear. I even made Beth come over to help me." She touched the side of her head. "She did my hair."

"Your friend is a true talent." He lifted his glass in salute.

"I'll tell her you said so. I wanted to look my best." Just when he began to feel flattered that maybe meeting him for dinner had something to do with her uncharacteristic fussing, in an awed whisper she added, "This place is so amazing."

Max swore he heard his ego deflate. "Isn't it, though?"

She was glancing around. "I didn't want to feel underdressed."

One side of his mouth rose. "And so you wore that itty-bitty number?"

Her gaze snapped back to his. "It's not too…you know."

"Oh, no. Not nearly, especially for my taste. You always look classy," he assured her. And he meant it.

A waiter stopped for her drink order then and she glanced over at Max's half-empty glass. "What is that you're having?"

"A vodka martini." On a wink, he added, "Dirty." She frowned.

"It's made with olive juice," he clarified.

"I'll have the same," she told the waiter.

Once they were alone, he asked, "Feeling adventurous tonight?" He'd never known Dayle to sip anything other than a crisp white wine.

"I guess I feel the need for a little kick of courage."

"You won't find that in a glass," Max told her.

"No, but then I won't care, will I?"

Nerves tingled again, causing his right foot to tap under the table. "Why don't you tell me what you wanted to talk about? My curiosity, among other things, is begging to be satisfied."

The suggestive comment earned no reprimand. Instead she asked, "Are you sure you don't want to wait until after we've had dinner?"

"That unappetizing?" He plucked up the small wooden skewer from his glass and ate one of the olives.

"Of course not." But Dayle's nervous laughter offered little reassurance.

"Come on. I'm all ears."

Max ate the remaining olive as he watched her moisten her lips. She'd painted them red tonight. Red, the color of passion. And the color that accompanied warnings of danger.

"Well, as you know, Ryan and I will be getting married this summer," she began.

A sharp pain lanced Max's breastbone. He'd felt its twin earlier that day, back at the office upon first hearing the news. This time he chalked it up to the vodka. He really shouldn't drink on an empty stomach, a couple of olives notwithstanding. Yet he raised his glass and sipped again after saying, "Unless I can persuade you otherwise."

"Right." Her gaze flicked toward the ceiling. "Well, one of the reasons we decided against a lengthy engagement is that he's accepted a new position. It's an excellent opportunity for advancement in his field."

Ryan was an engineer of some sort. "Good for him."

"Yes." She moistened those red lips again. *Danger! Danger!* his brain screamed as she added, "But it involves a move."

Both of Max's feet were tapping now. He thought he could hear the muffled thuds of his wingtips as they slapped the carpet. Or was that his heart? "Here in the city?" he managed in a casual tone.

"No." Dayle plucked at the linen tablecloth, her own nerves showing. "Actually in California."

The thuds had definitely come from his heart and it was now in Max's throat. He sought to dislodge it with a discreet gulp of his martini. "That's the other side of the country."

"Gee, Max, your grasp of geography is impressive."

Where he usually enjoyed her barbed comebacks, just now he was feeling too dazed for such repartee. "Are you moving, too?"

"Yes."

He stated the obvious. "To California."

No razzing this time. She nodded. "San Francisco."

"Am I really losing you, Dayle?"

Her brow furrowed. "Losing me?"

He took another liberal sip of his cocktail, giving him time to resurrect his easygoing façade. "You know, as a business partner. Are you asking me to buy you out?"

That was his major concern, Max told himself. He didn't need her. The company did.

"Of course not. We're partners, Max. I'm in for the long haul. It's just that I can do my job from anywhere thanks to technology and the Internet. Half the time you and I are on opposites of the globe."

It was true, but no matter where he went, he always felt connected to her, anchored in a way that he didn't care to analyze, especially now.

"Besides," she was saying. "We've talked about expanding again. This is the ideal time, not to mention that California is the ideal location. I can head up a West Coast office."

Dayle's proposal made perfect sense, he thought, while he listened to her expand on it for the next several minutes, during which time her drink arrived and he finished his. As always, she'd done her homework. She'd come armed with facts, statistics, ideas and her customary enthusiasm.

As a businessman Max knew she was right. Yet as his feet tapped faster under the table, the only thing that registered was that the one person he'd considered a permanent fixture in his life soon wouldn't be there to greet him when his wandering feet grew weary and brought him home.

CHAPTER THREE

OVER THE NEXT COUPLE of months, while Max concentrated on Globetrotter's expansion, Dayle concentrated on her wedding plans. That proved the more trying of the two endeavors, but only because her mother insisted on calling three times a day to find out what she'd come up with and then making contradicting suggestions.

Dayle wasn't exactly ecstatic to be relocating to San Francisco, her expanded duties at Globetrotter's aside. She was a born and bred New Yorker, and her friends and family were here. Which brought her to the city by the bay's key selling point: It was three time zones and a long flight from Lorna.

"I'm going to be in Italy in April," Max announced one morning in mid-March. He stood framed in Dayle's doorway like a piece of pricy artwork in his crisp white shirt and cashmere jacket. "I've got a meeting in Milan about Bruno's new fall line and I'm going to Venice to meet with a couple of potential clients, including a sculptor I met on the previous trip."

"Is this trip business or pleasure?" she asked, arching one eyebrow in speculation.

"Business." But then his tone turned sly. "And it's entirely my pleasure."

Dayle sighed. "How long will you be gone?"

"Missing me already?"

"Always," she replied, but without inflection.

In truth, though, she did miss Max when he was away. She enjoyed his company, the give and take of their banter. She even enjoyed his clever double entendres and endless flirting. His friendship was another of the reasons that the thought of moving to San Francisco was proving so difficult.

He entered her office as she called up the master calendar they kept on the computer. Instead of taking a seat in one of the chairs, he hiked up a pant leg and settled his hip on the edge of her desk, as was his habit. Pointing to the calendar, he said, "I'm thinking of leaving on that Monday, staying in Rome a couple days, and then heading to Venice. I should be back by the end of the week."

Dayle typed in the dates and ignored the way his cologne tangled up her hormones. God, the stuff was potent. Sex in a bottle. "Has Cara made your travel arrangements yet?" she asked, referring to the secretary they shared.

"Yes. I'll be at the Gabriella in Rome and staying at the same place I did last time while in Venice."

"The Marquis? Again?" That surprised her. Usually Max liked to mix things up. "Any special…reason?" It was code for woman and he knew it.

"Not how you mean. The rooms were first-rate and the service was excellent, especially with so much going on."

"A wedding, right?" Dayle said, trying to recall the old conversation.

They always went over everything when he came back from a trip. Sometimes, he even called her at home, regardless of the hour, just to tell her that he'd returned and to recap the high points. Not everything they discussed had to do with business. He told her about the sights, the sounds, the interesting people he'd met and the new foods he'd tried. She enjoyed his travelogues almost as much as he enjoyed telling them.

"A wedding? Oh, no." Deep laughter rumbled. "This was Bridezilla, a philandering groom and thirty-two temperamental guests, according to the concierge." He winked then, before adding, "We played cards one evening."

"Let me guess. Strip poker?"

"Please. The concierge was a man. Now, had I managed to talk a couple of the very lovely clerks from the front desk into joining us…" He let his words trail off on a wolfish smile.

"You work too hard, Max," she drawled. The leather of her chair groaned softly as she leaned back, subtly putting more distance between them. Even so, the scent of his cologne followed her and seemed to beckon.

"I do work hard, every bit as hard as you do. The only difference between us, Dayle, is that I play hard, too."

He had her there, so she picked up a fountain pen, a gift he'd brought her from London, and said nothing.

Max went on. "You needn't stay chained to your desk, you know. I've told you often enough that you're welcome to travel. In fact, as head of our new West Coast office, some buying trips might be inevitable, at least at first. I still haven't found a competent counterpart for me."

"That's because you're one of a kind."

A grin creased the hollows of his cheeks. "I'm glad you finally realize that, sweetheart."

Her telephone rang. Before she could reach for it, Max had snatched up the receiver. "Globetrotter's. We bring the world's goods to you and your goods to the world."

Dayle rolled her eyes. He seemed to come up with a new business slogan every week.

"Ah, Lorna. I was just telling your daughter how

sorry I was that I wasn't here yesterday when you stopped in."

Dayle rolled her eyes again, but didn't reach for the telephone. She was hardly eager to talk to her mother for what would be the second time that day. And it wasn't even noon.

"Dayle?" Max was saying. "Actually she's right here. Yes. I'm in her office, trying to persuade her to dump that bum she's engaged to and run off with me." He chuckled softly at something Lorna said, before adding, "We'd give you beautiful grandbabies."

He stroked the side of Dayle's face as he said it and she shivered. His eyebrows rose fractionally. She glanced away, busying herself with paperwork.

"So, what's new with the wedding plans?" he asked, eliciting a groan from Dayle. "Really? No, your daughter didn't mention that. Three hundred guests." He whistled between his teeth. She issued an oath and felt the headache she'd chased away with three aspirin a couple of hours earlier throb back to life. "Well, I'll let you speak to Dayle. Yes. Nice talking to you, too."

Before handing her the telephone, he said softly, "Deep breath and then exhale, sweetheart. And remember, the woman gave you life."

Hand cupped over the receiver, Dayle muttered, "Yes, and for that reason she feels she's entitled to run it."

"In and out, in and out," Max said, motioning with both of his hands as he stood.

Dayle sent him a black look and brought the telephone to her ear. "Mom, hi." She managed this in a cheerful voice that had Max nodding in approval before he slipped out of her office. Once he was out of earshot, Dayle snarled, "Three hundred guests! Mother, I thought we agreed to no more than half that."

"We can't exclude my cousin Arlene's family." Lorna's tone was reproachful. "They were so good to me after your father died."

"Yes, but I wasn't aware Arlene had so many children."

"Don't be ridiculous, Dayle. If we include Arlene, then you know we must include her neighbors, the Thompsons. They've invited us to all of their children's weddings. And then, of course, there are the Bakers. They're such nice people."

Dayle tuned out at that point. Now she remembered exactly why she'd opted to elope the first time around. Her wedding to Ryan was turning into a three-ring circus rather than the intimate and romantic affair she'd imagined.

After talking to her mother, she called Ryan with a summary of the conversation, eager for an ally.

"So she wants to invite people you haven't seen in a decade. Is that really so bad?" he asked.

His response wasn't what she'd hoped to hear.

"I want something small and tasteful. You, me, a couple of attendants, our folks and a smattering of close friends. I told her that. I've told her that repeatedly. Now I have three hundred people coming to watch me prance down the aisle."

"You don't need to prance," Ryan said on a chuckle.

Dayle ignored his attempt at humor. "She doesn't like the dress I picked out or the cake's design. She wants a band rather than the nice string quartet I interviewed. With three hundred people, we're going to need to find a bigger reception hall." She tapped the tip of her pen against the deck blotter in irritation. "I don't even know that I can get the deposit back at this point."

"Don't worry about the money," he soothed.

"It's not the money. It's…her. She's taking over just like she tries to take over everything in my life."

"She's just excited, Dayle. For that matter, so is my mother. From what I understand, they've had their heads together," he said.

She groaned and was half hoping he would take her seriously when she asked, "Can't we just elope?"

"No. Now that I've finally convinced you to be my wife, I want a proper wedding. Something we both will remember well into our golden years."

"This is promising to be memorable for all the wrong reasons."

Ryan sounded slightly impatient when he replied, "It's just one day, Dayle."

After she hung up, she wilted back in her seat on a sigh. "It's just one day. But it's supposed to be *my* day."

When she glanced up, Max was standing in the doorway. "Want to talk about it?" he asked.

She straightened. "How long have you been there?"

"Long enough."

"Were you eavesdropping?"

"Shamelessly," he agreed on an affable grin. "I came by to see if you wanted to go to lunch with me and heard you talking. Unfortunately I could only hear your side of the conversation. You can fill me in on the parts I missed over a glass of wine," he invited.

"I have a bottle of water in the fridge."

"I'll throw in a Cobb salad," he replied, upping the ante.

He had her attention, but she held firm. "I brought tuna made with light mayo on marbled rye."

He wrinkled his nose. "Save it for tomorrow or, better yet, take it home and feed it to your cat."

"I don't have a cat."

"Give it to a stray, then. I know this cozy little bistro that makes the best soups—the perfect accompaniment to that salad I mentioned."

Dayle gave in as her stomach growled. "Why not?"

THE COZY BISTRO turned out to be a gourmet restaurant in the theater district where the waitstaff knew Max by name.

"I'm a regular," he admitted on a shrug as they were led to their table. She didn't bother to protest even after catching a glimpse of the prices on the lunch menu, although she did mutter, "Nothing about you is regular, Max. Do you ever do anything halfway?"

"Why would I? Besides, only the best for you," he said lightly. "I'm trying to sweep you off your feet, remember? Only three months till your wedding. I don't have much time to make you change your mind."

"What would you do if I did?" Dayle couldn't believe she'd thought the question much less asked it. Silently she blamed stress, nerves…her mother, and then laughed aloud, hoping to turn it into a joke. Max laughed, too. Interestingly, though, he didn't have a comeback handy.

After the waiter took their order, Dayle poured out her frustrations, ending with, "And I can't talk Ryan into eloping."

"That's because he's a smart man. He knows there will be no living with Lorna or his mother, for that matter, afterward."

Dayle cast her gaze skyward. "Will no one agree with me about anything today?"

"It's not that I'm disagreeing with you. I just under-stand Ryan's point. And Lorna's. And his mother's."

"Max—"

"I'm not finished. I have a suggestion. A com-promise that might suit all parties involved."

She narrowed her eyes. "I wasn't aware you knew how to compromise when it came to personal relationships."

"I know how it's done. I simply prefer not to do it. Besides, we're not talking about me. We're talking about you. Are you interested or not?"

"I'm listening," she said.

"Your mother wants to showcase her only daughter's big day. So, let her."

"That's your idea of a compromise?" she sputtered.

His sigh was exaggerated. "You really need to learn patience, Dayle. You're always rushing things, pressing ahead."

"That's only because you take so damned long."

Brows arching, he replied, "I've never had a woman complain about that."

Heat suffused her face. It curled elsewhere in her body when, for just one moment, she allowed herself to imagine Max taking his time. "Mmm."

He glanced at her in puzzlement. Had she made that sound aloud? Just in case, she said, "This soup is heaven in a bowl."

His frown intensified. "You haven't eaten any of it yet."

"Well, it smells like heaven." She picked up her spoon and motioned with it. "Can you get to the meat of your compromise at some point before the dinner crowd starts to arrive?"

"No patience," he said again with a shake of his head. But he went on. "As I was saying, let your mother showcase your day. Inform her that you've decided you want to hold your wedding someplace special, at some romantic, out-of-the way destination that will give her supreme bragging rights, but be pricy enough to limit who she can invite."

"Sneaky," Dayle murmured. "And to think my mother trusts you."

"She doesn't just trust me," Max corrected. "She adores me. If she were a few years younger she'd be all over me, giving you stiff competition for my affection."

"Please." Dayle pulled a face and waved a hand. "I'm trying to eat here." But then she asked seriously, "So you think I should take the show on the road, so to speak?"

"Only a fool would presume to tell you what to think. I'm merely suggesting that an out-of-town site, someplace exclusive, would encourage a small and select guest list."

"Small and select." She smiled. "I like those adjectives."

"I thought they might appeal to you." He grinned in return. "No matter where it's held, I'll be invited, right?"

"Of course." Dayle dabbed at her mouth with her napkin before setting it aside. She'd been waiting for the right time to ask him something. This appeared to be it. "Max, I need a favor."

"Name it." His grin was magnanimous.

"You and I go back a long way. Besides Beth, I consider you one of my best friends," she began.

"Same goes. Of course, you're also the only female friend I haven't slept with." His grin turned wicked and his voice dipped to a husky whisper. "We could remedy that, you know."

She shook her head. "I prefer my status as the one who got away."

He nodded. "Smart. Makes you irresistible."

"Right." Dayle pressed on. "As you know, my father is gone. Mom wants me to ask my uncle Lyle to stand in on my wedding day. Uncle Lyle is a nice man, but honestly, I haven't seen him in half a dozen years and we were never what I would call close. And so I was wondering—hoping, actually—that I could persuade you to walk me down the aisle."

She finished with a smile. Max, however, was frowning. At the outset of her request he'd appeared touched, humbled even. Now he just looked surprised and not in a good way. His face had turned decidedly ashen.

"You're asking me to give you away?"

"Yes."

His voice was hoarse, although this throaty whisper no longer appeared to be intended as sexy. "But what if I want to keep you?"

Dayle blinked. Sure she hadn't heard him right, she leaned closer. "Max?"

Max sucked in a breath. It took him a moment to regroup, especially with her watching him, her Elizabeth Taylor eyes filled with confusion and even a little concern. Finally he managed his signature smile. "Of course, I'll do it. I'd love to. In fact, I'm honored to be asked."

Her expression brightened. "Terrific. Thank you."

"Don't mention it." He adjusted his French cuffs, needing something to occupy his hands. "Besides, it will give me an excuse to buy a new tuxedo while I'm in Italy. No one makes a penguin suit quite like Armani."

Dayle reached across the table and laid a hand on his arm. "It means a lot to me."

Max smiled in return, helpless to do anything but. Dayle looked so relieved, so pleased. She looked so damned grateful. He felt that familiar white-hot poker jab just below his breastbone. The pain seemed omnipresent these days. He really should go see a doctor. Maybe he had an ulcer. Maybe something was wrong with his heart.

The latter seemed more likely, since when he replied, "*You* mean a lot to me," the pain grew worse.

CHAPTER FOUR

"I'M COMING WITH YOU," Dayle announced.

Max's brows shot up at that. It was late on a Friday afternoon and he was just pulling on his overcoat, preparing to leave the office for the week-end. On Monday morning he would depart for Italy. "Where? Home?" he asked. Then he smiled. "Interested in giving me a private send-off?"

Her breath hissed out on an impatient sigh. "I'm talking about Venice."

It was his breath that hissed out then. "Venice?"

He must have been staring blankly at her because Dayle snapped her fingers in front of his face and added in a dry tone, "Yes, Venice. The city in Italy with all those canals."

"And you want to go with me," he repeated in an effort to buy some time, because for just a moment his heart had bucked out a few extra beats, thudding with the kind of robust intensity it did after he'd finished a particularly punishing workout...or a bout of passionate sex.

"Yes. I do," Dayle said on a nod.

I do. They were two small words that reeled in his libido, for soon enough they would make her another man's wife. As they stood in Globetrotter's tastefully decorated lobby, he jingled his keys and considered how best to handle this situation.

"But you never go on buying trips," he began.

She merely shrugged. "Never say never. Isn't that one of the mottos you live by?"

Dayle had him there. Sort of. His gaze lowered briefly to her mouth. Her lips were tinted their usual respectable shade of peach and curved in a smile. *Never* did apply in one instance. Or rather, *never again.*

"Besides," she was saying, "you told me I need to gain more experience in buying since I'll need to go on some trips for Globetrotter's West Coast office."

Yes, he had said that, but he hadn't intended for the comment to be construed as an invitation. In fact, he'd been looking forward to his trip to Italy precisely because it would put an entire ocean between him and Dayle.

The closer her wedding came, the closer her move to the West Coast marched, the more restless Max felt. Oh, he'd always been restless, unable to stay put in one place for long. He needed adventure, craved excitement. He was addicted to new sights, sounds, scents and tastes. He was like his old man in that regard, always eager to be off, to try something new. Always eager to spend time with new people…new women, though in his case one at a time and without breaking any sacred vows.

This restlessness, though, was different. Exactly how, he couldn't say. But it stemmed from his feelings for Dayle, of that much, he was certain. He liked her. No, he *adored* her, he admitted as he studied her lovely face. Admiration came into play, too. She was smart, determined. She'd picked herself up after the heartache and betrayal of her divorce, and had made a new and better life for herself.

"You're an amazing woman," he murmured.

She nodded impatiently, taking his heartfelt comment in stride. He supposed her reaction was to be expected since he was a serial flatterer as well as a shameless flirt. In this case, however, he was being utterly sincere.

It struck him then that in his own limited way, he loved Dayle. Well, as much as he was capable of truly loving any woman. Perhaps because of that, Max wanted the absolute best for her. And though he generally entertained an exceptionally high opinion of himself, he'd always known she deserved better than the likes of him. He couldn't give Dayle the one thing she required from a man: stability.

He would never be the nine-to-five sort, the kind of man who would punch a clock, carve out a life with a wife and two-point-four kids in suburbia, coach Little League, host neighborhood barbecues and, heaven forbid, wear synthetic fabrics purchased off the rack.

That was Ryan. Good old Ryan. The lucky bastard.

"I had an epiphany last night," Dayle was saying.

"Oh? Were you alone at the time?" He sent her a lecherous smile, feeling his footing return now that common sense had been resurrected. Love wasn't for him. Not the "till death do us part kind" anyway.

"Max," she warned.

"Sorry. Old habits."

Apparently mollified, she went on. "Remember how you suggested Ryan and I get married out of town? Someplace select to discourage the large guest list my mother has in mind?"

"I recall that," he said slowly as apprehension did a tap dance up his spine.

"Well, I was flipping through a bridal magazine while eating some takeout the other night, and it had this entire spread on destination weddings. It got me thinking. I've always loved Venice," she said.

"Understandable. It's a great city, but Dayle—"

She cut him off. "Really, of all the places you've

traveled for business, the only time I've ever felt the slightest bit of envy was when you've gone there. The canals, the palaces, St. Mark's Square…" She smiled dreamily.

Her soft expression tugged at him. How many times while he'd been in Venice—or other places, for that matter—had he wished she was with him, seeing the sights, savoring them alongside of him? "With the right person it can be incredibly romantic," he admitted.

"No doubt you have plenty of firsthand knowledge of that."

"I'm too much of a gentleman to say." He busied himself with the buttons of his overcoat. But he couldn't help wondering, did he? Oh, he'd found romance in Venice and other places around the globe, for that matter. Romance in its most earthy form. The interludes all blended together now. Not a single one, not a single *woman,* stood out. Romance with the right person? Apparently not.

Frowning, he shoved his hands into his coat pockets. What was wrong with him? That was what he wanted. That was how he'd planned it. He didn't want permanence, memories, ties. None of those suited his personality, his lifestyle. Unlike his father, Max trod carefully when it came to others' feelings and so he never made promises he wasn't capable of keeping.

"Getting married in Venice would be ideal," Dayle said. "It would be small and intimate, for the sake of logistics alone. My mother couldn't invite second cousins and neighbors I haven't seen since puberty."

"I don't know," he hedged, still feeling uneasy.

"Come on, Max. Venice is romantic, stylish. You said I deserved that."

He smiled weakly. Nothing like having one's own words tossed back in the face. They hit a bull's-eye, making it all but impossible to object. Still, he gave it his best shot.

"I'll only be there a few days, and if you're serious about going on sales calls with me, business will keep us busy for a good portion of that. Surely you'll need more time to make the kind of plans you're talking about."

"You're absolutely right," she agreed. But, damn, she was smiling. "Which is why I took the liberty of booking us rooms for another week and a half."

"Us?" he asked.

"You'll stay on in Venice with me, won't you? Please, Max," she pleaded. "You know the city so well."

"Like the back of my hand," he murmured as his gaze flicked to her left one and the ring that encircled her third finger. The diamond caught the light, shooting sparks. One seemed to land on his chest.

Damned heartburn. He reached into his pocket for the roll of antacids he'd begun to carry.

"I'm due a vacation," she said. "You're always after me to take off more time and go someplace exciting. Do you mean it or are you all talk?"

"I've never been accused of being all talk," he replied.

"Well?"

Neither had Max ever been one to back down from a challenge, but he chewed the chalky tablet and took his time answering, coming up with more questions instead. "What about Ryan? What does he say?"

"He's all for it." She laughed then. "He finally admitted to me that his mother is driving him to distraction, too."

"Will he be coming to Venice with us?"

"I wish," she said on a sigh. "Unfortunately he has a training seminar for his new position. But don't worry. He has complete faith in my judgment."

"Excellent."

"And he trusts you."

"He trusts me?" Max asked, unable to mask his surprise. Were the shoe on the other foot, Max knew trust wouldn't be forthcoming.

But Dayle was nodding. "He's well aware that you have impeccable taste."

Max worked up a smile. "Yes."

"And he knows that you know quality when you see it."

Max's gaze lowered to Dayle's lips again, lingering for a moment longer than he intended. "Quality," he murmured.

BETH SAT CROSS-LEGGED on Dayle's bed, drinking some foul-looking energy drink she'd picked up at a health-food store on her way to the apartment. She was half a head shorter than Dayle, with an athlete's lean body. She always seemed to be in training for some marathon or grueling fitness event. Not surprisingly, they'd met at the gym. Beth had been going through her own divorce at the time. As a person who had been there, done that, Dayle had held her hand through the painful ordeal.

Officially Beth was at Dayle's apartment to help her pack for Venice and go through the many files Dayle had downloaded from the Internet. Unofficially she was there to play devil's advocate. Beth had a law degree and worked in the district attorney's office. She also had a streak of romance as wide as the Atlantic. Put the two together and her imagination had been working overtime ever since Dayle told her she was jetting off to Venice. To meet Max.

"I still can't believe Ryan is letting you go." She slurped the last bit of unappetizing green goo through the straw and set the cup on the nightstand.

"I'm thirty-six, Beth. I stopped asking people for permission nearly two decades ago."

"You know what I mean."

"I haven't a clue," she said, opting to play dumb, even though her friend had long maintained that Max secretly carried a torch for Dayle.

"Mark my words, he's going to try to talk you out of marrying Ryan," her friend insisted.

"Max?" Dayle shook her head and snorted. "Yeah, right. Like he's interested in me that way."

"I've seen the way he looks at you," Beth supplied. "He wants you."

Her friend's blunt assessment made Dayle's hands shake. Even so, she took her time carefully folding a cashmere sweater set and setting it in her suitcase. Eyes downcast, she said matter-of-factly, "He looks at every female between the ages of eighteen and eighty the exact same way. He's a flirt, Beth."

"Okay. I've seen the way you look at him."

When Dayle glanced over, Beth offered her most confident litigator's smile. Dayle returned to the closet and began riffling through hangers in an effort to compose herself. After a moment, she turned, holding out a dress in one hand and a pantsuit in the other.

"What do you think?"

"I think you're avoiding my question."

Dayle tossed the garments onto the bed and folded

her arms. "Oh? Is this a cross-examination? I thought we were having a conversation?"

"It's a little of both." Beth shrugged, not the least bit contrite or intimidated.

The women had been friends for nearly a decade, offering encouragement, giving one another advice, whether solicited or not. They didn't keep secrets from one another. Which made Dayle feel especially guilty for keeping this one. The truth was, as much as she loved Ryan, as much as she appreciated his steadfastness, she'd never felt with him the smallest flicker of sexual satisfaction. Heaven help her, but Max could look at Dayle across a stack of invoices, smile in that debonair, dangerous way of his and spark more heat than Ryan could manage in a marathon of inventive foreplay. It wasn't right. It wasn't fair. But it was a fact.

Still, she said dismissively, "Max is harmless."

"We were talking about you."

"What's to talk about? I'm going to Venice to plan my wedding. *To Ryan,*" she stressed. "If I were interested in Max in any way other than professionally, I certainly wouldn't have accepted Ryan's proposal of marriage."

That was sound logic. She'd used it to quiet her own conscience. So she smiled confidently.

"About that," Beth began. "We've been friends for a long time and I like Ryan. You know I do."

"Of course."

"I'm glad. So, please, don't take this the wrong way."

Nerves fluttered and Dayle had the insane urge to stick her fingers in her ears and start singing at the top of her lungs.

Instead she opted to act like a grown-up. "Take what the wrong way?"

"Honey, are you sure about this?"

"About Venice?" Dayle asked, hoping that that was the "this" to which her friend referred. Of course it wasn't.

"No. About marrying Ryan?" Beth asked softly.

Dayle pushed away the niggling doubts that usually only crowded in late at night when she was alone and feeling the most vulnerable. In a brisk tone she replied, "Beth, honestly, Ryan and I have been dating for four years."

Unperturbed, Beth replied, "That's one of the reasons I ask."

"I didn't want to rush into marriage. You of all people should understand that."

"I understand caution." Beth nodded. "But there's a great deal of difference between rushing and moving at a reasonable pace. Four years is…well, glacial, especially at this point in your life. It's not like you were waiting for him to finish college and for you to get your career established. You were both doing well professionally when you met. So, ask yourself, what's been the holdup?"

"There's no need to ask myself. I know. The timing wasn't right. And it is now." Dayle insisted.

But later that evening, after Beth had gone home and Dayle had finished packing, she wondered if the timing felt right or if she'd felt cornered. The proposal had come out of the blue, their longtime relationship notwithstanding. Ryan had told her he was taking the job in California after it was already a fact. Dayle knew not many couples could make a go of a long-distance romance. So she had felt pressured to accept his offer of marriage. After all, saying no essentially would have ended their relationship, and that's not what she wanted.

Was it?

CHAPTER FIVE

DAYLE ARRIVED at Marco Polo International Airport early in the day, at least according to the clock. Her body was still operating on New York time, which meant she should be sleeping or at the very least just waking up. Oddly neither the long flight from JFK nor the three-hour layover in Amsterdam had drained her of energy. She'd been awake for both legs of the trip. Wide-awake and thinking. And she didn't care for the direction of her thoughts.

She blamed Beth. Her friend's well-meaning comments had Dayle second-guessing not only her engagement but her entire relationship with Ryan. Doubts were normal, she told herself as the Fasten Seat Belts sign blinked off. And these really weren't doubts so much as prewedding jitters. Every bride was entitled to those. Now that she was in Italy to plan her wedding without her mother's sniping or interference everything would be fine. So convinced, Dayle stood, retrieved her carry-on bag from the overhead compartment and took her place in the queue of deplaning passengers.

Inside the airport, she spotted Max easily enough amid the crowd of people eagerly awaiting loved ones. A man that classically handsome, that sophisticated and self-possessed was impossible to miss. Her heart did a funny little somersault when he spied her and a welcoming smile creased his cheeks. The jitters she'd just managed to quell staged a second uprising. She blamed these on jet lag and pushed through the crowd toward him. Max met her halfway. Ever the gentleman, he was reaching for the thick strap of her bag to transfer it to his shoulder even before offering a greeting.

"Hello, Dayle. Welcome to Italy." Max smoothed the hair back from her face, tucking it behind her ears. Then he kissed both of her cheeks. "I trust your trip was uneventful."

"Pretty much." She wouldn't think of those doubts now.

"You look lovely, as always. An absolute vision."

Max's comment was over-the-top, and Dayle couldn't help chuckling. "I look travel-weary and wrinkled. *You* look lovely."

His brows rose at the compliment.

"New suit?" she inquired. She brushed the coat's lapels before giving in to the urge to rest her palms flush against his chest. It was solid, warm and oh so inviting. She pulled her hands away.

"I got it while I was in Rome," he confirmed on a nod. "The tailor worked overtime to ensure it was ready before I had to leave." He took a step back. "So, what do you think?"

"Hmm, nice." It was more than nice, especially on Max. The man had a body that was made for suits. The soft wool gabardine of this one hung elegantly on his lean frame. She meant it when she said, "It almost does you justice."

"Now there's a compliment. You must be exhausted to so willingly feed my ego."

She hadn't been tired a moment ago, but she was now. So much so that when he put his arm around her shoulders and said, "Let's get your luggage," she leaned against him rather than trying to step away. At the baggage carousel, he asked, "How many suitcases do you have?"

"Just one in addition to my carry-on." That bit of news had him scowling until he saw it come around on the conveyor belt.

"It's a good thing I'm physically fit," he teased. "How on earth did you manage to get it to Kennedy airport?"

"It does have wheels," she replied pointedly. But then admitted, "I gave a very generous tip to both the cabdriver and the porter."

"Generous, hmm? I'll look forward to claiming mine later."

He offered a sinful smile that sent heat slithering down her spine before it coiled in her stomach, as dangerous as a snake preparing to strike. She sucked in a breath and relied on practicality to tame it.

"The suitcase is way over on the weight limit. I had to pay extra when I got to the airport, so be sure to lift with your knees. I wouldn't want your back to go out."

"That makes two of us." His smile remained wicked and he winked. Dayle felt snakebit.

They took a water taxi to their hotel, which was in a prime location on the Grand Canal. Despite the overcast sky, chilly April weather and her own growing fatigue, Dayle couldn't help but be enthralled as the boat chugged through the city that had defied the sea for centuries. She'd seen pictures of the place. Dazzling full-color photographs in travel brochures and on the Internet that paid homage to the ornate architecture and colorful façades. But nothing had prepared her for the reality that was Venice. The city exuded an intoxicating mix of charm, whimsy and decadence. Just like Max. And it was definitely romantic, sensual and seductive. Just like…

"Incredible, isn't it?" Max whispered the words in her ear. His breath tickled like a feather, which surely was the only reason she shivered.

She turned her head toward him. "Yes. I love it and I can see why you love it, too. The place suits you."

"Oh?" He arched an eyebrow at that.

Dayle chose not to enlighten him. Instead she changed the subject. "It's the perfect destination for my wedding. I can't wait to phone Ryan and tell him."

Frowning, Max glanced away. "So, I take it that Lorna is on board with the change in venue."

"More or less." She shrugged. No sense recounting the blistering, three-hour war of words that had followed Dayle's announcement that she and Ryan planned to exchange vows in Venice. Of course, with Max, there was no need.

"Sorry. I'll give her a call when we return to the States, see if I can't help smooth the waters."

And he could, too. Not a woman alive was immune to the man's charm. Well, except for Dayle.

"She wanted to come with me on this trip," she told him.

"How did you manage to talk her out of it?"

"Actually I didn't. Ryan came to my rescue. He told her that he needed someone to keep an eye on his apartment while he's out of town at his training seminar."

"The man's a saint," Max said dryly.

"He is," Dayle insisted. "Especially since my mother probably will have poked into every drawer and cubbyhole before he comes back. I'm sure she already has the contents of his medicine cabinet memorized."

"Remind me never to ask Lorna to housesit for me."

"Afraid she'd discover something that might change her high opinion of you?"

"We all have our secrets," he replied lightly.

What, Dayle wondered, were his?

They reached their hotel a few minutes later. Max was on a first-name basis with the entire staff, not to mention several of the guests. They greeted him with an enthusiastic *buon giorno*. The smiles of the women were far more frank than those of the men. Dayle tried not to be annoyed, especially since thanks to Max's familiarity she was checked in and ensconced in her suite in short order.

Her rooms were located next to Max's on the hotel's third floor. Both of their suites offered lovely vistas of the canal, a perk that was reflected in the price. Well worth the splurge, Dayle decided, as she let the sheer draperies fall back into place. The hotel would definitely make the list of possible accommodations for wedding guests. Not only was the view stunning, the interior was lovely. All of the furnishings were top-of-the-line reproductions that did justice to the building's architecture and Venice's storied history. A soothing color palette of soft rose and gold added to the sumptuous ambiance.

Dayle was just getting ready to kick off her shoes and lie down when a knock sounded at the door. Max was leaning against the frame when she opened it. He held a bottle of red wine in one hand and a foil-wrapped box of truffles in the other. His smile was as enticing as the chocolates. Dayle ignored it and the accompanying tug low in her belly. In a bored voice she informed him, "If you've come to seduce me, I'm too tired."

Having said so, she moved aside to let him enter. Not in the least put off by her tone, he fell in step beside her as she walked to the sitting room.

"You always seem to have sex on your mind, Dayle. I wonder why that is?" He didn't give her a chance to respond. He set the wine and truffles next to the flower arrangement on the entryway table. "Actually these are compliments of the hotel. I'm merely the messenger. I ran into one of the staff out in the hallway and told him I'd be happy to see that they got delivered."

"You're the soul of accommodation."

"What can I say? I aim to please."

She dropped down on the sitting-room sofa with a sigh. "I know it's not quite noon here, but I'm beat. And I can't wait to get out of these shoes and clothes."

"I'll be happy to help," he offered. On a wink he added, "It so happens I'm exceptionally skilled when it comes to assisting women in such matters."

"Yes, I'm sure you are. All that practice."

Max merely shrugged. "Practice makes perfect." Then his eyes narrowed. "Jealous?"

Because she felt an odd little prickle of possessiveness at the thought of him undressing another woman, she snorted. "Please, I'm engaged."

Max shrugged. "My father was married. That didn't stop him from being tempted. And acting on it. Again and again."

He said it flippantly, but Dayle knew him well enough to detect an underlying note of pain. Max had once confided that while he was growing up his father had betrayed his mother repeatedly. Rosalind Kinnick had stuck with him for years, hoping the man she loved would make good on his vows to reform. Finally she'd had enough. Max had been thirteen when his parents divorced—old enough to understand why Rolland had moved out, old enough to know why he had a place to move to.

Dayle was no therapist, but she didn't figure it took a degree in psychology to draw a correlation between Max's parents' fractured relationship and his inability to make a lasting commitment. Of course, people in glass houses… Dayle had enough issues with trust thanks to her previous marriage that she generally kept such observations to herself.

"How about I start with your shoes," Max was saying.

Before she could fathom what he meant to do he had scooped up her legs and settled onto the opposite end of the sofa with her feet in his lap. She was forced to turn sideways, which put the armrest and a decorative pillow under her shoulders. Her position was now one more of reclining than sitting. She was grateful to be wearing pants.

"Max," she began, struggling to sit up and take back possession of her feet. But he held them firmly.

"Relax, sweetheart. I promise to behave. Scout's honor."

"You were never a Boy Scout."

"Got me there," he agreed amiably. "Still, you can trust me."

Dayle was too tired to argue. Besides, he'd already divested her feet of their flats and had begun to rub her aching arches through the thin material of her socks. If she were a cat, she would have begun purring. As it was, she moaned softly. She chanced a glance at Max, wondering if he'd heard. His smile was smug and purely male. She had her answer.

Though she knew it wasn't wise, Dayle closed her eyes and gave in to the sensations. No doubt about it, Max was exceptionally skilled with his hands. He knew exactly which spots to knead, to stroke and caress to deliver the most pleasure.

Her mind had begun to stray into decidedly erotic

territory when Max asked, "Are you sure you want me to behave, Dayle?"

She kept her eyes shut. God only knows what they might reveal were she to let the lids flick up. "The only thing I know for sure at the moment is that if our business ever folds you would have a promising career as a masseur. I'd pay big bucks for this, and I'm sure I'm not alone."

"Oh, I couldn't do this for money." He removed her stockings then. His hands were warm on her skin and their heat seemed to transfer to her flesh. "I prefer other, more basic forms of compensation."

At his huskily spoken words the warmth spread, spiraling upward, spiraling out of control as unpredictable and dangerous as a brush fire. For one brief moment, Dayle felt consumed and almost welcomed her own combustion. Then, thankfully, sanity returned. She abruptly pulled her feet away and stood.

"I—I really need some sleep." She kneaded her forehead and muttered, "I'm not feeling like myself at all."

Max eyed her curiously for a moment before rising to his feet as well. "Sleep isn't a good idea. Give in to jet lag now and you'll pay for it later. It's better to stay awake and reset your body's internal clock to local time."

She nodded, knowing what he said made sense.

"All right. Just a long soak in the tub then," she replied. "I'll call you later. We can make plans for dinner."

But he was shaking his head. "We have a client to see before then."

"A client? Today? But I've only just arrived." She glanced at her watch. It was just after eleven Venice time.

"It's not for a few hours yet. That will give us plenty of time for lunch and a leisurely stroll along the canal."

She held out a hand in protest. "But, Max—"

He laid the stockings he'd removed over her wrist. "Go and freshen up. You have time for a shower." Cocking an eyebrow he asked, "Need help scrubbing your back?"

"I can manage on my own."

"Really?" One side of his mouth rose. "That must mean you're flexible. Flexibility is a vastly appealing trait in a woman."

On a strangled cry, Dayle wadded up her socks and tossed them in his direction. It was just her luck that even with one of them draped over his head he managed to look incredibly sexy.

"Leave me alone, Max."

He removed the sock, retrieved the other one from the floor and set both on the sofa. He sounded serious when he replied, "I'm trying."

MAX WANTED A DRINK. If it were later in the day, he would have been tempted to indulge in something far more potent than the sparkling water he'd swiped from the suite's minibar.

Sipping the water, he paced the sitting room. It was a twin to Dayle's, which was why he had a hard time even looking in the direction of the sofa. God help him, but when she'd moaned as he'd rubbed her instep he'd come close to forgetting she was his partner, his friend and the woman whose wedding he had agreed to help plan. He'd wanted to push her feet aside and find out what other spots on her body might be sensitive to his touch. Good thing Dayle had put an end to what had come awfully close to foreplay.

He finished off the water and began pacing again. Right. Good thing.

This was ridiculous. *He* was being ridiculous. But there was no denying he was feeling decidedly proprietary of the woman and as a result decidedly jealous that she was soon going to be another man's wife.

He wanted her to be his.

The unprecedented thought came out of nowhere, catching him off guard. The idea was crazy, not to mention appallingly selfish. Kinnick men weren't hardwired for commitment.

An hour later, when Max tapped on Dayle's door, his resolve was firmly in place. During the next

several days, when they weren't seeing clients, he
would walk her into every church, palace and reception hall in Venice. He would take her to every florist,
caterer and bakery. He would see to it that come June
she had her fairy-tale wedding.

Dayle deserved one…even if fate had decreed that
Max wasn't to be the groom.

CHAPTER SIX

DAYLE DESPERATELY needed something to occupy her mind after Max left her suite. It must be this place, she decided. Venice was so romantic, after all. Wasn't that one of the reasons she'd chosen it for her wedding?

She decided to unpack her suitcase, hoping the mundane chore would put an end to her wayward thoughts. She'd brought only a couple of dresses to wear for special dinners out. She hung those in the closet right away, as well as a few of the other garments that were prone to wrinkling. That left her with the rest of the big suitcase. Even as she lifted out the first neat stack of sweaters, fatigue had her yawning. She removed a few pairs of pants. They really should be put on hangers. And then she emptied the side pouches that contained her lingerie and other unmentionables. Much of it, she realized as she glanced down at the swatches of crimson, had come from Max.

Max.

She sank down on the free side of the bed and rubbed

her eyes. She really should call Ryan and let him know she'd arrived safely. Ryan was such a good man. So kind. So steadfast. So…not Maxwell Kinnick.

She leaned back and brought the feet Max had massaged up onto the mattress. She just needed a moment. She just needed to stop thinking. About anyone. About anything. She rolled to her side, pulled the pillow from beneath the duvet and when exhaustion beckoned, she gratefully fell into its embrace.

SHE WOKE to a lingering kiss that promised far more.

"I was lonely," a husky male voice whispered against her lips. "I've been so lonely."

"Me, too." At the admission, Dayle's heart began hammering, tapping so loudly that she swore she could hear its beating.

It took off faster when he began to undress her. He removed her clothes with agonizing slowness, lips kissing, teeth nipping at the sensitive skin his skillful hands exposed.

She'd never been vocal during lovemaking, but she was moaning now, begging actually, until finally the last of her garments was removed.

Then it was time for her to return the favor. She was far less patient, showed far less restraint. She was so ready for him, so unbelievably eager. The small, slippery buttons of his shirt slowed her progress. She tugged at the fabric, nearly rent the broadcloth when she grew tired of fumbling with them. His rich laughter rumbled, only to stop abruptly when she reached for his belt and unbuckled it. Then his breath hissed out as she lowered the zipper on his trousers. It was her turn to be slow, to be thorough. It was his turn to moan, to writhe and to want.

Finally neither of them could stand any more. Their bodies met in the center of the bed. Heated flesh molded together, burning hotter and brighter than the sun that had pierced the clouds outside and now illuminated the distinctive domes of St. Mark's Basilica through the window. She felt him slide into her, filling her so snugly that she let out a long, low sigh of contentment. Soon enough, however, she became greedy for more. She arched her back against the mattress and lifted her hips to make more room for each deep thrust. His tempo had been slow, but now it began to quicken as his breath sawed out.

"So good." She panted the words into the curve of his neck, kissing the pulse that beat in time with their movements. "So good."

And it was. Better, in fact, than it had ever been. That alone made her want to weep, but she blinked away the gathering moisture. Now was not the time for tears even if they were the result of triumph rather than the product of sorrow.

Together they rolled on the mattress, their legs tangling in the satin sheets as they traded places. She was on top now and sat up, bringing her knees to either side of his torso and bracing her hands on the solid wall of his chest. She could feel his heart hammering beneath her palms. It rapped as loudly and as erratically as her own.

A little thrill sneaked through her. She had never tried this position in lovemaking. It let her set the pace, to determine the depth of penetration. She savored the control, but she wasn't selfish. She used it to both of their advantages, alternately rotating her hips slowly and then pumping them faster up and down…up and down…up and down.

Sensations built. Her breathing grew more labored. She heard him moan. Then the hands that had been cradling her hips moved to her breasts. He flicked his thumbs across her nipples, causing them to harden, causing other places in her body to tingle before contracting. Delicious heat curled, taking her closer to the flash point.

Her movements grew faster, more urgent and far less controlled. Primal instinct kicked in as need wound inside her like a spring. It coiled tighter and tighter until finally she could take no more. She leaned forward, rose up until their intimate connection was nearly lost and then drove down on him. He said her name, his voice hoarse and barely recognizable, as she supposed was her own when she cried out on a shattering climax. It was the first real orgasm she'd experienced in years, a fact that once again made her feel like weeping. She smiled instead as she lay draped across his chest, sated and happy, at long last complete.

"I love you," she murmured.

"I love you, too."

When she finally found the strength to move she levered herself up, pushed the hair back from her eyes and smiled down at her lover. It was not her fiancé she straddled.

It was Max.

Dayle woke with a start and scrambled off the bed as if it were covered in molten lava rather than a satin duvet. Her body was still throbbing from what had been a very real, very lovely orgasm. She glanced down, half expecting to find herself naked, but she was completely clothed, just as she was completely alone.

"A dream." She exhaled heavily. "It was only a dream."

It took her a moment to realize the tapping sound was real. It wasn't coming from her heart but from the suite's door, and it had turned to pounding by the time she went to answer it. Max was in the hall, looking irritated, looking good enough to eat. Heat crept into Dayle's face, making it hard to meet his gaze.

"Are you okay?"

"Fine," she managed, fiddling with the cuff of her blouse. The very blouse he had removed with such maddening slowness in her dream.

He touched her cheek. "Are you sure? You look a little flushed."

"I'm…fine," she repeated. She chanced another look at his face. He was studying her.

"I know what happened here," he said softly. "I can read you like a book."

Dayle moistened her lips and felt her face burn hotter. "You can?"

"Always."

Dear God.

"You fell asleep, even after I told you not to."

She nearly laughed in relief. "Yes. I did." She bobbed her head. "I fell asleep."

"You're going to regret it."

Actually she already did. Because she couldn't look at him now without a totally inappropriate question nagging. Was Max as good in real life as he'd been in her dream?

"Are you sure you don't want to sit down?" he asked. "You seem a little shaky."

"No. I'm fine. Just tired. I started to unpack and

then decided to lie down for a minute. I was just planning to rest my eyes," Dayle said.

Max smiled. "Well, you rested them for nearly an hour."

"Sorry," she said again.

"You're only sorry I woke you." He stepped into the suite and nudged her in the direction of the bedroom. "Go take a shower. I'll finish your unpacking and pick out something sexy for you to wear."

"I can pick out my own outfit," she informed him.

Max was relieved to see some of Dayle's usual pluck return.

"That's fine," he replied on a shrug. Then he sent her a smoldering gaze. "I was referring to what you can wear beneath it anyway. That way I can imagine you taking it off tonight."

Where a moment ago her face had seemed flushed, now she looked positively pale.

"Hey, are you sure you're feeling okay?" he asked. "I can reschedule our meeting for another day."

"No. That's not necessary." She shuffled off in the direction of the bathroom.

MAX FROWNED AFTER HER. She was acting odd, but then he wasn't feeling quite like himself, either, and hadn't been since she'd arrived in Venice.

He wandered to the large bed. Clothes covered

half of it, neat stacks of sweaters, carefully folded shirts and pants. There was also a tantalizing assortment of lingerie, the majority of which was made of red silk. His doing. He grinned.

Max liked knowing that she wore the things he gave her. He liked knowing that he got the sizes of such intimate apparel right. And though he knew he was being sadistic, he picked up the lacy camisole he'd purchased the summer before in Paris and pictured Dayle wearing it. The mental image his fertile imagination produced had him groaning.

He dropped it back onto the pile and circled the bed. The opposite side was empty. Dayle hadn't turned down the covers to sleep, but she had pulled the pillow from beneath the spread. Max sat down on the edge of the mattress and placed his hand on the indentation her head had left. It was still warm. Because he heard the shower running, he gave in to temptation, leaned over and sniffed. He closed his eyes and sighed as her scent curled around him. The woman was going to be the death of him.

He stood and paced to the window. What was it about her that made him wish he could be a different kind of man? She was beautiful, smart, funny, interesting, but so were many of the women he'd dated, bedded. He'd never regretted it when their liaisons ended, but he still couldn't quite face the fact that he was losing Dayle, not just to another man, but to another city. He'd never really had her, of course. Maybe that was the issue here. The one who got away. Hadn't they once joked that that was what made her irresistible?

Max was still staring out at the canal traffic when he heard the shower switch off. A moment later Dayle stepped out of the bathroom wrapped in a fluffy white towel. Steam escaped along with her. His breath hissed out. She stopped when she spied him, her expression oddly vulnerable. More than anything he wanted to take her in his arms, hold her. Keep her.

Instead he crossed those arms over his chest. "You look good in terry cloth. Got anything on underneath it?" He bobbed his eyebrows and settled into the comfortable role of flirt.

"Wouldn't you like to know?" she retorted, her vulnerability vanishing along with the steam. "Wait out in the sitting room while I dress."

"And miss the show?"

"Exactly." When he stayed, she raised her voice. "Max."

He lifted both hands in defeat. "Going, going." But he stopped when she was within reach and wound one thick, wet curl tightly around his index finger, squeezing a little water from it. He wiped the droplet on her towel at the spot where one end was tucked bctween her breasts and took some satisfaction when she sucked in a breath and her eyes went wide.

He meant it when he said, "Ryan is one lucky man."

CHAPTER SEVEN

ENZA LEONI was a jewelry designer who counted European royalty and American celebrities among her clientele. Her one-of-a-kind pieces commanded outrageous sums, but more recently she'd started a signature line she wanted to sell through select stores in the United States. The line wouldn't be inexpensive, but it would be within splurging distance for the less affluent.

If everything worked out as planned, Globetrotter's would be the importer that handled Enza's entry into the trendy boutiques of Rodeo Drive and Fifth Avenue.

Her studio was in Venice's interior, well away from the city's main tourism arteries. It was tucked amid the slim alleyways and tiny canals that Venetians traversed in their daily lives and that lucky travelers merely stumbled across. Max seemed to know exactly where he was going. Dayle followed him, literally, since some of the alleys were so narrow that she and Max were required to walk single file.

After what seemed like an eternity, they entered a small *piazza*. The weather had cleared, much like it had in her dream. Dayle focused on the sunshine that danced on the water pooling in a fountain in the middle of the square. She wouldn't think of that dream. No. She would think of Ryan, of their wedding, of their life together. He was going to like Venice. In the summer, when she returned with her intended, flowers would be spilling from the city's many window boxes and planters. It would be warmer then, steamy or so she'd read. Ryan didn't like the heat. She frowned, as the dream and it's too real heat, beckoned.

"Here we are," Max announced, stopping in front of an arched doorway at the far end of the square. "Enza's studio." He opened the door and ushered her inside.

He spoke too soon, as far as Dayle was concerned. They didn't officially arrive at the studio for three more flights of stone steps. Despite the low heels of her shoes, her feet were begging for relief by the time they finally reached their destination. Her mind reeled back to the foot rub Max had given her as she'd reclined on the sofa. Desire curled at the memory. She swallowed and sought to banish it, as well as that intimate dream. That was easily accomplished when they reached the studio and Enza came to greet them.

The woman wasn't as tall as Dayle, but she was poised and self-assured, with the most amazing green-brown eyes set in a face that would have stopped Manhattan traffic at rush hour. Dayle felt positively plain in comparison.

"Maxie, it's so good to see you again," Enza cooed in a lyrical voice.

She kissed him enthusiastically on both cheeks, resting her ample bosom against his chest during the time that it took. Then she turned her attention to Dayle. A pair of dark, finely arched brows tugged together and lush, full lips pursed. Dayle recognized that scrutinizing look. She'd been on the receiving end of it often enough from the women in Max's life. It said, "Back off. I've got dibs."

She'd never grown accustomed to it, but it particularly grated now.

"Enza, this is Dayle Alexander, my business partner," Max said by way of an introduction.

Since the woman wasn't quite done inspecting her, Dayle decided to go first. "It's nice to meet you, Enza." She held out a hand.

"*Si.* Yes. It is nice to meet you, too." But Enza continued to frown. "Forgive me for my rudeness, it's just that when we had dinner together the other evening Maxie neglected to mention that his Dayle was a woman."

His Dayle. The words held an accusation. Max seemed to know that, too, for he cleared his throat.

"It must have slipped his mind," Dayle replied dryly.

To which it sounded like Max murmured, "Never."

Both women turned to study him. He fiddled with one of his gold cuff links. "Dayle can be a man's name. Perhaps that's where the confusion came in."

Enza's scrutinizing gaze cut to Dayle again. "Perhaps," she allowed after a moment, but her tone resonated skepticism.

Dayle opted to show her hand, literally. She let the diamond engagement ring flash. "I don't usually travel with Max, but I couldn't resist coming to Venice. My fiancé and I will be getting married in June and we want to have our wedding here. Max knows the city so well. He's agreed to help me find the perfect location."

Enza's smile bloomed. "You're engaged. Congratulations. Maxie didn't mention that, either." She sent him a pointed look. He shrugged by way of apology. "May I see your ring?"

Dayle held out her hand. The diamond was just over a carat and set in platinum. She'd picked it out herself after accepting Ryan's proposal. That had taken some of the romance out of the moment, as far as she was concerned. But then Ryan never seemed to get her preferences right. Whereas Max...

"A solitaire," Enza said. "A very traditional setting."

"Dayle is a very traditional woman," Max said knowingly.

Both women frowned at him. Enza was the first to speak. "The ring is beautiful, don't you agree, Maxie?"

"Stunning." But he didn't look at it, and it struck Dayle then that he'd never asked to see her ring, though he was a self-described connoisseur of beauty in all its many forms.

Dayle decided it was time to get down to business. "Max tells me your designs are unsurpassed, especially your hammered gold pieces. We believe Globetrotter's can ensure they receive the right positioning in the American market."

"So Maxie says."

The nickname was starting to grate. Dayle continued. "I've seen some examples of your work, but I'd love to see more."

"Certainly." Enza waved a bejeweled hand. "Right this way."

AN HOUR LATER, to Dayle's relief, they were shuffling down the steps from Enza Leoni's studio.

"You might have mentioned that you're sleeping with our client, *Maxie*," she drawled.

She knew Max flirted outrageously with all women, even those who were Globetrotter's clientele, but she'd always assumed he knew where to draw the line. That was why his apparent intimacy with the very lovely Enza Leoni had her so incensed, she told herself.

"Actually I met Enza before she became a client. There's nothing going on," he said as he held the door that opened into the square.

"Now." She brushed past him. He didn't correct her and so Dayle figured she had her answer. Fury swept in from nowhere. "God! I should have known."

"Known what?"

"She's female," Dayle snapped. "So, of course you've slept with her."

"Are you saying I'm indiscriminate?" He had the nerve to sound puzzled and to look almost wounded. Dayle lowered her chin and sent him a pointed look.

"I'm not indiscriminate," he mumbled, reaching for her elbow.

But she pulled it away. "Oh, that's right. You'll flirt with anyone female, but in order for you to sleep with them they have to be stunning, sexy and have a flair for fashion."

"I appreciate a good sense of humor and some intelligence, too," he inserted with his trademark smile.

Dayle was beyond being charmed. God, what was wrong with him? For that matter, what was wrong with *her?* Even as she silently asked the question, she was snapping irritably, "I don't find this situation amusing."

She lengthened her stride and stalked ahead of him.

"Whoa, whoa!" Max caught up to her and grabbed her wrist, forcing her to stop and face him. "What's gotten into you? Since when do you care who I spend my personal time with?"

"I don't care." She didn't. No, of course she didn't. If she cared that could be construed as jealousy, and a soon-to-be-married woman had no right—*absolutely* no right—to jealousy when it came to a man who was not her groom-to-be. It was that damned dream. That damned foot rub. It was Venice and jet lag, prewedding jitters and Beth's off-base musings. Dayle shook her head vehemently in a bid to clear her mind. Images she could have done without stayed, stubborn as burrs. Even so, she claimed, "I couldn't care less as a matter of fact."

"Uh-huh." Max ran his tongue over his teeth. She gritted hers. But at least he wasn't looking smug at the moment. She couldn't have tolerated that.

"I just don't think it's very professional of you to blur the boundaries between your bedroom and Globetrotter's bottom line." Yes, that was the issue. Professionalism was *exactly* the issue that had Dayle feeling so damned agitated.

Max gaped at her. "You're being a little melodramatic, don't you think? Enza and I had a brief…" He waved a hand, as if a suitable description of their coupling escaped him.

"Fling," Dayle supplied succinctly. "You and Enza had a fling."

He wrinkled his nose. "I prefer the term interlude."

Of course he did. Interlude made it sound gauzy and strewn with rose petals.

"You can use a prettier word, *Maxie,*" she drawled. "But it doesn't change the facts."

He frowned. "Well, here are the facts for you. My relationship with Enza was one between two, mutually consenting adults who were both well aware that it wasn't going to be anything more than what it was."

"And it was?"

"None of your damned business."

He was right, absolutely right, but that didn't make his words any easier for Dayle to hear. Even when Max added, "Besides, that relationship was over long before she contacted Globetrotter's about the possibility of becoming a client."

His explanation should have mollified her. It didn't. Quite the opposite.

"Relationship?" Dayle spat. "You don't have relationships, Max. You have flings." She shook her head. "Oh, sorry. That's right. *Interludes.* In the dozen years I've known you you've had too many *interludes* for me to count."

His eyes narrowed, making it clear she wasn't the only one irritated now. "And that's suddenly an issue for you because?"

His words had her blinking. "I-it's not an issue for me."

"Okay, then what are we standing in the middle of this charming little square arguing about?"

More than irritated, now he looked confused. Dayle was confused, too. She had been since that dream, which perhaps explained why she said the first thing that sprang to mind.

"Sex."

Max's eyebrows notched up, taking one corner of his mouth with them.

"S-sex with a client," Dayle added, but she wasn't sure if the clarification was for his benefit or her own.

His expression sobered on a sigh, and he rubbed his forehead with the thumb and index finger of his right hand. "As I believe I've already made abundantly clear, Enza and I are not sleeping together."

"But you aren't sleeping alone. Or at least you won't be for long." Something inside of her twisted violently. Dayle decided it was because the bald statements crossed a line that she had drawn very carefully herself.

Max seemed to know it, for he stepped closer, metaphorically putting one designer loafer over that line as well. His voice was pitched low and held not a hint of its usual teasing when he asked, "Does it bother you to imagine other women in my bed?"

Dayle knew she should back away and reestablish

the old boundaries. She needed to redraw the rigid line that had served her so well all these years. Or maybe it was time to erect a high, impenetrable wall in its place. But she stayed where she was, captured, captivated by his sensual and very serious expression.

"Yes, it bothers me," she admitted softly.

Their faces were mere inches apart now. Their breath mingled in the charged air of the square. Max ran his fingers down her arm. When he reached her hand, he clasped it within his. "Why? Why does it bother you?"

She answered with what she knew was only part of the truth, but the rest wasn't something she was ready to explore at the moment…if ever. "Because I want you to be happy, Max."

"Ah, Dayle. My sweet, sweet Dayle." He leaned in and his lips brushed hers for one brief, torturous moment. In the time it took him to back away, his mouth had already curved with a familiar, cocky grin. "There's no need for you to worry about me. Happiness is my middle name."

Dayle begged off on dinner that evening. She couldn't face Max again. She felt too exposed after their bizarrely intimate talk in the square. She wasn't sure what had gotten into her, saying the things that she had…and suddenly seeming to want the very things that she couldn't have and knew would ultimately bring her heartache. Whatever the reason behind these rioting emotions—Beth's probing questions, jet lag or Dayle's cheating subconscious—she was sure that some time away from Max would help her make sense of them.

So, she ordered room service, put on some comfortable clothes and curled up on the sofa with a bridal magazine. She had just flipped it open to an article on rehearsal-dinner etiquette when the telephone rang. Dayle eyed the phone a moment before answering it, worried it might be Max. But the voice on the other end belonged to Ryan. Oddly she felt disappointed.

"Missing me?" he asked.

"Of course." She ignored the guilt that nipped at her.

"So, how's Venice?"

"It's lovely and absolutely perfect for our wedding. I wish you were here with me to see it." And she did. If he were in Venice, everything would be…normal. For hadn't she long known that Ryan was the perfect antidote to Max?

As if she'd spoken that thought aloud, Ryan said, "Is Kinnick behaving himself?"

She cleared her throat. "Oh, you know Max."

Ryan chuckled. "Yes, I do, which is why it's also a good thing that I know you."

This time guilt didn't merely nip. It snapped down hard and sank in its razor-sharp teeth. Coward that she was, Dayle opted to change the subject.

"So, how's your training going?"

Twenty minutes later, after ending their call, she was once again convinced that Ryan was the right man, the right choice. So what if she experienced no fireworks, felt no delicious urgency during their lovemaking. She could do without those things. He was a good life partner, a safe choice. Unlike her ex—and unlike Maxwell Kinnick—Ryan would never break her heart.

He can't break what he doesn't have.

CHAPTER EIGHT

FOR THE NEXT COUPLE of days Max and Dayle had business appointments that took up many of their mornings. Max let her take the lead in wooing a couple of new clients, getting her feet wet for when her new duties kicked in on the West Coast. She was very persuasive at laying out the benefits of signing with Globetrotter's. He sat back and watched her, pleased and proud. Even though she'd always been content to stay in the shadows, he'd known Dayle would shine at whatever she tried.

Though neither of them mentioned it again, it was clear to Max that their argument—or whatever the hell it had been—in the square on her first day in Venice, remained on their minds. For a moment, he'd almost sworn she was jealous of Enza, maybe even jealous of all the other women in his life, past and future. It had scared him to death, but at the same time it had stirred something he dare not think of as hope.

He wouldn't categorize their personal dealings

since then as strained. He still flirted with her. She still put him in his place with a glib reply or a pointed look. That had always been the give-and-take of their dealings. He supposed one could call it their routine. Even so, something was different, something was…off. Dayle seemed on guard around him. He scrubbed a hand over his eyes and called himself a fool. Perhaps that was what his ego needed to believe. More likely, she was preoccupied. After all, she was in Venice to plan her wedding.

Before arriving, she'd researched possible sites for the ceremony on the Internet. In typical Dayle fashion she'd made a detailed list of those sites, what amenities they offered, how many guests they could accommodate and so forth. Max suggested a couple of other places that would match the mood and tone she was seeking. They would require him to cash in some favors since they were privately owned, but so be it. He'd promised her a romantic and stylish Venetian affair and he was determined to be a man of his word, no matter what it cost him personally.

The price was proving to be quite steep. He hadn't slept well since her arrival. How could he when his mind kept picturing her in that big bed in the adjacent suite clothed in silky bits of crimson he'd picked out himself? She was so close, yet farther than ever beyond his reach. He comforted himself with the knowledge that soon enough their time together would be over, and he and Dayle would return to the normalcy of New York. That meant she would be in their Manhattan office and he would be jetting off again.

Max already had begun laying the groundwork for his next trip abroad. The Far East, he'd decided, for at least one week, maybe two, with stops in Hong Kong, Shanghai and Taipei. For the first time in his life, though, he wasn't looking forward to traveling. Perhaps it was because this time his plans seemed more about the need to run away than a remedy to restlessness.

DAYLE MET HIM in their hotel's restaurant at nine as he sipped espresso and glanced through an English-language newspaper. He'd been up since dawn after another fitful night's sleep. Two espressos later he'd still been dragging, until he caught sight of her. The woman sent the blood pumping through his veins at lightning speed. A man didn't need caffeine when she was around. The casual black pants she wore drew attention to the long line of her legs, especially since she'd apparently decided to ditch comfort for the day and had donned a pair of heels. He loved it when she wore them, the higher the better.

He folded the paper and set it aside. The tingle of attraction wasn't so easily dispatched. He opted to ignore it. "Good morning, beautiful. I trust you slept well."

"Fine, thanks." She signaled for the waiter to bring her an espresso and settled into the chair opposite his. "And you? How did you sleep?"

"Like hell. I tossed and turned. Visions of you wearing red kept me awake all night long."

It was the truth, but she rolled her eyes. "Right."

He shrugged. If she only knew. "So, what's on the agenda for today?"

They had wrapped up the last of their business meetings the morning before, meaning her and Ryan's wedding plans would receive their undivided attention from here on out. Max's stomach burned at the thought.

Dayle pulled the small notebook from her handbag and flipped it open, consulting her lengthy to-do list.

"Let's see. We took care of flowers yesterday afternoon." She made a little check mark next to the entry.

"After what seemed like a lifetime of indecision," he remarked dryly.

"Don't start," she warned.

He held up his hands, palms facing out. "I'm just saying that someone who is as picky as you are has absolutely no right to label me high maintenance ever again."

Her utter fussiness still surprised him. It had almost seemed like foot-dragging. But what reason would Dayle have to drag her feet?

"I wanted white calla lilies."

"Yes and the blooms had to measure a certain number of inches in diameter and be uniform in all other aspects."

"I like uniformity." She shrugged.

"And the stems all must be wrapped in rose-colored ribbon. Not pink, not mauve. Rose." He mimicked her voice as he spoke.

"There's nothing wrong with knowing exactly what you want," she replied.

Max couldn't argue with that. Still, he felt compelled to point out, "But as the song says, you can't always get what you want."

And didn't he know it?

She glanced up from her notebook. Dark eyes studied him a moment. Oddly Dayle sounded resigned when she said, "No. You can't always have what you want. That's why it's good to have a Plan B."

"So, you settle." When she frowned, he added, "That's what you're really saying, isn't it?"

They weren't talking about flowers or ribbon colors any longer. Max was sure of it when Dayle said quietly, "Sometimes the backup plan is the wiser choice." She moistened her lips before adding, "The safer choice."

Her words surprised him. "Safer?" he asked.

"Infinitely." She cleared her throat then and went

back to her notebook. "I'd like to place the order for my cake today. I have a list of bakeries near St. Mark's Square that I'd like to visit, but I'm open to other suggestions if you have any."

Apparently she'd decided that the previous topic of conversation was now closed. Probably just as well, he decided.

Safer.

The word echoed in his head. Max ignored it and worked up his patented smile. "Cake it is."

"I'd also like to pick out some gifts for the wedding party. Perhaps we could get that out of the way first. I'm thinking jewelry, maybe something that can be engraved."

"You can't go wrong with jewelry," he said. "It's the perfect gift for any occasion."

"I thought that was red undergarments." She made a sound that was half laugh, half harrumph.

Max shook his head. "Oh, no. Those are only acceptable when you are particularly fond of the person."

"Then you must buy undergarments often—perhaps you even purchase them in bulk quantities." She smiled sweetly after issuing the dig.

"As it happens, I hand select each item and I only buy them for a certain someone when I've been away."

"I'm the only one?" Her expression was doubtful,

although he noticed that she had edged forward in her seat, as if anxious to hear his response.

"The one and only," Max confirmed. But because the words left him feeling unmasked, he added a wink.

Dayle shook her head on a sigh and settled back in her chair. "So, can you recommend a place where I can find some quality pieces?"

"Of lingerie?" he asked, purposely misunderstanding her.

Her eyes narrowed. "Of jewelry."

"Well, as you know, Enza Leoni does exceptional work." It was petty of him, but Max took a perverse amount of pleasure from watching Dayle's upper lip curl at the mention of the other woman's name. "Her pieces are expensive but since she's a client she'll probably cut you a sweet deal."

"No, thanks. Her work may be exceptional, but it's a little too ostentatious for my taste."

Max sipped his espresso to hide his smile. Dayle might not be jealous, but she gave a good impression of it and his ego needed that at the moment.

With it sufficiently bolstered, he said, "It was just a thought. I know a few other places. Venice has no shortage of jewelry stores."

A couple of hours and several shops later, Dayle had purchased a lovely glass-bead necklace for Beth, whom she'd asked to be her maid of honor, and a watch for Ryan's best man. With a little prodding from Max she'd also picked out a strand of pearls for herself and a beaded handbag for Lorna as a make-peace gesture.

Finally, she had ordered favors for her guests. *Bombonieras* were an Italian tradition. Since the wedding was to be held in Venice, he'd suggested that hand-blown glass roses would make the perfect gift. After some dithering she'd agreed. Foot-dragging, he'd thought again, only to change his mind when they'd walked past another shop and she'd said, "I bet I can find something for Ryan in there."

Max shrugged and opted to wait for her outside with her bags full of the day's other purchases. The minute she ducked inside, he was digging into his pocket for the roll of antacids.

For small swatches of time as he showed her around Venice, it was easy to forget the true purpose of their visit. But it always came up, followed by heartburn. Max thumbed off a second tablet and popped it into his mouth, scowling as he chewed. He'd worked his way through half the roll by the time Dayle finally exited the shop.

"All set," she announced with an enigmatic smile.

When they reached the famed Rialto Bridge, he put his hand on her lower back, guiding her progress. The bridge was bustling with people, many of them tourists snapping pictures of the distinctive structure or the gondolas gliding on the canal beneath it. At the elevated center of the span, Dayle surprised him by taking his hand and drawing him to one side.

"Do you want to take a photograph?" he asked.

"No. I have something for you." She pulled a small, gift-wrapped box from her shopping bag. "I was going to wait to give it to you, but I can't. It's to thank you for all of your help."

"Oh, there's no need for that." Max meant it. Gratitude was a poor substitute for what he really wanted.

But Dayle shook her head. "I think there is. You've even agreed to stand in for my dad."

Max blanched at that. "Please, comparing me to your late father makes me feel perverse given the very vivid sexual fantasies I've entertained about you." He wasn't quite joking. They both managed tight laughter as people jostled past them chattering away in a variety of languages.

"How about this? You've agreed to give me away."

"Better," he murmured, though those words didn't sit right with him either.

"And you've been a huge help, showing me around Venice, helping me make decisions. Honestly, Max, I don't know what I'd do without you," she said.

"You'd be fine. You're a born survivor."

He, on the other hand, was becoming increasingly worried about how he was going to manage the day-to-day act of living after she married Ryan and moved away.

Dayle pressed the box into his hand. "Go on. Open it."

As he untied the ribbon and began peeling off the paper, an odd sense of anticipation built. She'd given him gifts before, jewelry even, which he figured this was. But the mood surrounding this gift was different. Or maybe *he* was different. Not a changed man, but a changing one, and the reason for his metamorphosis was standing opposite him, smiling.

The last of the paper was removed. He wadded it up and stuffed it into his jacket pocket, wanting to draw out the moment. Finally he lifted off the lid and looked inside the box. It held a gold chain and a medallion of some sort. He pulled them out, laying the medallion flat on his palm.

Dayle edged in closer. "I saw it and I thought of you. It's a St. Christopher's medal," she said.

"The patron saint of travelers." He stroked the face of the medal with his thumb.

"So you'll always return home safely."

Max attempted a laugh, but it caught in his throat. *Home.* He frowned. Where exactly was that for someone like him? First-class on an international flight? A suite in one of the world's choicest hotels? The Manhattan apartment that he kept but didn't quite live in?

Home is where the heart is.

The old saying plunked into his mind, sending out ripples like a pebble in a pond. He glanced over at Dayle. She was smiling, her expression open and inviting. Welcoming.

Home. Maybe Max did know where that was after all.

CHAPTER NINE

MAX WAS QUIET during much of their lunch at a charming café in St. Mark's Square. He was wearing the St. Christopher medal she'd given him, and when he didn't think she was looking, she'd seen him finger it through the fabric of his shirt.

Dayle had stumbled across the medal as she'd scoured the shop for something for Ryan. She'd come up empty-handed for her fiancé, but not for Max. If Beth were there, Dayle knew what her friend would say about that, just as she would have something to say about Dayle's uncharacteristic indecisiveness over even the most basic of her wedding plans.

But Beth wasn't in Venice, leaving an ostrich to her sand.

Max was touched by the gift if his initial reaction was any indication. Indeed, Dayle wasn't sure she'd ever seen him look quite so moved, even when she'd given him pricier or more practical things. Since then he'd been lost in thought. He seemed to snap out of it when they started on their quest for the perfect wedding cake a little later.

She consulted her notebook as she waited for him to pay the bill. "I think Salvatore's is just on the other side of the square," she said when he joined her.

"I have another place in mind. It's not as well-known as some of the places here, but no one in Venice can outdo Franca Celli when it comes to dessert," he promised her.

They took a water taxi part of the way and then shuffled down a labyrinth of narrow passages. All the way, Dayle braced herself to be greeted by another curvaceous Mediterranean beauty, but when they reached the bakery that wasn't quite the case. Signora Franca Celli was a pleasantly plump widow who was pushing sixty. It was also clear from the way she patted Max's cheek and then came around the counter to wrap him in a robust hug, that she adored him. What woman didn't? But at least Franca didn't call him Maxie. No, she called him by his full given name, with the fond lecturing quality of a parent. For this reason alone, Dayle liked her.

"Maxwell, you stay away too long," Franca accused.

"I know. My apologies. But I'm here now and I've missed you," he said with his usual charming smile.

Franca shook her head and laughed. "You cannot

fool me, Maxwell. You miss my cannoli. You miss my tiramisu. You are not pining for an old woman."

"You're not old. You're experienced."

"Bah!" But she laughed. Then she turned to Dayle. "And who might this be?"

"This is Dayle Alexander, my business partner."

"Bella," she murmured and sent a wink in Max's direction. While Dayle's grasp of Italian was sorely limited, she did understand that word. Beautiful. She felt her face heat when Max smiled and nodded in agreement.

"Buon giorno," Dayle said in greeting.

"Buon giorno," Franca replied. "It is nice to meet a friend of my Maxwell."

Where Enza's possessiveness had been annoying, Franca Celli's was endearing. Dayle smiled warmly in return.

"It's nice to meet you, too. Max tells me that this is the place to come for the best sweets in all of Italy."

"Ah, Maxwell." She patted his cheek again before asking Dayle, "What woman can resist such a charmer?"

"Actually *that* woman," Max murmured. "Which is why we're here."

"Scusi?"

A little louder he said, "Dayle would like your suggestions for her wedding cake."

"Wedding!" The woman's eyes widened first in surprise and then in excitement. She wrapped him in another bear hug. "Oh, Maxwell, so you are finally going to settle down."

"Oh, no. No, no." He sent an apologetic glance in Dayle's direction. "It's not what you're thinking, Franca. I'm not the groom. Come to that, I'm not even the best man."

Was that regret in his voice? She didn't have time to ponder it now. Franca ushered them to a table, calling over her shoulder for the young girl at the counter to bring them some espresso. For the next two hours she came out of the kitchen with one calorie-laden confection after another. All of the dishes were traditional to Italian weddings and vastly different from the icing-coated cakes that Dayle had been expecting. Not that she minded. These were feasts for the eyes and palate.

"First, you will try my *crostata di frutta,*" Franca said, setting a slice of fruit-covered tart in front of them. A decadent vanilla cream voided out any of the fruit's nutritional qualities, but it was a worthwhile trade in Dayle's mind. If one was going to have dessert, why skimp?

Next Franca brought them a sponge cake filled with Bavarian cream, and then one topped with thick whipped cream and white chocolate shavings. All of the desserts were excellent, melting in her mouth. But Dayle knew she'd found the perfect one when she bit into a puff pastry filled with Chantilly cream.

"Oh, my God, Max. You've got to try this one."

Max had relaxed enough to start enjoying himself, but then he heard Dayle moan. If that weren't bad enough, she'd held out her fork and offered him a bite off of it.

"It's heaven," he agreed, though the flavor didn't register. In fact, background noises and the bakery's scrumptious scents fell away. The only thing he was aware of at that moment was Dayle and how she looked smiling at him in expectation while sunshine streamed through the window behind her and teased highlights from her dark hair.

That stabbing pain lanced his chest again. God help him, but Max welcomed it. At least he knew he was alive.

"Are you sure you like it?" she asked. "You're frowning."

"Sorry." He worked up a convincing grin to go along with his lie. "Just thinking of how long I'll have to spend in the hotel's fitness center to work off all these calories. I'd hate to have to have my new tuxedo altered so soon."

After leaving the bakery, they took what Max intended to be a scenic detour back to their hotel. The weather was mild for April, nudging up near sixty degrees, and he thought Dayle might enjoy strolling amid the shops and boutiques. He knew he could use the air. But she walked at a New Yorker's pace, brisk and purposeful with her shoulders squared, her head up and her eyes focused forward.

He reached for her elbow. "You're going too fast. This is Italy. They believe in taking their time here."

She glanced sideways. "Sorry. Habit." And though she modified her pace and began to glance around some, she continued to walk as if she were late for something. Her feet had to be killing her in those heels. Maybe he'd offer to rub them later. He recalled the last foot rub he'd given her and the lingering effect it had had on him. Maybe not.

He was wrestling with his demons when she all but skidded to a halt on the uneven cobblestones.

"Ooh, look at that." She pointed to a mannequin in the shop's window. It was clothed in a pale blue silk dress accented with tiny darker blue beads around a low-plunging neckline.

"Do you want to go in?" he asked, somewhat amused by her uncharacteristic reaction. Unlike most of the women Max knew, Dayle wasn't the sort who enjoyed shopping. Yet despite laboring through a long day of it, she apparently was game for more.

"Do you mind?"

"Anything for you."

He followed her into the shop, hanging back a couple of steps in the hope of finding his footing. He needn't have bothered. The rug was pulled out from under him completely when he caught up with Dayle several minutes later. As he stood at the back of the boutique looking around for her, she stepped out of a fitting room clothed in the dress that had been on display in the window. It looked far better on her than it had on the mannequin. It flowed over her soft curves in a waterfall of blue silk. He balled his hands into his fists, which he stuffed into his trouser pockets.

"What do you think?" she asked.

Words he couldn't possibly give voice to piled up on his tongue. He swallowed every last one, grateful when he caught a glimpse of red peeking from her décolletage. The sexy distraction was just what he needed to regroup.

"I think you'll need different undergarments if you plan to wear that dress."

"Could you take your eyes off my chest for a moment and give me your honest opinion?" She tugged the neckline higher. Max sighed dramatically. Then he was left without pretense.

"It's lovely, Dayle. You're lovely."

"You think so?" He saw her swallow. Nerves?

"Stunning." The moment stretched. Finally he

cleared his throat. "So, are you thinking of wearing that to your rehearsal dinner?"

For a brief moment he swore the question had her puzzled. But then she nodded. "Yes. The rehearsal dinner." She fussed with the fabric that gathered at her waist. "Ryan says I look good in blue."

Max managed a smile even as his molars ground together. "Well, it's what Ryan thinks that matters."

DAYLE STRETCHED on the bed the following morning. She and Max had stayed out late. They'd dined. They'd danced. They'd drunk a toast to Italy, to life, even to love. She'd been a little tipsy after that, but as she recalled, Max had been a perfect gentleman. He'd issued no off-color comments. He'd made no inappropriate advances. He'd walked Dayle to her suite's door in the wee hours of the morning and, after unlocking it, he'd handed her the key. He hadn't asked to come inside. He hadn't even kissed her on the cheek. She should have been relieved. She'd felt disappointed. When she should have been sleeping, questions had bubbled like the champagne they'd drunk.

Just what was going on? Not only with Max, but with her? Ever since her divorce Dayle had been able to keep foolish needs and damning desires in a box. But the lid was off now and no matter how hard she tried, she didn't seem to be able to stuff them back inside.

CHAPTER TEN

MAX SLAPPED at the alarm clock when it began to beep. Not that he needed the thing to rouse him. He'd been awake most of the night. Again. He'd pulled plenty of all-nighters thanks to a woman in the past, but those had left him satisfied afterward, relaxed. He was far from relaxed now. He was growing more frustrated, sexually and otherwise, by the hour.

And another day of helping Dayle plan her damned wedding loomed. On the bright side, the woman's lengthy to-do list was growing shorter, although she had yet to pin down the actual site for her nuptials. That was on the agenda for today. He rolled out of bed and stumbled in the direction of the bathroom. He'd take a shower, a nice long cold one. Then he'd wash down some breakfast with a carafe of espresso.

Who knew? Maybe the day wouldn't be as bad as he assumed.

By noon, he knew he'd been right. It was worse.

They'd only visited two sites from her list with three more scheduled before they called it a day. In both cases the people they met naturally assumed that Max was the groom-to-be. He and Dayle were quick to set them straight, tight smiles and forced laughter accompanying the explanations.

We're old friends.

We're business partners.

The benign descriptions of their relationship had really started to grate. Was that it? Was that all they were to one another after all these years? Maybe it was just as well that he wasn't feeling brave enough to discover the answers.

Max braced himself for more uncomfortable misunderstandings as they headed to the Palazzo Cavalli just before noon.

"It's a city-owned palace complete with eighteenth-century furnishings and it's considered a premiere venue for a civil ceremony," Dayle said, consulting her notebook.

"Lovely," he mumbled.

They were in a gondola, hips touching as they sat side by side. Their gondolier, a young man named Fabrizio, called out cheerful greetings to the other gondoliers they passed as he used a long pole to guide the vessel down the canal.

Buon giorno. Good day. What was so good about

it? Max thought sourly. He reached up to loosen his necktie, only to discover he wasn't wearing one. Dayle glanced sideways at him in question. He abandoned the open collar of his shirt, folded his hands in his lap and ignored her.

When they reached the palace, though, he wasn't immune to her enthusiasm or to the building's impressive façade.

"Wow. It looks like something out of a fairy tale," Dayle mused.

She looked like something out of his fantasies with her hair floating loose around her shoulders and her cheeks turned rosy from the chilly air. Max stepped out onto the landing to help her from the gondola. He offered Dayle his hand, though a part of him wanted to offer much more.

"This would make pretty picture on your wedding day, no?" Fabrizio said in halting English. "You helping your lovely bride from my boat."

"She's not my bride," he replied.

"Just good friends," Dayle added.

Max was thankful that her grasp of the language was limited when Fabrizio continued in Italian. "What bad luck that you are in love with her, too."

Max opened his mouth to deny it, to explain that someone like him wasn't capable of the kind of love that marriage required. But his stock spiel about the wayward Kinnick genes never made it past his lips. He nodded instead.

"Very bad luck," he agreed in Italian.

"What did he say, Max?" she asked, smiling politely at the gondolier.

"He said…" Max glanced down. He was still holding her hand. What would she do if he told her the truth? He chose a safer version of it. "He said your fiancé is a fool to trust you alone with me."

"Max."

He offered a negligent shrug. "He also said you'll make a lovely bride."

"Oh." She smiled then, looking a little embarrassed. "Tell him thank you." She turned and added her own, *"grazie mille"* before starting inside.

Max caught up with her and a guide as they climbed the palace's restored marble staircase to a large hall replete with frescoes and antique paintings. He usually appreciated fine art, but he barely spared these a glance. He needed a few minutes. While Dayle peppered the guide with questions, Max slipped out onto a balcony, sucking in air as he gazed sightlessly out over the Grand Canal. By the time Dayle joined him, the façade he'd worn as easily as a Venice carnival mask was once again firmly in place.

He nodded in the direction of the formal reception

hall. "So, what do you think? Will this palace do for your 'I dos'?"

"It's lovely, but something's not right. I'll know it when I see it." She bobbed her head for emphasis. "I'm sure that I will. When it's right, it's right. You know?"

"Absolutely."

But Max felt certain of nothing as they made their way to the villa outside the city an hour later. The estate dated back several centuries and was located in an area where Venice's nobility had once passed their summers. The charm grabbed him instantly, despite the building's imposing façade. As had happened previously, the person showing them the villa's many amenities assumed Dayle and Max were the couple to be wed.

"You will find our honeymoon suite very luxurious and exceedingly private," the man told them with a smile.

"This is gorgeous." Dayle sighed and walked ahead of them.

"I'm sure the two of you will be most comfortable here," the manager said. If she heard him, she didn't let on. I should correct him, Max thought. But he didn't.

They went outside then, Max growing more uncomfortable with each sexy ooh and aah sound that Dayle issued. She found the site's storied history and its old world charm appealing, but the possibility of a garden ceremony had her looking enraptured.

"The gardens are resplendent in June," their guide assured them as they walked the curving path between box row hedges to a vine-covered pergola in the center. "Many of our guests have had their ceremony performed here."

"I can see why." Dayle turned in a semicircle underneath it, taking in the expansive view. "This is it. This is the one." She turned to look at Max, her grin fading by degrees as she whispered, "It's…it's the right place."

It was. He felt that, too. He could see it, a little too clearly for comfort. In his mind, the current brown foliage greened and the small lawn area beyond the pergola filled with formally attired guests. The wedding march, a tune that he'd long likened to a death knell, played. It filled Max with anticipation rather than dread as he studied Dayle. She was a vision in pale ivory against a backdrop of wisteria and roses.

You may kiss the bride.

He obeyed the imagined command, leaning forward and kissing her not on the cheek as he'd been so careful to do all of these years, but on the mouth. When he heard her sexy sigh, he closed his eyes and surrendered what little remained of his sanity.

DAYLE DIDN'T PULL AWAY, at least not at first. She blamed her delayed reaction on shock. But need played a role, too. The desire she'd subjugated for so long staged an all-out insurrection when Max wrapped her in his arms. One of his hands was at the small of her back, pressing her body snuggly against his, though she needed no encouragement in that regard. His other hand was buried in the hair at her nape.

His body was solid, unyielding, and his mouth was proving to be every bit as erotically skilled as it had been in that dream.

"Dayle." He whispered her name against her lips. It sounded like a plea. When she opened her eyes, he was watching her. For the first time in all the years she'd known Max, he looked lost.

A discreet cough broke the spell. Belatedly she remembered they weren't alone. The villa's manager stood to the side, his smile indulgent and knowing, though he didn't have a clue about the true inappropriateness of what had just occurred.

"It is a romantic place, no?" he asked.

She wanted to believe the idyllic setting was the impetus behind that forbidden kiss, but she knew better. God help her. She knew. For when she had turned to Max to tell him that the site was exactly what she'd been looking for, a panicky inner voice had whispered that her groom-to-be was not.

"I will let you talk in private." The man gave a sly wink.

Dayle felt her face grow warm as he walked away, leaving her to face not only Max but her own worst fears. When she turned, however, Max had his back to her. His shoulders were held at a rigid angle and his hands were stuffed into his trouser pockets. She thought she heard the faint jingle of loose change. I should say something, she thought, but was at a loss as to what.

Max broke the silence. Without turning around, he said, "I'm sorry, Dayle. I had no right to do that."

His words were heartfelt, his tone sincere. She'd wanted him to treat the incident differently, she realized. She'd wanted him to joke about it, turn on the old Kinnick charm. This reaction was far too damning, especially given the insinuations her subconscious was making.

"Max—"

"I had no right," he said again, this time a little more emphatically, making her wonder which one of them he was trying to convince.

Fairness demanded that she point out her own culpability. "Neither did I. I'm hardly innocent in this matter."

He turned. "Nothing is your fault."

She'd never seen him like this, so open, so off his game. He was no longer a smooth player, his every

word and move calculated in advance. He was un-
guarded, utterly exposed. If she'd thought the man
dangerous before, he was deadly now. And that was
before he admitted, "I wish I could say I was merely
caught up in the moment, but the truth is I've wanted
to do that for quite some time now."

Her heart tripped. Guilt? She twisted the engagement ring around her finger. *Please, please let that be
guilt.*

"Well, Venice is a very romantic city," she began.

His gaze was direct, his voice husky. "I'm talking
before Venice. *Long* before Venice."

She twisted the ring again before fisting her hand.
The diamond solitaire bit into her palm. "But…but
I'm engaged."

"I know." Max shoved a hand through his hair and
swore ripely. "Believe me, Dayle, that fact has not
escaped my notice." Half of his mouth rose in a smile
that never reached his eyes. "You know, you're the
only woman I've ever met who's made me wish I
were a better man."

She frowned. "I…I don't know what you mean."

"I wish I could be good enough for you." He shook
his head then. "Sorry." And before she could say
anything in return, he was walking back up the
cobblestone path.

Dayle's heart tripped again as she watched him go. She had a name for the emotion that was causing the sensation. It wasn't guilt. No. Not guilt.

The question was: What was she going to do about it?

MAX CALLED HIMSELF a coward and an unchivalrous one at that. He'd left Dayle at the villa with only a note of apology and money to make her way back to their hotel. He'd needed to get away before he said anything else. As it was, he'd revealed way too much.

The pain was back in his chest. He didn't bother with antacids or excuses. He knew its cause now.

He'd always been determined to steer clear of emotional entanglements with women, telling himself he was doing it for them, for their good. He was a confirmed bachelor and a Kinnick. He was like his father. Or was he?

He'd made it a hard and fast rule never to cheat on a woman. Each relationship was exclusive no matter how casual or short-lived. What if the heart he'd been so driven to protect from being broken all these years was his own? Well, if that were the case, the joke was on him. It was breaking right now.

When he arrived back at the hotel, Max called to see about getting a flight out of Marco Polo airport.

The destination didn't matter. While he waited on hold, he started packing his bags. His hands stilled when he heard the knock at the door. Dayle. He knew it would be her, but he didn't answer it. A moment later, he spotted the slip of paper on the carpet just inside his room.

Max,
We need to talk. Please come by my suite when you get in. I'll be waiting.
Dayle

He crumpled the note in his hand, determined to ignore it. But an hour later, as he wheeled his bag past her door, he slowed. One last goodbye, he decided. She deserved that. When Dayle opened the door, she was wearing the blue dress. Max sucked in a steadying breath. He could do this without making a fool of himself.

"I got your note."

She glanced past him to the suitcase. "Going somewhere?"

He nodded, but didn't elaborate.

"So, you stopped to say goodbye," she guessed.

"Yes."

Her expression dimmed. "I was going to see if you wanted to go out for dinner to that fancy restaurant by the square, but…" She tilted her head to the side. "Got time for a drink?"

"Sure."

He parked the suitcase just inside the doorway and followed Dayle to the sitting room. A bottle of wine sat breathing on the low table in front of the sofa. She poured them each a glass.

"What shall we drink to?" When he said nothing, she said, "I know. How about happiness?"

"To happiness," he agreed somewhat warily.

"Yes." She smiled. "Your middle name."

He lifted his glass and clunked it against hers before taking a sip. The Chianti's mellow undertones soured. *Happiness.* It was all Max could do to swallow.

"Sorry about leaving you today. It wasn't a very gentlemanly thing to do."

"And you're always a gentleman," she said.

"I try." He set the wine aside and walked to the far side of the room. Outside, the sun was setting. Apropos since something inside of him seemed to be dimming, too. "I hope you didn't have any difficulty getting back to the hotel."

"None. I'm a big girl, Max."

"I know. But I am sorry."

Dayle sipped her wine and regarded him over the glass's rim. "Is that all you're sorry about?"

He kneaded the back of his neck. "I believe I already apologized for kissing you at the villa."

"Yes, you did. But that's not what I mean." She set her glass next to his and started toward him. The dress's skirt swayed along with her hips. She wore her hair up. Diamonds caught fire in the light and shimmered on her earlobes. Thanks to her heels, they were eye to eye when she stood in front of him. "Why are you leaving Venice, Max?"

He cleared his throat. "Business—"

"Is an excuse."

Yes, but excuses were all he had at the moment. So he offered another one. "Well, you know me, Dayle. I can't stay in one place for long. I thought I'd pop back to New York before heading out again."

"Running, Kinnick?" It was too close to the truth. Max said nothing. His silence didn't appear to bother her. She went on. "You're not who I thought you were, or rather who you've let me believe you are."

The words left him feeling vulnerable.

"Something occurred to me today when I was standing in the garden at the villa," she began. "I said I'd know it when I found the right place for my wedding."

"Yes, and the villa's garden was perfect," he said tightly.

"I'm not finished."

Max motioned a hand, urging her to go on. Wrap it up, already, he thought. He couldn't stand much more.

"Yes, the place was perfect, but something was off. Something was absolutely wrong. I'd known it for a while. I just had a hard time admitting it to myself. And then you kissed me." She brought her hands up to his face. "Like this."

Dayle placed her mouth over his, slid her tongue along the seam of his lips until he allowed it inside. But then he was pulling away. "Wait a minute. Hold on." He shoved a hand through his hair. "What are you saying? What *exactly* are you saying?"

He looked terrified, confused…hopeful. Dayle knew those feelings. She was experiencing the same ones at the moment.

"Do you really need to ask, Max?"

"I'm usually not slow, but—"

"Actually, slow is good for what I have in mind."

"But Ryan—"

"I called Ryan when I got back to the hotel. I told him I couldn't marry him. I'd been feeling that way for a while, but standing in the garden with you, I knew it for sure. I'm not in love with Ryan." She tipped her head sideways. "It turns out I've fallen for someone else."

"And that would be?" But he was smiling now.

She kissed him passionately for an answer and sighed afterward. "Sparks. I love sparks. I love you, Maxwell Kinnick."

His expression was as sincere as his words. "I love you, too."

"So, I take it this means you no longer need to catch the first flight home?"

"No," he said, walking her backward in the direction of the bedroom. "I'm already there."

REQUEST YOUR FREE BOOKS!
2 FREE NOVELS PLUS 2
FREE GIFTS!

HARLEQUIN ROMANCE®

From the Heart, For the Heart

YES! Please send me 2 FREE Harlequin Romance® novels and my 2 FREE gifts (gifts are worth about $10). After receiving them, if I don't wish to receive any more books, I can return the shipping statement marked "cancel". If I don't cancel, I will receive 4 brand-new novels every month and be billed just $3.32 per book in the U.S. or $3.80 per book in Canada, plus 25¢ shipping and handling per book and applicable taxes, if any*. That's a savings of over 15% off the cover price! I understand that accepting the 2 free books and gifts places me under no obligation to buy anything. I can always return a shipment and cancel at any time. Even if I never buy another book, the two free books and gifts are mine to keep forever.

114 HDN ERQW 314 HDN ERQ9

Name	(PLEASE PRINT)	
Address		Apt. #
City	State/Prov.	Zip/Postal Code

Signature (if under 18, a parent or guardian must sign)

Mail to the **Harlequin Reader Service:**
IN U.S.A.: P.O. Box 1867, Buffalo, NY 14240-1867
IN CANADA: P.O. Box 609, Fort Erie, Ontario L2A 5X3

Not valid to current subscribers of Harlequin Romance books.

Want to try two free books from another line?
Call 1-800-873-8635 or visit www.morefreebooks.com.

* Terms and prices subject to change without notice. N.Y. residents add applicable sales tax. Canadian residents will be charged applicable provincial taxes and GST. Offer not valid in Quebec. This offer is limited to one order per household. All orders subject to approval. Credit or debit balances in a customer's account(s) may be offset by any other outstanding balance owed by or to the customer. Please allow 4 to 6 weeks for delivery. Offer available while quantities last.

Your Privacy: Harlequin Books is committed to protecting your privacy. Our Privacy Policy is available online at www.eHarlequin.com or upon request from the Reader Service. From time to time we make our lists of customers available to reputable third parties who may have a product or service of interest to you. If you would prefer we not share your name and address, please check here. ☐

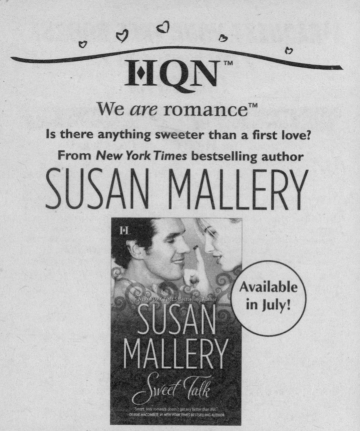